# PROMISE ME, LORD HEARTWOOD

## Z.M. CELESTAIRE

DREAMING IN COLOR

# CONTENTS

# Content Warning

This book contains magical violence, depictions of trauma, themes around substance abuse. Reader discretion is advised.

# Roster of Named Lilydale Residents

Ingrid – High Fae, Ruby Daughter

Chamomile – goblin

Syabira – gnome, Micah's gardening mentor

Leif – satyr, partner to Spirulina, musician

Spirulina – pixie, pink wings, partner to Leif, musician

Wex – sprite

Reave – pixie, moth wings

Thorn – pixie, blue skin and yellow hair

Spinn – goblin triplet

Gwynn – goblin triplet

Brynn – goblin triplet

Nox – satyr, goat pupils

Maeve – wandering dryad

Cosmos – dryad, auntie to Fionna

*Folk Who Visit*

Andrew

Micah

Fionna

# CHAPTER ONE
# THE QUESTION

"COME ON! WHAT DO you mean, you won't give me any?" cried the boulder of a woman beneath layers of sweatshirts, scarves, and a floppy winter hat. Thin tangled hair clung to her reddened cheeks, which were hollowed out by cravings and desperation.

"I mean," said Micah Stillwater through his teeth, "that Lilydale's foods will remain in Lilydale. Go back the way you came and tell your friends the supply is dead." He was shirtless in sweatpants and boots, the muscles of his back dotted with rapidly cooling beads of sweat from his exercises.

The woman's dark eyes flooded with tears. She braced herself against a naked oak tree with the backdrop of Saint Paul behind her, cloudy with a heavily falling snow. "You don't understand what you're doing," she hiccupped. "We need those foods."

Micah shook his head, wincing as Andrew Vidasche's fingers dug into the underside of his bicep. "You need *help*."

"What can help us?" the woman insisted, her voice rising.

"Go back the way you came," Micah ordered. "You will get nothing from me."

Drawn to the raised voices and the smell of Andrew's fear, the wolf Fionna slipped between broken cobblestones in the fence around Lilydale, tawny hackles raised like thorns between her shoulder blades. Her black lips peeled back in a silent snarl of warning as she brushed against Andrew's leg and remained there, protective and on edge.

The woman looked briefly alarmed, but then her eyes roamed past Fionna, searching the copse of trees past the fence for any glimpse of the food she was yearning for. "What about that little white child with the braids?"

"Wex," Micah said under his breath. Loudly and decidedly, he said to the woman, "Nobody will give you anything today." He straightened, taking a slow, deep breath that made his shoulder tense with a lightning bolt of pain. "You will leave the bluffs and tell your friends the supply is dead." Andrew's shoulders tingled when Micah spoke, the scent of sweet mulberries clinging to the frozen air and making him light-headed.

The woman blinked, eyes darkening, her jaw going slack. She let go of the tree and moved away, arms swinging, boots crunching through a heavy snowdrift, beginning a laborious trek through the snowy, desolate bluffs back towards Cherokee Park.

"Shit," said Micah, hand on his face. "That worked?" Charming the woman felt easy and intuitive, especially while holding onto his birchwood staff, its point stuck in the snow near his duck boots. Because of the staff, he could now access so much more of the power that stirred like twining ivy beneath his sternum. It was no longer a tiny seed lost in a wasteland. Now it was a whole wilderness. Foreign, exhilarating, and...terrifying.

When Andrew remained silent, Micah looked up to find a drawn, carefully neutral expression wrung onto Andrew's face. Finally, after Andrew had explained the shape that his depression and trauma took, Micah knew what that face meant.

"Hey." He lifted Andrew's chilled hand and set it on his bare chest. "Babe, talk to me."

"I'm..." Andrew was about to say he was good, but he knew Micah wouldn't believe that. Hanging onto Micah's hand, he lowered himself onto the cobbled fence, tucking his scarf into his chin and brushing his auburn hair back from his cheeks. "Shit." His thoughts were on his mother and the ache in her bones she'd described even though it had been over a decade since she'd last consumed Fae-spelled foods.

*And* how he'd left her two weeks ago at her cabin in the North Shore, ruefully and without mercy. He found the Superior agate in his palm, cool and smooth and grounding. It did that a lot: jumped from his pocket to his hand without prompting, particularly when he became untethered.

Fionna whined and nudged her wedge-shaped head through Andrew's elbow. Dropping an arm around her neck, he looked up at Micah. How his bonds had changed in the past seven years. Sam first. Steady and easygoing. Micah, sweet and tender and devoted. Micah's people here in the bluffs, feral and loyal. And Fionna, like a familiar, ancient yet childlike, fierce yet vulnerable.

Micah picked up his sweatshirt where it sat next to Andrew and struggled into it, his features screwed up when his head popped through the hood. He still wore a square of gauze taped to the stab wound near his shoulder blade, and, since he'd just finished a physical therapy regime, there was a spot of blood framed in the center of it. The Folk had been vastly helpful as he healed, with plenty of experience among them on healing wounds without the use of modern Western medicine.

Andrew asked, "Are people still coming up here all the time looking for Fae-spelled foods?"

"From what I understand," said Micah, grabbing his injured shoulder and rolling it carefully, "a lot of the Folk stopped giving out food when I came around two years ago. I have made a point to advertise what the Redwood Queen did to my father, and how I feel about that. But, yeah, Wex..." He trailed off. The chalky-skinned sprite had a bit of an attitude with him, and he thought this might be why. If the sprite was trading an apple or a heel of bread in exchange for one of the human contraptions they liked, then they would be angry Micah was discouraging such commerce with humans.

Andrew said quietly, "She looked about my mum's age. What if she'd been the supplier back then, too?"

"Yeah. I don't know, babe. Could be. You said your mum never came up to Lilydale for the Fae-spelled foods she got, which meant she could have gotten them from anyone down in the city. And anyway, what would knowing do for you?"

"You don't think I can go on a little vigilante mission?" Andrew grinned sidelong at Micah with a hard glint in his half-lidded eyes. Truthfully, his mother's words were heavy on his thoughts. She'd been so...desperate when she expressed that she thought Micah as a half-human had a responsibility to end the abuse of Fae-spelled foods by humans. Andrew didn't want to impose his agenda on Micah, but based on the way Micah's hand went up to his hair, he'd had no trouble sensing Andrew's thoughts.

Micah's sage-green locks were the only color in the bluffs right now, especially under the shale sky and the fat snowflakes that fell. He threaded his fingers through his hair like it was sweet summer grass. "We'll keep working on it, okay?"

"Yeah." Andrew pulled Micah onto the fence next to him so he could lay his head on his shoulder. "It's for the best. I can imagine putting an end to the Fae-spelled foods down in the city will be devastating for a lot of people."

Fionna stood up, stretched her front legs into a bow, and peeled off her wolfskin. It was still unnerving watching her do it; it looked fuzzy and gruesome, and yet as simple as discarding a blanket. Micah's nose twitched before he sneezed suddenly, which made him clutch his shoulder with a pained laugh.

"I know," said Andrew, rubbing the small of Micah's back. "It tickles when she shape shifts."

Drowning in one of Julian's sweatshirts, Fionna scrambled onto their laps and nestled between Andrew and Micah. Her cheeks shone bright as apples and the golden coins of her eyes glittered. Micah stretched his arm around her to Andrew's waist, pressing a warm kiss to Andrew's winter-cooled forehead.

When Micah went down to his brownstone a few days ago, Julian had done his best to contain his worry. Fionna helped. She stayed in her girl form and fawned over Julian, tried all his cooking with vigor, gawped at photographs and computer screens and stereos, and curled up in his lap by nightfall. It seemed like Julian would be a good intermediary between the bluffs and the city. It made Andrew wonder about what Ingrid had said—about fate. All these threads, all these souls that were once so impossibly distant, now woven together into some blessed tapestry, with Andrew and Micah the moon and sun at the epicenter.

Another two weeks of calm and healing passed. Clutching steaming paper cups from Amore Coffee, Andrew and Micah loped down toward the Smith Avenue bridge. Derelict houses were crowded among small business storefronts, cars lining the curb next to the sidewalk. Dirty, shrinking snowbanks encircled the street signs. Fortunately, it hadn't snowed for two weeks. The kind of high pressure that came with the snow made Micah's shoulder ache and he was happy for the break. After a month since his athame injury, he was almost, nearly, practically whole again. Except for the nightmares of women in black, and his tingling fingertips, and the general feeling of disaster lurking just out of sight. Aside from that.

Despite the horror of the ambush at Diana's house, Andrew's trip to the North Shore and subsequent return had completely repaired the damage between him and Micah. In fact, they were better than ever. Andrew had seen his therapist a couple of times, and had concocted a non-magical narrative for the events that transpired so he could still try to process everything.

Andrew sipped his spicy chai as he peered at the white domed state capitol building nestled across the river in the hills straight down Smith. They were just reaching the top of the Smith Avenue bridge, which cut determinedly across the Mississippi and pointed toward the modest skyscrapers of the business district downtown. He glanced down at Micah, his breath catching in his throat.

After a month with a sallow, washed out hue to his skin, Micah's hazelnut complexion was finally restored to its former glory. His hair was tucked under a chocolate-brown beanie that partially obscured the shiny gold plugs he wore in his stretched lobes. The shoulder injury had improved his posture, since he couldn't slump anymore or it would pull on the healing stab wound. Plus, the month of strength training to ensure his left arm didn't weaken meant he was more toned than before. The sleeves of his fleece pullover stretched taut over his biceps. Rosy lips pursed, Micah lifted his latte and took a drink that sent a little puff of steam across the stubble on his cheeks. Since he was spending so much more of his time in Lilydale, he finally felt bold enough to let his facial hair grow into a mossy shadow some days.

He felt Andrew staring and coughed into his drink, wiping foam off his upper lip when he glanced. "What?"

Andrew shrugged, his knees growing weak at the sparkle in Micah's lilac eyes. "You're beautiful. Can't help but stare." He switched his chai to his other hand and put his arm around Micah's shoulders. Micah hummed happily, holding onto Andrew's waist and nestling into his chenille scarf. The sweet sound of Micah's voice, like wind in the reeds, made Andrew's next few steps feel like he barely touched the sidewalk.

Andrew pulled out his phone and, tilting it slightly away from Micah, he sent a group text to Julian, Sam, and Chamomile.

I'm doing it!

As they passed a community garden and crossed the street, Andrew steered them toward an overlook with a bench tucked into a grizzled topiary plot. Micah went happily to the ornate railing to gaze at the park clinging to the riverfront below. He was precisely represented by the scene spreading out before them: the toothy gray bustle of the city and the quiet, relentlessness of nature impassively watching over.

His limbs going numb and just as quickly turning to fire, Andrew rocked on his heels and reached into his pocket. "Micah, I...I've been wondering something." His voice strained with anticipation.

Micah blinked at the tremble in his voice and turned from the view of the city as Andrew dropped to a knee, cupping a small wooden box in his hands, eyes bright with tears held back.

Gasping, Micah fell against the railing. "Andrew? What're you doing?"

"Ever since I came back from the North Shore," said Andrew, "it was apparent to me that I had to make my devotion to you as clear as day. Screwing up like I did was the kick I needed to realize that I want to be by your side every day until I die, which will probably be long before you, I know. But all of the struggling will be worth it if I get to spend my days with you. So that's why I'm hoping you'll marry me, Micah Stillwater."

With a little *clack*, the wooden box popped open. Frantically, Micah tried to clear the tears leaking from his eyes so he could crouch to see the ring on the velvety green pillow. It was a frothy green moss agate, which looked like there was a tiny forest suspended in the stone. The crystal was ensconced in golden branches dotted with rough leaf-like emeralds.

"Oh, Andrew!" Micah mopped his face dry with his sleeve. "It's perfect!"

Andrew gave him a strangled look. "And—?"

"And of course! Yes. Get up." He drew Andrew to his feet and wrapped him up in a strangling embrace until he pulled back and captured Andrew's narrow face between his hands to kiss him. Nudging him back after a moment, Andrew picked up Micah's left hand and slid the ring onto the finger next to his pinky. It was a perfect snug fit that made Micah start crying all over again. A pair of runners paused at the top of the bridge, a woman with a bobbing ponytail clapping and the dark-haired man with her calling out congratulations. Though Andrew usually despised attention like that, the couple made him grin and blush as he gave them a wave.

"I never imagined you could be so secretive as to surprise me with this." Micah held his hand close to his face, turning it this way and that as he intensely scrutinized the new adornment on his finger, heart swelling.

Andrew gave a little bow. "Yes, thank you. It wasn't easy. I'm not sure that I could have if you hadn't been recovering. You slept a lot more than usual." He tipped Micah's chin up with his finger, inhaling the smell of sun-ripened strawberries and basil that rolled off Micah's lips as they kissed again. They swirled their tongues together, soulful, hopeful, Micah leaning back into the railing as Andrew leaned over him.

When they finally separated, cheeks flaming with deep color, Andrew brushed aside Micah's fringe and told him sheepishly, "Now, the gesture was important to me, but uh...picking a date, or having a big production is less the point—"

"Ostara!" Micah blurted. His face somehow lit up even more. "Holy shit. How perfect would that be?"

Andrew blinked. "Um. The spring equinox is in five weeks, isn't it?"

"Well, yeah, but...c'mon, babe. Renewal, new beginnings, planting seeds. It's practically begging to be our wedding day." Micah adjusted the knot of Andrew's scarf, his brow crinkling as he sighed, "Our *wedding* day. I'm gonna *marry* you."

Unintelligible screeching split the air, making both of them jump and cling to each other as a small blur of a woman launched herself onto their shoulders as though they were a jungle gym. In their ears, Chamomile screamed as she showered both of them with kisses. Micah pried her free of them, holding the short goblin out at arm's length as she flailed with glee.

Ingrid stood behind her, a long and thin shadow relative to the bouncing sunspot of the goblin. She wore a gauzy red dress that made her bound burgundy curls look darker, but her scarlet eyes brighter. Her slender lips were spread in a smile; she padded silently over to Micah and embraced him.

"Wait, wait!" Micah squirmed out of his taller sister's hug. "You guys knew?"

Feet clad in fuzzy sandals back on the ground, Chamomile flipped open a small pad of paper bound with pink ribbon. "Sam and Julian are mobilized, but will need about three hours to prepare. The Folk will be ready for you by dusk, though the triplets are quite stressed out." She paused, shooting Andrew a glare with sky-blue eyes before adding, "Since *someone* couldn't agree to a specific time for a proposal." Andrew shrugged, unapologetic. Chamomile continued with a sharp-tipped finger pointing at them, "Don't overeat at Saint Claire, since you'll be due back at moonrise for your engagement party in Lilydale."

Micah's jaw dropped. "So much planning, Andrew!"

With a squeeze of Micah's newly ornamented hand, Andrew said wryly, "Well, since the wedding is on Ostara, it seems we're only getting started."

"Ostara!" Ingrid and Chamomile shrieked, talking over each other, sharing disbelief and outrage over the closeness of the date, yet breathlessly agreeing that the symbolism was extraordinary.

"Aw, we're doing it?" Micah wrapped his arms around Andrew's waist, leaning into him to kiss his chin.

"I would do anything for you," Andrew said softly, his eyes slipping shut as he met Micah's lips with his own.

A blue-skinned pixie with pink flashing dragonfly wings flitted in the air over Lilydale. Spinning like a suncatcher, Spirulina trilled a warm, wordless melody while Leif strummed a lyre where he sat on a mushroom underneath her. They played for the Folk who pranced joyously in celebration around the enormous roaring fire that overlooked the river valley and the city of Saint Paul to the north. On such a clear winter's night, the distant shape of Minneapolis rose in the northwest.

Someone had thrown a capsule of herbs into the fire so that the scent which rose from it was sweet and complex, so that the air in Lilydale was almost intoxicating on its own. The men for whom the Folk danced were seated on a log tossed with blankets and cushions before a broad, flat-topped toadstool that held an array of foods—mostly human-made from the city or from Julian—and several bottles of open champagne. For Andrew, Wex fetched a large selection of take-out food from a fancy restaurant in the neighborhood up the hill. As a sprite, they could pass as human well enough with chalky white skin, round pupils in big green eyes, and textured hair in braids, the hue an iridescent silver that just looked professionally dyed. When they wore loose clothes, you couldn't see how inhumanly bony they were.

Half-teasing, Andrew asked, "Did you enchant this?"

Eyes gleaming fever-bright, Wex presented Andrew with fistfuls of take-out bags. "No. You are fortunate to be under the protection of Lord Heartwood. Nobody wants to fall under his ill will, so we all obey when he says we cannot play tricks on you."

"What makes you think you could trick me?" Andrew asked them softly. He smiled sweetly when their eyes widened slightly.

Disgruntled, Wex sniffed and pranced off to the fire.

Micah watched the sprite leave as he rubbed his chin. For the last two weeks, he'd been monitoring Wex closely to see how often they disappeared with fruit or bread or jugs of honey mead. So far, they'd only left twice. So if they were bringing the foods to trade with humans, it was about once a week. Micah wasn't confident enough that he could make Chamomile or Ingrid care about this as much as he did, so only Andrew knew that Micah was keeping an eye on Wex.

Leaning forward, Andrew put himself in Micah's line of sight with a bright smile and flushed cheeks. He had on a sheer cream-colored shirt with a collar and bow that made him look like an old-fashioned magician. It highlighted his lean torso and displayed the scars from his duel with the

Redwood Queen as a reminder to all how capable he was for having survived.

"Tonight is not the night for worries, my love."

Micah scoffed. "Right, right." He tried for a smile. "Yeah. Sorry."

Andrew frowned, brushing his knuckles along Micah's defined jaw. Micah relaxed under his touch, wishing not for the first time since Andrew had been away that drinking hadn't become so problematic. Being sober all month had been...grueling. Recovering from his injury and the constant anxiety of the witches might have been more tolerable if he'd taken a finger of whiskey every night or something. But after how sloppy he'd been with Andrew gone, sobriety seemed necessary.

"We're all right," Andrew whispered. "You're safe."

Micah kissed the delicate blue veins on the underside of Andrew's wrist before he nodded. "You're right. I should be focused on us—" He looked up at the Folk and declared, "Because I'm *getting married!*" The Folk cheered and hollered and clinked crystal glasses of honey mead. A dance began, chaotic yet orchestrated, like the coded steps of honeybees.

Micah took a forkful of chocolate cake from a crystal platter in front of them. Julian had attempted three cakes before it but wasn't satisfied, despite Andrew's insistence that each were divine. This one had pale purple buttercream frosting and real yellow buttercups decorating the top. He glanced at Andrew, whose eyes followed the fork and traced Micah's open lips with heat and hunger, a blush shooting up the nape of Micah's neck and into his cheeks. Andrew's lips quirked, his tongue flicking out briefly to wet them—heavens, how he made them glisten—before he cleared his throat.

"You put my childhood romantic fantasies to shame, Lord Heartwood." The sound of Micah's newly acquired title on Andrew's supple lips sent a shiver up Micah's spine.

Humming and swaying her hips, Ingrid sauntered closer to them. "You know..." Her tone was conspiratorial. "If we were in the Redwoods, there would be no reveling for an engagement. I knew one couple that were so frightened of their romance being found out that they simply fled. But the Queen caught wind of this and turned them both into doves."

Andrew grimaced.

"I know, Red." Micah gave her a sad smile. "But you found a way to teach me how to be loving anyway."

"Did I?" Doubt wedged between her eyebrows as a slender crease in her skin.

Despite the way she had traumatized Andrew after he injured her seven years ago, Andrew firmly believed in Micah's sentiment. It was impossible to miss how deeply the woman cared for her younger brother. She'd murdered a witch to save his life just a month ago. And any efforts Ingrid made to look stoic or fearsome evaporated like mist in morning sunlight whenever she laid eyes on Micah. No matter what other instincts the Redwoods had taught the siblings, they learned from each other how to fight for the ones they loved.

"What are you doing?" Ingrid glared down at where Andrew's fingers curled around her hand.

Embarrassment heated Andrew's already flushed cheeks as he let her go. "Feeling...sorry for you?"

Micah choked on his sparkling water. While Andrew *might* have risked such a gesture when he was sober, he really went for it with all that champagne turning his blood to honey.

"Hm," was all Ingrid said, eyes slitted as she took another two spears of asparagus off Andrew's plate before drifting off like a cat that lost interest in him.

Andrew's gaze drifted away from her; she left a residue in his vision like he'd been gazing at the sun. He found Chamomile watching Ingrid like the goblin also thought she was a star.

When the goblin's lips turned down in a rueful frown, she glanced over to meet Andrew's eye and gave him a glare as if regretful he'd caught her pining. He crooked a finger at her, beckoning her over, and against her better judgment Chamomile came to him, climbing a stump beside Andrew and swaying into his arm. She was wearing a jagged spruce crown, her loosely tied silk robe fluttering open over a provocative peek of flesh when she moved.

"What do you want?" Chamomile's birdsong voice warbled slightly.

"I have a question."

"You always do," remarked Chamomile. She began braiding Andrew's hair with deft fingers that made his scalp tickle. Past her, Leif had set aside the lyre to blow bubbles for Fionna while she wore her wolfskin. When the iridescent spheres popped, they became colorful pansies. One of the blossoms landed on her nose, and the wolf gave a great sneeze that scattered the petals to a roar of Fae laughter from the spectators.

Andrew watched Ingrid fiddle with the hoops in her ears. "Am I missing something, or are there really no other faeries like Ingrid here?"

Chamomile lost her balance, her chest squishing into the back of his neck.

Andrew winced. "All right—"

"Whoa!" Micah exclaimed. "Bad goblin. Get your boobs off his head." He hefted her off Andrew and let her hang onto his wrist when she lost her balance. "And to answer your question, there are many fewer Folk like Ingrid than like those here. Most call her High Fae."

Andrew giggled. "Sorry, what? I was just watching your sexy lips move."

"Oh, boy," Micah sighed.

Bright-eyed, the goblin deftly resumed braiding Andrew's copper hair before she added, "I just call her a Tall One."

Chewing thoughtfully on a pretzel bite, Andrew watched Ingrid nearly float up the limestone steps to sit by herself in the kiln throne. "It's descriptive," Andrew agreed. He paused. Twisting around to look at Chamomile—she glowered when he pulled his hair out of her fingers—Andrew asked quizzically, "But isn't that what you called me when we met?"

Chamomile's expression clouded. She opened and closed her mouth, her eyebrows hitching lower. Finally she echoed cryptically, "It's descriptive."

"There you go, babe. You go to sleep, hm? Do you want some water?"

"I want some cuddles." Andrew's words were a muffled mess; he was already nestling into their blankets with a contented sigh. All that remained was a tuft of glinting ginger hair.

"I'm going to stay up a bit longer." Micah found Andrew's knuckles over the edge of the blanket and pressed a kiss to a caramel-colored freckle. Andrew murmured something affectionate in Irish—all Micah caught was *grá*.

All the Irish language books stacked next to the bed had done good for Andrew, but Micah had no gift for languages, as much as he liked to listen to it. Especially with how it seemed to roll off Andrew's tongue like he was meant to speak it.

Realizing how easily Micah could get derailed just watching Andrew sleep, he stepped back and dimmed the faerie lights dangling from the ceiling with a flick of his fingers and a tingle of magic. He picked up his staff and then backed through the tent flap.

Outside under a dome of pristine onyx dotted with diamond stars, Micah turned his staff in his hand with a sigh through his nose. It was so bulky; even when he brought it with him to the brownstone, it was knocking over lamps and scaring Cinnamon and clanging into pans in the kitchen. Yet he felt odd when it wasn't nearby, like if he didn't have any gauges in his ears and his lobes were just floppy loops of skin.

Confidently, he marched down to the fire pit and rejoined the Folk. Their dancing had tapered off and Spirulina and Leif were beside each other playing a slower ballad, Leif's baritone voice rumbling like gravel on a rustic trail and woven with the silky ribbon quality of Spirulina's singing. By their feet, Fionna was laying on her wolfish side, eyes closed, enormous furry paws twitching slightly. But he was looking for Syabira, and she wasn't with them, so he left the bonfire pit and went toward the evergreen garden where her bed was. Up here, away from the warmth of the fire, the thin air held a chill and muffled the sound of the music from below.

Syabira turned from her little abode tucked into the fencing around the garden and raised an eyebrow at him. She was gripping a thick blanket of quilt squares sewn together with glinting golden thread. "Do you need something, Lord Heartwood?"

"Bee, please. You've always called me Micah."

"You're different than you were." She draped her blanket over the loam and moss of her straw bed. "What is it?"

Swallowing, he gestured with his staff. "What am I supposed to do with this? Just go around Saint Paul looking like Donatello?"

The gnome stared at him.

"Um—can I change it?"

"You can do whatever you desire with it," Syabira answered, in true Fae fashion. "It is part of you, like your hair."

Well, this was a dead end. Micah suppressed a sigh, turning on his heel to leave. "Thanks, Bee."

She smiled faintly, turned away, and picked up a wooden spade from a tray of gardening tools. "I want you to sit down—" He obeyed at once. He always obeyed Syabira. She had a matronly air to her, despite her small stature. She had begun telling him what to do as soon as he arrived in

Lilydale when he was twenty, asking her to let him help her garden. "—And close your eyes."

Micah was now level with the small gnome's eyes, so he knew she caught his skeptical pursed lips. He tugged on the collar of his sweater as if to distract before he forced his eyes shut. The garden swaddled him in the smell of fertile soil, the strawberry blossoms and bee hive touching his tongue with delicate sweetness. Though the ground underneath him was chilly and firm, he still felt the pulsing of water in roots crossing intricately like a net cradling Lilydale.

Syabira stole back his attention although he could neither see nor hear her. She was doing something to her spade, directing her energy to the slivers and cells in the wood, merging with it till Micah sensed her and the wood as one entity, flowing in tandem. Their life was an even exchange. When he opened one eye, Syabira held a complicated knot of wood where the spade had been, and it twined around her arm like a serpent before returning to her hands and settling comfortably into its spade shape.

"Syabira, that's so cool!"

"Micah, I am but a garden gnome." Syabira's voice swelled with feeling, her eyes gleaming with the distant light of stars and bonfires. When she spoke, her doe ears quivered on the sides of her head. "You are the son of the Redwood Queen. You are capable of leagues more than a transformed spade." He frowned. "I see you trying to trust yourself but you keep tripping yourself. Nobody can stop you from doing so. You battle your own scars."

Micah's throat tightened. He gripped his staff to try to fight off the burning of his eyes. How Syabira had managed to grasp such a deeply buried root inside him and rip it out with medical precision was beyond him. But she was bound to speak truth, and he recognized it.

"Wh-what should I do with it?" His tongue felt thick and dry.

Syabira didn't answer, twirling her spade in her hand instead. She took a seat across from him, leaning against her bed, picking at a protruding needle of straw.

"Oh, I'm on my own now?" Micah narrowed his eyes at her, though his irritation was halfhearted. He just felt so...intimidated by his own power, by the fact that his power came from his mother. It was like when he was face to face with Tom last month, smelling the man's fear and wondering what he could do to heighten it. It was like any step toward being formidable he took made him more dangerous. More wicked.

But the birchwood staff wasn't wicked. Not on its own—it was his anger that had made him wicked. The staff arrived in his time of need, like some sort of priest's tool, and he knew it had helped him heal more swiftly. And that was what he wanted from his Fae side, he realized. Life and healing. And he had a funny feeling that the birchwood did, too.

The birchwood staff across his knees shone like pewter in the darkness, etched with slivers and whorls of midnight. He wasn't sure what he could have done without it this last month. And yet he needed a better understanding of his relationship with it. Its place in his day to day life, when he was pretending to be an average human to protect Julian and the kids at To a Tea.

Maybe like Syabira had turned her spade into a rope, Micah could wear it as a necklace. He frowned. Maybe the birchwood had an opinion on the matter. He took several deep breaths, in through his nostrils and out through his lips, stroking the staff as he let his eyes slip shut. The wood shivered like a dreaming cat under his touch and slowly turned pliant. It reached for his hand, and he invited it to his wrist as one would beckon a skittish wild beast. No, he realized. Not so coyly. It was like communing with an old friend. A fraternal twin. Come along, other self.

He felt the hairs on the back of his wrist catch as the birchwood raced to loop around it. Micah peeked as it formed itself into a pretty bark cuff. It was unbroken, one continuous bracelet that felt at once like armor and a second skin.

"Would you look at that," he breathed. He rubbed an admiring thumb on the wood. "How stylish."

"Well done, Lord Heartwood. See how easy it is when you approach it cooperatively?" Syabira's dark eyes gleamed.

"I never even thought of that," Micah admitted. He gave the bracelet a gentle nudge and it unwound to reshape into the staff, tickling his knuckles as it passed over the peaks and valleys. "We always think of asking nature for favors. But this was like seeing what it wanted to do with me." It arrived back to its full length with an excited shiver.

"You're finally approaching it like a faerie," agreed Syabira.

"Weird." He grinned. "Ten years ago, I'd have been terrified at that thought."

"It would have been hard for you to make your magic your own when you didn't know who you were." Syabira absently plucked off a wilting leaf from a strawberry plant. "If I may be so bold."

"I would expect nothing less from you." Playfully feeding off the eagerness from his staff, Micah called it back to his wrist, back and forth the birchwood went, leaving a mist of dewy green in its wake. "I've been fortunate to have someone with a similar gift as mine. It's just a pity I waited so long to figure my shit out."

"Folk don't often believe that things happen at the wrong time." Syabira stood up, stretched mightily, and sipped water from a large rhubarb leaf. "If you don't mind, my dear, I'm bound for sleep."

"Sure. Yeah." Micah clambered to his feet, the staff jolting back into his hand so he could support himself on it. "I knew you were the right person to look for. I owe you one,

Bee. I owe you a lot. And now I think I can finally make good on my debt. You just name it, okay?"

The gnome smiled patiently before she gave him a slight nod. "Sure, Micah."

# Chapter Two
# The Run

THE SKY WAS AN empty gray and the air was warm in Cherokee Park. Andrew loped along with Fionna, who wore her wolfskin. Wearing tightly laced running shoes and compression leggings under his Columbia jacket, Andrew ran with the ease of experience and well-developed stamina. Fionna's tongue lolled out between her savagely sharp fangs, her ears swiveling eagerly.

Behind them, Micah huffed and puffed as he tried to keep up, his face bright red with cold and exertion. The closest he had to running gear was a windbreaker and striped joggers with Nikes that were rubbing painfully into his heels, unfamiliar beneath the soles of his feet.

"You're not even out of breath!" exclaimed Micah. "We've been running for like, an hour!"

Andrew glanced at the screen of his watch. "We're at six minutes."

Micah cried out and stopped with his hands on his knees, dropping his head. "This is the worst! Why do you like this?" Fionna bounded up to him and leaned her weight against the back of his legs. Micah moaned tremendously but allowed her to nudge him forward.

Andrew laughed. "I love running. Running computers, running from trauma." He slowed down. "It's about all I did in college." He touched the small of Micah's back, which was warm and damp. "Now, you told me you'd complain, but I wasn't allowed to let you stop."

"Past me is an idiot!" Micah yelled to the heavens. He dragged his feet and they continued around the back curve of Cherokee Park with little to their western side but the skyline, and the bluffs sloping toward the river. "Why couldn't we do more strength training? I'm getting *muscular!*"

"Oh, trust me. I've noticed."

"Flattery will do nothing for these blisters."

Fionna shot into the underbrush to chase a squirrel, her tail a flag straight over her back. Andrew sharply yelled in Irish, "*Stad!*" and Fionna froze, whining. "Not here." Andrew's feet tramped in sync with Micah's on the salted pavement. A man walking with a stroller gave Fionna a particularly long look, prompting Micah to give him a charming smile that had the man flustered and blushing as he scuttled away. Fionna turned to watch the stroller, her tail thumping and her canine tooth poking out goofily through her lip. Andrew glared at the eager gleam in Fionna's eye and cautioned, "*Aon cailín.*" Her golden gaze slid to him with a disgruntled glare, and Andrew nodded in satisfaction and started off again. Not quite before Micah managed to pinch his rear and elicit a yelp of surprise that had Micah giggling. They both picked up their pace, Fionna settling begrudgingly between them on silent paws.

The best part about running with Andrew was the look on his face. Rarely did he look so at ease. Rarely did his cheeks have that pleasant redness, rarely were his shoulders so straight, or the lines of his face so smooth. Micah used that expression to bolster himself and briefly he was able to forget that he should have let Andrew go running alone like he usually did.

Micah tried to distract himself with wedding plans so he'd focus less on the burning of his throat or the pressure building in his temples. It worked for a few moments, but as his heart kept pounding, it turned from exertion to anxiety that prickled along his shoulders and concentrated in his athame scar. He glanced again at Andrew, debating on what he could say, or should say, or how stupid he would look if he bailed on their run.

Andrew's dark gaze shifted off the path and found Micah's face. "You all right?"

"Um—"

Fionna suddenly crashed forward between their legs, tripping them both. A wet, snarling growl broke from her jowls and all her hackles rose along her spine like tawny thorns. She stopped with her narrow snout pointing toward the cluster of bare trees and dead, drooping underbrush.

Blood pounded in Micah's ears, deafening. Andrew gripped Micah's wrist in his right hand and unsheathed his seax from its holster between his shoulder blades, crossing it over them so the black blade glinted in the gray light. Warily, they stepped off the path into the thin, dirty layer of snow and the shadows of the forest.

"The oak." Micah's whisper caught around his heart in his throat.

Fixed to the bark of an oak tree, a naked action figure had been painted black and tied up with twine. It had a sprig of stiff-looking hair sprayed bright kelly-green. A wilted lily hung from it, orange petals drifting down to the muddied snow among the roots. Bound with the lily was a small bleached bone.

"The hell is that?" Andrew muttered, stepping into the underbrush to inspect the object closer. He held his sword out first, probing, like the whiskers on a cat.

"Don't—don't touch it." Micah lifted both hands, stomach clenched. "It feels...disgusting."

"It feels like a threat." Andrew tapped the point of his sword against the bone, which clacked drily against the bark of the oak with a cursed sort of rhythm.

"Against me," Micah murmured.

Andrew straightened, brow furrowing. His profile was sharp and serious as he surveyed the area around the oak tree, looking for footprints or other indicators of how the doll had been arranged. Interrupting their tense silence came the grating caw of a crow. Andrew looked up into the branches of the oak and met its beady black as it shuffled its sleek feathers.

Fionna threw off her wolfskin. She jumped for the lowest branch in the tree and scrambled up toward the crow with a war cry. Branches and dead leaves rained down below her. The crow rasped angrily and flapped off into the sky. Fionna straddled a branch and peered down at them, her heavy brows furrowed over golden eyes.

Her coarse voice tumbled down from the heights like a rockslide. "Bad for Micah."

As Andrew fixed Micah with his harrowed gaze, Micah grimaced, scraping his hair off his brow and grinding his cheek between his molars. "Shit."

Fionna suddenly tipped off the branch and fell in a tangle of limbs and snapped branches. She yelped in alarm, Andrew and Micah both lunging to catch her. The girl landed in their outstretched arms but squirmed free of them, thumping onto the dirt and rolling off her back as she pulled on her wolfskin. The men stepped back slightly as Fionna shook herself vigorously, her hackles still spiky on her back as she tottered on her feet. Whining, she swiped her paw furiously over her snout and shook her head.

"Fionna?" Andrew said loudly. He exchanged a glance with Micah and said, "We need to get away from here."

Micah nodded. "C'mon, Fionna. Walk, darling."

Fionna lifted her large head, her black lip parted slightly over her sharp fangs, drool stringing off beneath her maw. She stumbled forward, away from the tree.

"Can you take off your wolfskin?" Andrew asked hurriedly, heart in his throat. "Let me carry you." Not looking at him, Fionna lunged at Micah, snapping sharply at his knee. Micah leapt away and then stepped quickly further back, onto the trail, his expression going blank. It was still impossible not to notice, however, that Micah crossed his birchwood staff protectively in front of himself. Andrew crouched and looped his arms around Fionna's chest, her damp fur overwhelmingly smelly and somehow off, some kind of smoky grunge rising off her coat that wasn't there before. He dragged her away from the tree and said again, "Wolfskin!"

When his sneakers hit the trail, Fionna obliged. She dragged off her wolfskin and clung to Andrew with both her arms and legs wrapped tightly around him as he hauled her off the ground and against his chest. As soon as he had a hold on her, Andrew took off at a run from the tree with the doll hanging off it, heading back toward Lilydale. He heard Micah's feet pounding on the pavement behind him. When they were out of sight of the accursed oak tree, Fionna's grip on Andrew loosened and she lifted her head off his shoulder. Her face was wet and smeared with snot and tears, but her eyes were clear and focused.

Andrew skidded to a halt, leaning her back on his hip, wiping her face with his sleeve. "What happened?" he asked her. "You tried to bite Micah."

Fionna's face crumpled. She slid off his hip and onto the ground, hurrying to Micah right behind him and flinging herself around his waist. "Sorry," she wept.

Micah blinked, his gaze still dark indigo as he patted the girl's hair. "I'm not hurt," he assured her. He fussed with the zipper on his purple windbreaker, glancing up at Andrew before looking back at the girl. "Did you want to bite me?"

Fionna shook her head urgently. "No, no!"

"What happened, then?" asked Andrew again.

Burying her face in Micah's windbreaker, Fionna cried, "Witches!"

The once-borrowed tent where Andrew and Micah took up residence in Lilydale had transformed into a sturdy, nearly completed brick house with a thatched roof. The Folk had a few rows of bricks yet to add but it was a far cry from the canvas-sided cone it had been that first night when Micah had been injured. An ornate Persian rug spread out over the limestone ground, banishing the chill from the space. Next to the doorway, a driftwood bookshelf was bursting with gifts the Folk had given them. Deeply personal, unique trinkets welcomed Andrew and Micah to Lilydale. Stone earrings, turkey feather quills, pearlescent hair beads, and handsome handmade parchment kept appearing at their door. It made Andrew almost happy to return there, though this complete transformation of his life continued to surprise him. He often thought about that first journey into the bluffs seven years ago by himself, what he'd expected the Folk to be like with their poisonous flowers. He wasn't *that* far off. He just didn't think he'd end up getting along with everyone quite this well.

Andrew unfolded a leather satchel tied with thick dyed twine and tenderly touched the wooden staves inside. Maeve, a solitary dryad who lived in Lilydale when she wasn't traveling, had gifted Andrew the staves last year for his birthday. She hadn't offered him an explanation, just handed him the satchel and climbed into a knotty hole in a willow tree to go to sleep.

There were twenty twigs each roughly finger-sized, burned with a variety of tic marks long and short that comprised an ancient alphabet used in Ireland called Ogham. Each symbolized a different type of tree, each with a different spiritual meaning. Much like other divination methods,

Andrew had played around with layouts to create different types of readings to serve his purposes.

Much in the same way that the birchwood staff felt familiar to Micah, so did the twenty staves Andrew was using. Micah could confidently identify each of the twenty different trees used to make them. The branches smelled different—rowan had a sharper, more lethal smell than the cheery sweetness of the apple tree stave, the holly branch like a winter breeze whereas the yew tree felt like autumn. It made Micah wonder if his sense of smell was all that different from an animal, but it seemed only so finely attuned for plant life.

Running the tip of his tongue over his slender lips, Andrew glanced up. The faerie lights toyed with the color of his eyes, so they turned to syrupy amber each time he blinked or looked away, slipping to midnight black when his brows shadowed them. On the cross sectioned stump that made up their low table, he indicated three columns. "My reading will focus on insight around Emotion, Spirituality, and Physicality."

Micah nodded, legs tucked into his chest, resting his chin on his knee. He liked seeing Andrew this focused; he practically had an aura right now, faint maple-hued light rebounding off his pale skin. Even his voice sounded different, coarse like shale but as insubstantial as a whisper of wind in leaves.

Andrew blinked as Micah's orchid-tinged eyes swirled lighter and lighter almost to periwinkle. With a curl of his lips, Andrew pinched Micah's nose. "Hey. Focus."

Swatting his hand away, Micah scowled at the ceiling. "I refuse to apologize for admiring you."

Andrew cleared his throat, looking at his staves and pretending they both didn't know he was blushing. He gathered up the staves, rolling them gently in his palm, sinking his pelvis into the limestone floor, which was hard and unforgiving even under the thick rug. Sitting so close to the stone was helpful for grounding, though, physically and spiritually. He rolled his agate across his knuckles, smooth and cool as if his fingers dipped into the relentless waves of Lake Superior. The clatter of the goblins' cauldron traveled through the gaps in their walls like the sounds wanted to become waves striking iron ore cliffs.

He blinked open his eyes, shaken by just how far away he'd suddenly become. Awestruck, Micah stared at him across the table with slightly parted lips. Andrew had looked like stone for a moment, rusty red and sharp, but then the illusion had faded. Andrew rolled his shoulders back with a little scoff, blinking a few more times.

"Something you learned Up North?" Micah inquired, admiration obvious in the way his hazel cheeks rose to crinkle his eyes.

"Um—I guess. Close your eyes," Andrew said firmly, partly to deflect the strangely magical moment dangling between them on a string of unanswerable questions. Micah obliged, making Andrew pause to admire the sweep of his long green lashes against his supple cheeks. And in the tight, slightly sheer tee that Micah was wearing, his nipples were pert and his abdominal muscles swelled as he took in a deep breath. This blasted man made it just as impossible for Andrew to stay grounded now as he had when they first met. Bothered in more ways than one, Andrew pushed his shoulders back and then lifted Micah's wrist to set his hand on the staves.

"Choose your first."

Micah's fingers trailed over the branches as confidently as if he was fluently reading Braille. The air around the staves became charged, making the hairs on the back of Andrew's hand stand on end.

"Wait, wait." Andrew snatched the staves back. "Can you tell which branch is which?"

Micah's eyes stayed closed, but his lips twitched as he tried to fight a smile. "No."

"Bah." Andrew pushed his hand back and then shut his own eyes as he slid the staves onto the table. His fingers closed on the first just as he felt the tickle of his loose hair brushing against his throat. Eyes snapping open, he flinched away from Micah's reaching hand which was about to clasp the side of his neck. "Micah! Do you want me to help or not?"

"Oh, yes," said Micah, shameless, gaze unwavering. "I want you."

With a scornful sigh, Andrew covered the staves with a corner of the satchel. Micah's smirk faltered briefly before Andrew reached across the table and hauled him closer with a fistful of shirt. Micah growled as he came to him, their lips crushing together with breathless fervor and their chests and thighs close behind.

Andrew tipped over, landing on his back with Micah caging him in between flexing biceps. Micah caught Andrew's hand within his own and pinned it over their heads while he stooped to graze his lips along Andrew's throat, nipping his jaw. Andrew purred beneath his touch, digging his fingers into Micah's hip when their mouths found each other again.

Andrew caught Micah's lower lip between his teeth and tugged until Micah moaned and released his other hand only to get tangled up in Andrew's hair. Andrew gave him a push toward the bed and sat up as he sucked on the balsam-scented skin of Micah's muscular neck.

They clambered onto their cinder block bed frame, which was deceptively plush and luxurious all things considered. The bed absorbed their hardly stifled moans as their tongues danced and hands roamed. Andrew tore off Micah's shirt, scraping his hands across the antlered bobcat tattoo as if he could collect the magic beading within the inked lines. Micah rewarded him with a devilish grin and his thigh slotted between Andrew's legs, the pressure of which sent shivers down Andrew's arms as he slid his eyes closed and twined around Micah's muscular leg.

Huskily speaking around a gasp of pleasure, Andrew said, "You know what you get when you irritate me." Then he sank his teeth into Micah's pectoral, but the sound that resulted was anything but agonized. Andrew lapped at the wounded flesh with his tongue but then bit him again right below his collarbone, delighting in the goosebumps that rippled out across Micah's chest.

Micah flipped Andrew easily onto his stomach and pulled him free of his bottoms, using his lips and his teeth to push up Andrew's shirt before planting a line of kisses up his neck and onto his jaw. He let himself out of his own pants and gave Andrew barely a chance to suck in a breath before entering him, lifting up his hips as he did so. Tears sprang into Andrew's eyes, which were closed as he covered his own mouth to muffle himself.

Micah slowed down as soon as he saw the tears, drawing Andrew's back against his chest and kissing the dot of salt on his cheek in an apology. Twitching against Micah, Andrew grabbed his hand and guided him down his navel and beyond, unbothered, urging him on with a half-formed word that was nevertheless clear in its meaning. They found an all-consuming, rocking rhythm, only interrupting it when Micah flipped Andrew once more. He enjoyed how much easier it was now to throw the lithe, skinnier man around after this month of strength training, and Andrew's cry of delight said that he enjoyed it too. Hooking Andrew's knees through his elbows, Micah leaned down as he thrust forward, sucking on Andrew's porcelain, freckled chest before making his way up to crush their mouths together as they reached the crescendo.

Soon after, they collapsed onto the blankets, shining with sweat, hair sticking to cheeks and foreheads but laughing with their noses touching, panting hot clouds against each others' faces.

"It's the biting," Micah said by way of apology. "You don't do it often enough."

"I'd have thought you had enough pain this month," Andrew rasped.

Micah shook his head. "That's not pain."

Andrew nodded, brushing his hair off his cheeks before sighing and flopping onto his side. "I can relate."

Micah pushed onto his elbow, kissing Andrew's collarbone. "Sorry for the intermission. I'll pay better attention now."

Ochre eyes glittered. "Oh, will you now?" Expression softening, Andrew trailed a finger across Micah's damp brow, unsticking his mossy hair from his skin and running the pad of his thumb over the bristles of his eyebrow. He swallowed, his throat dry and hoarse. "It's all right. I think it's this hut. Sex is great wherever we have it, but this place...this bed...it's *ours*."

Micah's eyes gleamed lavender as he leaned into Andrew's hand. "The whole future is ours, little fox." The nickname wasn't one Micah used for him very often, and only then in private. But it had lost its sting since Ingrid called Andrew that in his apartment before they went to the Redwoods. "Let me get you some water."

Micah climbed over him and yelped when Andrew pinched his ass. He helped Andrew upright and pressed his lips to his sweat-salty shoulder, neck, and jaw while Andrew drank deeply from their steel water bottle. Andrew passed him the bottle when he was finished before slipping the glittering black hair tie from Ingrid off his wrist to bind his hair in a messy bun. As soon as he put his hands down, Micah tugged the tie back out and gripped a fistful of his auburn hair, tilting back Andrew's head to graze his teeth against his throat, grinning when Andrew groaned in annoyance and pushed him off.

"Let me try braiding it," said Micah as he reached for Andrew's hair again. Andrew stuck his elbow into Micah's bare stomach before scooting off the bed and to his feet.

"After," said Andrew. "I think we should do this stave reading."

"I can multitask," Micah whined.

Shaking his head, Andrew held out his hand for the hair tie. Instead of giving it back, Micah caught his hand and pressed a kiss to his palm, not missing the goosebumps that made the deep red hairs on Andrew's freckled arm stand on end. Andrew shivered, pulling at his hand that remained fast in Micah's grip. Grinning over his fingers, Micah relented with a sigh. He let him go one finger at a time, and then finally slid the hair tie onto his pinky.

"Chaotic man," Andrew grumbled as he pulled back on his underwear and pants. Micah looked wildly unapologetic, a satisfied smirk on his shining lips as he watched Andrew dress before slowly following suit. When Andrew sat back down on his knees at the table, he tugged Micah down behind him and held the hair tie out for him between two fingers. Micah purred appreciatively and picked up Andrew's boar bristle brush from their little stump nightstand, gentle as he teased out the tangles he'd made there himself. Andrew allowed the soothing rhythm to help him find his center again. He was about to close his eyes when the flap to their tent burst open.

Fionna appeared in the opening, her tawny hair up in twin buns that were speckled with tiny white flowers. "Cosmos says they heard," she said expressionlessly, likely referring to the pixie who did her hair.

Andrew's eyes widened. Micah stifled a snicker.

"We all heard!" someone—it sounded like Chamomile—called over the trill of several accompanying wolf whistles. Andrew felt his ears heat up.

"Then finish the walls already!" Micah shouted, laughter in his voice.

Fionna sniffed the air, glanced at the bed, and then shrugged indifferently. "Can I run with Cosmos outside?"

Leaning his forearms on Andrew's shoulders, Micah watched him silently, yielding.

"Do you think she'll be all right, after this morning?" asked Andrew softly.

"In the bluffs? She couldn't be safer," Micah answered with a nod.

Andrew glanced at a cuckoo clock on the bookshelf, taking a moment to calculate. "Have her back before dusk!" he called.

"Yes, Uncle Fox!" returned Cosmos's musical voice.

Fionna gave a hop of excitement. She scrambled over to Andrew and licked his temple despite how he cringed. Looking up at Micah, she pawed his cheek with her fingers, grinned, and then turned and trotted out of the tent.

Andrew dropped his face into his hands, but relaxed when Micah gripped his shoulders and kissed the curve of his ear.

"All right," Micah murmured. "We've been side-tracked long enough." He leaned his hips against Andrew's back and resumed brushing his hair until he felt Andrew grow heavier against him as the remaining tension melted away. As Micah clumsily began braiding, Andrew let out a long breath, shut his eyes, and ran his fingertips over the staves.

He placed three of them on the table before him while Micah hummed and focused on his auburn locks. Andrew took three more measured breaths before he looked down at the table, hunching slightly, Micah easily echoing the movement so he didn't pull his hair.

Andrew gently rolled the stave on the left so he could see the mark etched in the chunk of wood whittled flat. "Emotion is *Beith*. Birch," he said, laughing. He moved onto the middle, already with its mark faceup, smiling again. "Spiritual is *Duir,* oak." Andrew paused over the third stave, his shoulders tingling. Micah's fingers stilled as if he sensed the same thing. As Andrew turned it so the mark faced up, he saw it pointed away from him, reversed. He bit the inside of his cheek as he said more slowly, "*Gort.* Ivy."

"Why does that scare you?" Micah asked quietly.

"*Gort* reversed is...inhibited growth," Andrew said, choosing his words carefully. "Life, or...or spirit, being threatened."

"The fuck?" Micah muttered. "Isn't the third spot Physicality?"

"Aye," Andrew agreed.

"Is that talking about what's already come to pass?" Micah reached back and clutched the healing athame wound. The scar felt tender still, stinging as he rolled his shoulder.

Andrew shook his head. "It should be future-oriented." He swallowed and looked up, watching Micah's ribs expand and a muscle jump in his jaw. Grasping Micah's hand, Andrew pointed at the middle stave and said more lightly,

"*Duir* is for leadership, though. You're coming into your own."

"Great..." Micah sounded dubious, eyes on *Gort.*

"Sometimes the message isn't very literal," Andrew assured him, rubbing Micah's pronounced knuckles. "It could be a metaphorical threat. The doll." He paused and then added, "I'm not an expert, either. The trees speak to you more than me."

With a resigned sigh, Micah nodded and tapped the first stave, the chunk of birch. "What about my little birchwood friend here?"

"Ah." Andrew grinned, lifting Micah's hand to plant a kiss on his wrist. "*Beith*—for emotion—is new, joyful beginnings. Prosperity, overcoming challenges, symbolizing love magic and union."

"Stop!" Micah cried, hugging Andrew's neck. "How perfect."

Laughing, Andrew nodded and nuzzled his arms. "Literally our marriage is your emotional waypoint. Whatever else is in store, let that guide us."

Kissing his temple, Micah sank onto the floor next to Andrew and sighed heavily, touching *Gort* again.

Sobering, Andrew offered, "We can talk to Ingrid. Tell her about the doll."

Micah picked up the piece of ivy, rolling it between his fingertips, considering. Finally, he shook his head. "Not yet. I...part of me wants to, yes. Because she's my big sister that can fix everything." He tapped the piece of ivy against the piece of oak. "But shouldn't I deal with this on my own? It's my mess with Diana and those bitches, so really what we should do is figure out a plan ourselves. Especially if Fionna's somehow at risk."

Andrew nodded. "Okay." He chewed on his thumbnail, staring at the Ogham symbols for so long his eyes went blurry.

Micah paused. "Do you think I can do it?"

Andrew's gaze sharply returned to his fiancé, whose skin was molten bronze and hair was seaglass beneath the faerie lights. "What? Yes. Obviously."

"It isn't obvious." Micah grimaced. "I handled nothing in the Redwoods, Andrew. I was powerless. And when we settled here, I was a disaster. I hardly made it through school. Hardly got the brownstone." He shook his head slightly. "This is all new to me. Having to handle shit."

"Good thing you aren't alone," Andrew said quietly, cupping Micah's cheek.

Eyes bright with restrained tears, Micah nodded, covering Andrew's hand with his own. There were days when he was younger that Micah wouldn't have believed that anyone would want to see him grow. That they'd prefer to see him fall. His life was so different now, especially since they started spending nights in Lilydale this last month. He could hardly recognize it. "Good thing."

Later in the day, the temperature was too warm for it to snow, but too cold to hold off the precipitation, turning everything to wet sludge. Andrew slid through slush towards Magic's Repair to put in a few hours of work with Sam, wearing a thin wool jacket over one of Micah's trendy hooded sweatshirts in hot pink.

When he pulled open the red door to the shop, Sam looked up from where he sat on the counter talking to a head of platinum blond hair. His companion lifted her head.

Outraged, Andrew yelled, "Gross! I remember you."

The heavyset woman narrowed her dark eyes lined with thick black makeup. "Oh, yeah!" She sneered. "The lame old man."

Andrew planted his fists on his hips. "Super lame of me to be pissed at you for stranding Sam in Lilydale by himself."

"What's the big deal? You know your way around there plenty, don'tcha?" She winked.

Sam was blotchy red from his forehead down to his neck. "Cirrus and I have just kept running into each other...it felt like fate, I guess?"

"Bummer though that he's still stuck with you," Cirrus said sweetly. She wore a black sweater dress accessorized with platform sneakers. Andrew hoped she would faceplant in the street in those shoes.

He sneered at her, "And what do you have going for you? 'Permanently stuck in your goth phase?'"

Cirrus straightened, crossing her arms and swaggering up to Andrew. She was so short it was as if she'd grown horizontally rather than vertically, like run-over chewing gum.

Glaring up at Andrew, she said to Sam, "Looks like I'm gonna go. Don't want this guy's bad vibes spreading to me." She shuddered and made a flicking motion at him. "Begone."

Andrew scowled at her as he watched her leave the shop in a cloud of incense. His boot squeaked as he turned his scowl on Sam. Very deliberately not looking at him, Sam resumed quietly working on a programming project on the iMac. Andrew gave him a growling sigh. "Come on, Sam. We live in the second largest city in the state. You can't find someone else to chill with?"

Sam glared at him with unexpected heat. "Andrew, you're hardly ever here. Why do you care who I'm hanging out with?"

Andrew grimaced. Sam slumped into his desk chair, heaving a ragged sigh, guilt tugging his lips down.

Andrew came around the counter and sat down in his chair next to him, the leg under him squeaking as he turned to face Sam. "You're right."

Arwen jumped onto the counter under his arm, twining her tail around Sam's neck and purring deeply in her chest. Sam mumbled something and tapped on his keyboard, eyes glassy with tears.

"And I haven't been helping with orders as much," Andrew added. "And that's unfair. This is my business and I can't dump it on you. At least not without your consent." Arwen padded up to Andrew and touched her nose to his.

"I mean, Micah got stabbed." Sam's voice was barely louder than his clacking keys. "It's a good reason to take a leave."

"But still." He reached out to scratch Arwen's chin but she dodged away, retreating to Sam's other side. Andrew tried to pretend like that didn't sting.

Sam lifted his head and stared at the ceiling tiles. "You just don't realize how boring being a human is till you're seeing all the crazy shit that happens to magical people like you."

Andrew sat back and blinked. "I'm not magical."

Sam snorted. "Yeah. Because non-magical people effortlessly bond with shapeshifting wolves."

Pausing a moment, Andrew let a small sigh out his nostrils. This was his first time realizing that maybe Fionna wouldn't have attached herself to just anyone she met in the woods. Shaking off the odd feeling the thought prompted, Andrew scooted his chair so he could bump their elbows together. "You're an outstanding guy, Sam. But Cirrus?" He curled his lip. "A big old dick."

Sam shot Andrew a quick and halfhearted glare. "You can be too, you know."

"Ouch." Andrew rubbed his neck. "Fair point."

Sam clicked his mouse and murmured, "I have to keep making friends. You're marrying a faerie prince. You're not gonna be around here forever."

Andrew leaned his cheek on his fist. He had a rebuttal on the tip of his tongue, but he sensed that wasn't Sam's point.

Sam took a short breath, more like a gasp than a sigh. "Can you look over this code for me before I execute?"

"For sure. Did you finish the Karan order?"

"Yeah. There's a new one you can start, the Franklin file."

"Roger that." Andrew wheeled over to Sam and started tapping down through his program file. Sam let him sit with their arms touching, and Andrew hoped that was enough for now.

# Chapter Three
# The Rift

The residents of Lilydale woke to the terrible roar of the ice wall fracturing like a calving glacier.

Tearing out of her hut still tangled in blankets, Ingrid reached the western wall before the thundering of the ice even echoed away. She watched the massive lip of her ice wall crumble, turning to white snow as it cascaded onto the cobblestone fence below. The magical seal between Lilydale and the winter night popped like a soap bubble. Cold air gusted inside, screaming through the jagged crack in the ice, blowing back Ingrid's loose red curls and making her instinctively shield her face in her blankets. Fionna howled in alarm, bursting out of the tent flaps followed closely by Andrew and Micah. In the frenzy of alarmed and confused Folk, Andrew slid barefoot down a slope of snow to reach Ingrid. He had his seax in hand, no shirt on, and hastily pulled on sweatpants.

Blade at the ready, he exclaimed, "What the hell happened to your wall? Oh my god, it's so cold!" Goosebumps raced up his arms and chest, shaking a deep shudder out of him. Micah, birchwood staff sparking bright spring green in the dark, spun in a circle on a limestone landing over them with his eyes on the heavens. Ingrid looked eastward and spotted Chamomile on the roof of her hut. Bow in hand, the goblin scanned the horizon, the edges of her cardigan flapping over silk pajamas. Her arm whipped up; she aimed an arrow toward the stars, shooting it off with a whistle audible across the compound. Faintly on the wind was a female cry, bit off as soon as it began.

Ingrid strode quickly away from Andrew and the other Folk examining the fractured ice wall. She rushed past her brother, who turned to watch her with a furrowed brow and his mouth in a thin line.

As Chamomile dropped to the ground outside her door, Ingrid demanded, "What did you see?"

Chamomile shook her head gravely. "Only a silhouette."

"But in the air."

Without confirming, Chamomile glared past Ingrid down at Micah and Andrew by the wall. "Hey, Heartwood!"

Micah straightened when Andrew nudged him. He twirled the staff in his hand and watched Chamomile stalk down the compound toward him with Ingrid a step behind her. Folk skittered out of their path.

Chamomile jumped on a wooden apple barrel. She grabbed Micah by the nape of his neck, yanking him close despite protests from both Andrew and Fionna. Level with his face, Chamomile snarled, "Did you forget to tell us something, Your Lordship?" She spat his title with a sneer.

"Back *off*." Glowering, Micah swiped his staff against her arm to break her grip on his neck.

"What is going on?" demanded Andrew, one hand raised toward Chamomile in warning.

"I just shot a witch on a broom." Each word from her mouth was sharp as the broken ice littering the compound. Chamomile slapped Andrew's hand down. "And Lord Heartwood here just looked a little *disappointed*, not terrified like the rest of us."

"What." The word dropped from Ingrid's mouth like a sword clattering.

"A witch did that?" Andrew pointed at the fissure in the ice wall.

"How was I supposed to predict their next move would be attacking Lilydale?" Micah shot back at Chamomile.

Ingrid stiffened, eyes narrowing. She looked down at Fionna, prowling in a circle around them with hackles still raised. Ingrid made a short, sharp noise, and Fionna lurched into action. She snapped her jaws at the Folk still gathered near the damaged wall. The signal was clear, and the gawking faeries slunk back to their resting spots and left the four of them alone.

When her job was done, Fionna discarded her wolf-skin and clung to Andrew's leg, eyes on the jagged ice overhead like it was going to fall to pieces until the whole thing crumbled.

Ingrid gazed coolly at Micah. "What do you mean, their 'next' move?"

Still scowling with her bright blue eyes fixed on Micah, Chamomile dug into the deep pocket of her cardigan. She pulled out the black-painted doll and thrust it into Ingrid's hands.

Ingrid gasped and dropped it as if burned. She stared at the doll in the snow, flexing and extending her fingers with her shoulders hunched. "Where did you find this?"

"Northern corner of Cherokee," said Chamomile. "Clearly you two found it as well, since I saw your footprints." She took a step on the barrel so her bare toes curled over the edge, chest to chest with Micah. "Now, I'll tell you how you could have predicted this, Lord Heartwood."

Micah straightened, the muscles in his jaw working and the grip on his staff tightening. He remained silent only because of the hand Andrew placed on his shoulder.

"If you hadn't kept that obvious threat a secret," she said, pointing at the doll, "I would have been able to tell you that Lilydale has gone up against the witches in the city before."

Micah's brows rose quickly, and then lowered again. "Th-these witches are my problem. I'll take care of them."

Chamomile's rosy lips curled back from jagged, silver-bright teeth. "You only get to say that when it's clear you *actually* will!"

"Hey." Ingrid held up a long hand. "This isn't productive."

"Tell us what to do next," said Andrew hurriedly.

Chamomile stepped off the barrel and thumped onto the ground. She pulled her cardigan further up on her shoulders, keeping her furious gaze on Micah. "I think we should ask Micah what to do next. Since he's going to take care of them."

"Chamomile, spitefulness is also not productive," warned Ingrid.

"It's not spiteful! I am angry because my village has been threatened and I wasn't prepared. I could have been, if someone my people now see as a leader hadn't kept critical information to himself." Her voice suddenly dropped and her expression cooled. She tilted up her chin in a challenge. "So don't stop now. Lead."

Ingrid remained silent and still as a winter night.

Micah ran his tongue over his lips. "I was going to go find the barista I fired." He managed to keep the tremor out of his voice. "She turned the attention of these witches on me, so she's going to take some responsibility for this."

"Good." Chamomile nodded once, sharply, and Andrew thought he noticed the goblin's shoulders relax slightly. "Are you bringing anyone besides your knight?" Her eyes flicked briefly toward Andrew. Micah shook his head. "Fine." Chamomile spun in the snow and trudged eastward up the stairs.

"Chamomile," Micah called after her.

She paused, but did not turn around to look at him.

Glancing at Ingrid to include her, he said, "I messed up. I'm sorry."

"Don't be sorry." Chamomile's icy blue eyes flashed at him. "Be *better*." Chamomile disappeared into her hut, a glow of light rising in her round paned windows.

Ingrid tucked a burgundy curl behind her ear and then crossed her arms. She lifted her gaze back to the fractured wall, releasing a quiet sigh through her nose. Then she turned away and went back to her hut, the bronze door echoing as it closed behind her. Her departure served as a silent reprimand to Micah, making his skin prickle with shame. Scraping his hair back off his forehead, he surveyed Lilydale without speaking. He wanted to kick something, or spew profanities. But when he glanced toward the baskets in the trees, he spotted one, two...five, six sets of eyes blinking, shining, staring down at him, watching him, waiting to see what he would do next.

As if he had any goddamn clue.

Andrew stuck his sword in a snowbank and propped a hand on his hip, absentmindedly stroking Fionna's hair. He looked up at the height of the ten-foot ice wall. "Do we know how Ingrid made this?"

"Of course not," grumbled Micah. "I don't know anything, clearly."

Andrew raised his eyebrows. "I can't imagine Chamomile would bother with a conversation like that if she thought you were an idiot."

"Also—" Micah's voice came out sharp with frustration. "I thought you said earlier that the *Gort* stave was a metaphorical threat, Andrew." He jabbed at the wall with the end of his staff, more to jab at something than to investigate.

Andrew set his jaw, eyes narrowing slightly. "There's no need to lash out at me. I was very upfront about the inexactitude of the staves."

Micah glared up at him, shoulders hunched in the manner of a cat braced for a clawed strike. His throat bobbed. Scoffing, he looked away. "Sorry." He brushed his palms over the wall, bending to scoop up a handful of the ice shaved off.

Andrew's gaze didn't shift as he stared at Micah for several more moments. Micah sounded about as sorry as a child forced to apologize, and it made his muscles clench in his shoulders. Andrew imagined what he'd get to say if he were still a hot-headed teenager with a big mouth. *"How did a woman half your height wound your fragile pride?"* was on the tip of his tongue, second being a reminder that Andrew had suggested telling Ingrid about the doll mere hours ago.

He shut his eyes, running a strand of Fionna's coarse hair through his fingers to collect himself. He just hadn't expected to be teaching his partner how to hold emotions respectfully, especially when Micah was eight years his senior. Then again, Andrew thought, perhaps Micah was quite young by Fae standards. Perhaps that's what the *duir* stave suggested: forthcoming growth into leadership. But forthcoming meant not *now*, which made Andrew wish he was petty enough to be snide.

Micah glanced Andrew's way with wine-splashed irises still boiling with frustration. But the longer he held Andrew's gaze, the more his shoulders slumped. "I am. Sorry. You wanted to tell her."

Andrew's own anger melted away like an ice cube inside Micah's sun-baked voice. He shrugged. "Live and learn."

Micah's brow crinkled slightly. "'Live and learn?'" he repeated. "Is that really what you were thinking just now?"

Andrew paused. "I...kind of."

"Kind of."

"I know you're trying," said Andrew carefully.

"All right then." Micah grinned, humorless, a little bit feral, like the Cheshire cat. "Forget it."

He turned his back on Andrew and his focus to the wall. He was *going* to do something about this. There was no way he would sleep before Lilydale was in better shape than this—unprepared for the cold and exposed to the elements because of...whoever broke the wall. Imagining Diana going *this* far was difficult, but then again, he hadn't anticipated she would try to have him murdered by her coven, either.

Mind racing, Micah looked up the hill behind the firepit. He turned on his heel and hurried past Andrew, whose face contorted in confusion. Micah had neither the interest nor the patience needed to communicate.

Using his staff to take large and loping steps up the limestone amphitheater stairs like his sister did, he climbed over the picket fence around the evergreen garden, startling Syabira on her bark and moss bed tucked behind the kiln throne. Even though she was wrapped in a heavy wool blanket, she shivered with a red cold-bitten nose as she surveyed Micah with curiosity. Giving her a quick nod, he leaned over the blanket of English ivy growing near her and dug his hand inside, feeling around for a large cluster of aerial roots and gently coaxing them off the bricks of the kiln.

Down below, Andrew stood watching Micah while Fionna hung onto his waist. He slowly took a step toward the ice fissure. Promptly, Fionna howled, dropping her weight and holding him in place, tightening her hold on him and squeezing her eyes closed.

"Fionna?" Andrew gasped. "What is it? Are you all right?" He tried to pry her arms off him—her grip hurt like a tourniquet—but she wailed louder. "Hey, hey, hey. Breathe, little pup." Awkwardly swinging his leg around and bringing Fionna with him, he changed routes, moving up to the steps past the fire pit. Thrusting his seax through a slat in a hollow log, he dropped onto the limestone and started to rub Fionna's back. "Come here, *a stór*," he murmured. Fionna lifted her flushed and soaking face, then climbed Andrew's leg to curl up in his lap, trembling wildly.

Shushing and rocking her, he said softly, "What is scaring you, little pup?"

"Witches," yelped Fionna. Choking on snot and tears, she gasped and hiccupped, "Witches want Micah hurt. Like Big Fionnas hurt."

"'Big Fionnas?'" repeated Andrew. "Your parents?"

Still shuddering, Fionna blinked around tears and nodded. "Parents. Witches say, 'parents, obey us!'" She bared her teeth. "Parents say no." Fionna shrank into herself, vibrating on his lap. The golden coins of her eyes dimmed into cautionary yellow.

Andrew thought immediately of the *faoladh* his grandparents rescued. Was it possible...? He swallowed. "Fi, did they...did your parents die?"

When she blinked, a tear flicked off her lashes. The question seemed to push her into a place void of feeling, a place where she was too frightened to cry anymore. "Parents hide Fionna, fight witch. But...witch use, uh—sharp." She mimed the hilt and blade of a weapon. Maybe an athame. She mimed spurting, trickling. "Blood."

Resuming his rocking, Andrew let out a sigh of, "Oh, little pup."

She was stiff now in his arms, eyes round and expression blank as a single shudder wracked her body. "Fionna sat and sat, maybe parents awake. But..." She hiccupped. "Just blood. Just cold." The last sound whimpered away as she began to sob again, covering her eyes.

"I'm so sorry, *a stór*," Andrew said, gently coaxing her head onto his shoulder, pressing his lips into her wiry hair. "We'll keep you safe, aye? You're safe with us. I promise." She choked and snuffled and let out gasping cries but they slowed and trickled away as he rocked her and hummed into her hair.

Halfway back down to the fractured ice wall cradling an armful of ivy roots, Micah muttered, "I need someone with wings," as he swung his head up toward the grove of trees where most of the nimble or winged Folk slept. "Hey, Thorn!"

A blue head popped out of a basket hanging from a high branch of a fir tree.

"Can I get your help?"

Thorn burst out of his basket. Several other heads prairie-dogged into view, curious or jealous as they watched the pixie buzz on minty green wings down to Micah.

Drifting onto the limestone, Thorn said in his wispy voice, "Name it." He wore a cardigan backwards so it buttoned under his wings, which were webbed with thin golden veins. He was a little too small of a pixie to fill out the cardigan, so the sleeves fell over his hands, and it looked almost like a shirt dress. He had lemon-yellow hair cut asymmetrically.

Micah held the ivy roots out to him. Thorn shook his sleeves back from his hands and then plucked the plant from Micah's fingers. Micah instructed Thorn, "Can you please line the crack with these? You might need to hold them in place until I say so."

Thorn nodded, flicking his wings, which whirred as they carried him straight up in the air like he was on a bungee cord. He pirouetted in the air and then tried to balance the leaves and roots on splinters of ice, but they started to fall. Thorn snatched them back and held them against the ice, looking over his shoulder through his wings at Micah.

Micah lifted his birchwood staff, took a slow breath in through his nose, and let it back out through his pursed lips. Then, eyes on the ivy roots, Micah sent out the magic twining inside his veins to speak to the ivy, inviting the two to play and grow over the fissure.

Something from the crack in the ice pushed back, rejecting his attempt to bring more life. Micah scowled. Thorn used his foot to scratch his leg as he awkwardly waited. Micah scanned the land at his feet, scuffing at the thin dusting of snow with the end of his staff. Dropping down, cross-legged, he dug his fingers through the snow and into the hard soil underneath, asking for it to join him and help the ivy sprout. Winter made the ground sluggish, slow to wake. Micah clenched his jaw, laying the staff on the ground by his knees. "I need your help," he whispered. "Please."

Thorn yelped and released the clump of roots as they exploded with newborn leaves that wriggled and sparked with light, but haltingly. Micah shook his head in frustration and pushed his will into the leaves. They yielded, unfolding, budding into a full rustling curtain of emerald-green ivy. Micah climbed back to his feet with both hands on his staff, which sparked and pulsed with a lively shamrock-green light. All else in his vision was a blur except what he was growing, demanding more from the ivy so that the vines raced forth in looping spirals, the leaves crowding into each other in a thick blanket.

He wasn't satisfied until the ivy bulged out of the fissure like insulation. Then he tucked the staff under his arm, pressed both palms to the wall, and imbued it with a final burst of life. Green light shot from his hands into the ice looking like the delicate veins in a wrist, sprouting seedlings which turned to velvety moss as it raced to merge with the ivy scar. With a groan, the magic border of the ice wall closed like a door on the winter. The cold seeped out of the air.

Light danced in Thorn's wide eyes. "Lord Heartwood, that was so great!"

Micah smiled. The corners of his lips trembled. His chest rose, and then he collapsed.

Thorn dove with a yell just as Andrew and Fionna shot off the steps toward Micah. The pixie caught Micah's bicep so he rag dolled under Thorn, head lolling until Andrew knelt beneath him and they could lower him into Andrew's arms. Micah's breathing was shallow and erratic, eyelids twitching as if his eyes were still moving underneath. It immediately sent an uneasy shiver up Andrew's spine. Hooking his arm underneath Micah's knees, Andrew struggled to stand until Thorn landed and helped him up with spindly hands. Fionna scooped up the birchwood staff and tucked it through Andrew's arm before pulling on her wolfskin. Thorn's slitted pupils were large and fearful as he hovered along beside Andrew as they made their way up the stairs toward Andrew and Micah's tent. Fionna stayed on Andrew's heels, ears pinned to her head. Thorn drew back the flap of their door as Andrew ducked inside, laying Micah on their mussed blankets. The staff rolled onto the mattress to rest against Micah's prone arm.

"What else can I do?" asked the male faerie.

"Nothing more. You helped a—" Andrew stopped when his voice warbled, betraying him. He swallowed the lump in his throat. "A lot. We're fine."

Nodding, brow furrowed, Thorn let the flap close. Once alone, Andrew tried to catch his breath while he knelt on the blankets next to Micah and touched his slick forehead. Isolation struck like a hammer. Tears leapt to his eyes. This must have been what it was like for Ingrid and Chamomile to nurse Micah after he'd been stabbed. Frightening and uncertain, like he was beneath the shadows that fell during a solar eclipse. Andrew stared forlornly down at Micah, worrying his lip between his teeth, resisting the instinct to try to shake Micah awake.

Fionna nosed open the tent flap and slunk inside, her head low. She crept up to the bed and nudged Andrew's leg until he reached out and scratched her ear. Then she climbed onto the bed and lay against Micah's calves, sniffing his hand with a whine.

Shuddering, Micah groaned. He squinted up at the faerie lights, eyes watering.

"Micah," gasped Andrew.

"Did I swoon?" asked Micah, blinking, taking in the worry creasing Andrew's brow and parted lips. He reached for Andrew's waist, which was chilled from the cold. At least that told him he hadn't been out for that long, if Andrew hadn't warmed back up yet.

Relief making his heart float, Andrew's lips twitched in a smile as he brushed aside Micah's bangs. "I wouldn't strictly call it that. You overexerted yourself—even though we all appreciate it. We'd have frozen overnight if you hadn't thought of that."

"My mess, my clean-up." Micah tried to sit up, but his arm buckled and he landed heavily on his shoulder. Hot tingling accosted his skin. Micah growled. "Literally, my magic is such a joke. Why can't I do more? You should have seen how fast someone in the Redwoods would have been able to do that. Easy as a sneeze."

"Were they half-human?" Andrew asked with one arched eyebrow.

Micah cast his arm dramatically over his eyes. "Whatever." Fionna stretched and planted a lick on his jaw, forcing a smile to curl his lips as he threw his other arm around the wolf's neck and scratched her scruffy jowl.

"How do you feel?" Andrew tucked Micah's humming birchwood staff under Micah's hip, wondering if it would help revive Micah a bit more.

"Sweaty," Micah grunted.

"Oh, you are." Andrew reached for their water bottle on the stump nightstand. He unscrewed the lid and helped Micah drink deeply. "We'll head back to Saint Claire in the morning."

Micah nodded. There were dark bruises under his eyes that hadn't been there when they went to bed. "I feel like a husk," he said. "What did I do wrong?"

"You need to give less of yourself next time," Andrew told him gently. "Ask for more help from the earth. You're not an infinite store of power, great as your reserves may be. The earth is much more bountiful than us."

With a glimmer in his eye, Micah pulled Andrew down into a kiss, the tickle of Andrew's auburn locks on his cheeks making Micah shiver. When Andrew leaned back, confused but smiling, Micah explained, "It's sexy when you talk like a wizard."

Andrew snorted and propped himself up with his cheek on his fist. "You should rest."

"So should you." Micah's eyes slid shut at the mere mention of rest.

Melting at the sight, Andrew smiled and pressed a kiss to Micah's damp brow. Fionna peered over Micah's chest through one slitted eye before shimmying closer, nuzzling under Micah's arm and huffing as she fell asleep.

Andrew remained as he was, buzzing with the electric fear of seeing Micah faint, knowing it would be a while before he could sleep. He gently combed his fingers through Micah's moss-green hair until Micah stopped that feline habit of leaning into his caress. It had been difficult in the beginning to tell when Micah was sleeping, since he twitched like a cat having a dream, always just a little bit restless. His tell was his breathing growing louder, more like sigh after sigh. When he hadn't stirred between sighs for a while, Andrew climbed back to his feet. Fionna remained fast asleep, curled protectively around Micah in their blankets. Smiling fondly down at both of them, he stood there for a moment and then reached for the jar of faerie lights on the ceiling and tapped them until the glimmers inside dimmed and became dark. He pulled on a fleece zip-up and one of Micah's slouchy beanies, and finally slid into his moccasins.

As Andrew emerged back into the night, he saw Ingrid outside her bronze door, hands on her hips, staring at the repairs in her wall. His movement drew her eye, and she pulled her patterned shawl tighter around her shoulders as Andrew approached her. They stood in silence beside each other for a few minutes. Andrew noticed the wall still glowed faintly green, as if holding a piece of Micah's power within it.

"How did you make the wall?" Andrew asked after a while.

"Agassiz," she replied.

"Gesundheit." Andrew snickered.

Ingrid cast him a disdainful glance.

"Sorry. Low-hanging fruit. What is Ag..."

"Ay-guh-see," she said slowly, like a teacher, a mocking smile curling her lip.

Andrew glared at her. "What is Agassiz?"

"It's what was here before, when there were glaciers."

"But you made the wall this winter."

Ingrid nodded, moving in a slow circle, as if checking the rest of the perimeter of the walls like she didn't trust it was intact. "What was on the earth before still remains long after it physically fades. We have at our fingertips a millennia of natural wonders."

Andrew was silent, gazing through the almost transparent wall down toward the frozen Mississippi. The barren trees clawed toward the dark sky, illuminated by the glow of the city encroaching on it. He tried to imagine such a significant change: hulking glaciers in Minnesota. Like the flood plains didn't exist, and the bluffs simply cupped the frozen mountains. If that were the case, all Ingrid would have had to do is carve the ice back into reality.

The thought was overwhelming, staggering, and yet he also felt the truth of it in the soles of his feet. On the North Shore, his mum had been teaching him similar lessons. Ingrid only confirmed what he already thought to be true.

Andrew glanced over at her, scrutinizing her fair, sharp profile for a long moment while she blinked dark lashes. He asked, "Are all Tall Ones as in tune with natural magic as you?"

Ingrid shrugged. "I don't know. I've never talked about this with anyone."

# CHAPTER FOUR

# THE WITCH

MICAH CHARMED THEIR WAY past the librarian without needing a student ID. He murmured a joke to the bespectacled woman at the front desk, gesturing vaguely. Andrew took his cue and shuffled around him with his hand around Fionna's shoulder. Fionna's eyes were wide with wonder and glued to Andrew's phone screen as she tapped at colorful pieces of fruit in a game. Most folks would probably think she was just a normal girl, with her hair braided neatly—Andrew was getting quite good at it—and a little sequined sweatshirt over leggings. They'd gotten her a sturdy pair of duck boots (purple, of course, per her request) that helped compensate for her human feet and kept her safer when she was scrambling over snowdrifts and splashing in puddles.

Envy gnawed at Andrew's chest as he listened to the quiet murmur of students and the dry hiss of pages turning in textbooks. This library didn't quite compare to the

University of Minnesota, but it still made him miss the simplicity of academia. And the solitude. And the absence of life-threatening magic, even if his fiancé had more of it than their enemies. He suppressed a sigh. If he was ever going to get the chance to get back into academia, he'd probably missed it. Now he had Lilydale to worry about, and Fionna. Not to mention a business he was sorely neglecting.

Andrew glanced down as Micah slipped into step beside him, the smell of mulberries coming with him as Micah's nightshade eyes scanned the crowded library. They leaned into each other; Andrew draped his arm around Micah's shoulders as he steered them further into the space. The best tables in his opinion were near windows furthest from the information desk, so Andrew wanted their search to start there.

After a long sleep and a hot shower at the brownstone, Micah was trying to make himself sit with the discomfort and shame he felt around Chamomile's lecture. That was the worst part about being lectured by a faerie. You knew they weren't exaggerating anything. So to be told off by Chamomile—she was truly more formidable than she had any right to be at four and a half feet tall—meant that Micah had well and truly failed. And that was...uncomfortable, but okay. It meant he was trying, at least.

He hadn't gotten told off much in his life because he was typically busy letting things happen around him. Not making them happen. The positive of Chamomile snarling at him was that it gave Micah quite a bit more direction than he'd had before. Chamomile confirmed what he'd been feeling, but had been reluctant to admit. That the Folk in Lilydale were paying more and more attention to Micah. That his actions held weight, and they were waiting to see what he'd do with it. At least he'd been successful fixing Ingrid's wall, but not without fainting dramatically. Andrew's usual strategy when Micah screwed up was to show him extra kindness and not actually say anything about what transpired. Micah still wasn't sure if that worked for him or not. This wasn't the time to ask him to make an adjustment, but it was going to need to be said sooner or later.

Micah glanced up at Andrew and quickly confirmed to himself that Andrew could do just about anything to him and get away with it. He was particularly attractive in the winter, Micah thought. It was his skin colored pale as the soft insides of fresh bread, his hair back in a bun, the sharp cut of his dark double-breasted pea coat, and the complicated way he tucked his wool scarf into his collar.

Micah used a hushed library voice. "The scarf is an heirloom, right? County...er...county Loud?"

"Close. County Louth. It belonged to my granddad, Phalen."

"Isn't that your middle name?"

Andrew gave him a sidelong smile. "Aye," he said, copying his mum's brogue.

Micah blushed immediately, wishing he could pounce on Andrew right then and there and lap that delicious accent off his tongue. "Are you gonna wear a kilt to our wedding?"

Andrew laughed soft and rough. "No, I've never even been to Ireland."

"Aw." Micah's shoulders sagged.

Andrew grinned and tugged Micah's hat down over his eyes, making him protest and bonk into him. Micah whipped it off with a scowl and fixed his hair.

"Do you smell that magic?" Andrew whispered, peering around a tall bookshelf. Fionna nodded first before Micah' nostrils flared and he pressed his full lips into a line. Most of the library was...dry and lifeless—except for Micah—but something nearby flickered like a dying lightbulb. Andrew sat Fionna in a plush chair under a window. "*Fan*," he told her, indicating for her to stay in the chair. He pinched her cheek lightly between his fingers.

Fionna gave Andrew a dismissive glance with her golden eyes. "Aye." She pulled her skinny knees up on the seat and stuck her tongue out between her lips as she tapped away at the game on Andrew's phone.

Micah smirked. "So?"

"What?" Andrew looked pointedly away.

"How long before you let her call you Dad?"

Andrew's ears warmed. It wasn't like he hadn't entertained the same thought. He was the first person she answered to, even though she was affectionate with Micah and reverent with Ingrid. She regularly fell asleep in his arms, and her pudgy little hand fit perfectly in his palm. But he deflected. "Does a shapeshifting wolf girl really need a dad?"

"Maybe not a normal dad," said Micah. "But definitely a 'you' kind of dad. She seems to fit into our world."

Cheeks burning, Andrew gazed down at Micah with the overwhelming sense that everything was exactly as it should be. Micah had fixed his hair in such a way that a few strands fell across his forehead like blades of grass, his eyes vibrant as summer lilacs despite the cold outside. The girl with the vanilla-scented magic was somewhere in here, but she wasn't going anywhere—at least not so quickly that Andrew couldn't spare a minute to crush his mouth to Micah's.

When they receded into the shadows of a secluded aisle
of books, Andrew pushed Micah by his hips against the

bookshelf. Micah's eyebrows rose in bewilderment and then hitched lower, tilting back his head to rest against the shelf where Andrew braced himself. Grasping Micah's chin, Andrew brought their faces close so they almost kissed, but he stopped short before their lips touched, hovering over him and grinning when Micah opened one silver-bright eye to glare at him. Enjoying the torment, Andrew ghosted his teeth against the hinge of Micah's jaw, his lips brushing slightly against the apple of Micah's throat, where a barely audible growl vibrated. Micah wound an arm tightly around Andrew's waist, pulling him into his chest, nosing Andrew's cheek until their lips finally connected in a kiss that still wasn't as firm as Micah wanted. He teased open Andrew's lips with his tongue, but then Andrew pulled away, his laughter deep and rumbling as Micah gave a whine of protest.

"Yas, boys. Love is love."

They both turned sharply as a young student gave them a peace sign at the end of the aisle, the half of their hair that wasn't buzzed colored lime green, large black aviator glasses perched on their nose. The student scurried off as soon as they were seen.

Micah cocked his head. He looked back at Andrew, who was still watching the end of the aisle with embarrassed color on his cheeks making his freckles stand out. Since he was distracted, Micah pushed onto his toes and planted a kiss on him, catching his face between his hands so he couldn't pull away. Andrew finally gave in, mouth opening to allow Micah's tongue to flick against his, offering him a musical moaning sigh. Micah let him go with a smirk of satisfaction, slipping his hand under Andrew's jacket to pinch the soft skin of his navel and forcing him to surrender another sigh-moan.

Ochre eyes glowing like embers, Andrew's gaze roved hungrily over Micah. "God, you'd have tanked my GPA."

"Why?" Micah looked offended. "I was a great...er...I was an average student."

A crinkle creased the skin under his eye. "I'd never do any homework. Just you. All right, back on that vanilla trail."

Far in the back corner of the library at a table by a window, a brunette lifted her head when the couple appeared from an aisle of history books. Her gray eyes bugged. Diana slammed her book closed and started to stand up until Micah lowered himself silently into the seat across from her. Andrew leaned casually against the edge of the table, giving her a brittle smile, rolling his polished agate between the fingers of his left hand.

She sagged back into her chair, her complexion paling. "Shit. You guys, I don't want any trou..."

"Hush," ordered Micah.

Obedient, or charmed, she clamped her mouth shut. No scent rolled off Micah, leading Andrew to believe she acquiesced voluntarily. The girl who kissed his fiancé was a pretty young woman with round cheeks and a narrow chin, and she stared up at Andrew like she wanted to crawl out of her skin and die. Diana's hair was loose around her shoulders under a white beanie. She had dark eyeliner on and a mauve sweatshirt.

"Your little coven has pissed us off up in Lilydale," Micah told her, elbow on the table and chin in his hand. He wasn't masking his eyes anymore, Andrew noted; they were nightshade-purple now as he gazed coldly at Diana.

"My—" Diana's brow furrowed. "I haven't seen any of those women since...since..."

Micah narrowed his eyes. "Say it."

"Since I helped them try to kill you." She swiped her fingers across her wet lashes. "Micah, I wish I hadn't—"

He shook his head to silence her. "I don't care what you wish. It was insightful for me, honestly. And you all would have been disappointed anyway, because I'm half-human. If you'd tried to...make yourselves immortal, or something, you'd probably just have gotten indigestion."

"Oh." Diana blinked. "That explains a lot."

Micah glared at her.

"N-not in a bad way!"

Carrying on, Micah said casually, "Well, it's too bad you've fallen out of contact with those witches. It makes your job a lot harder now."

"My...my job?"

"Yeah." Micah lowered his hand and leaned toward her. "You're going to get us some information. You're going to find out which of your nasty little witch friends attacked Lilydale last night."

Her eyes widened. "Lilydale was attacked? Are you okay?"

Micah leaned back sharply, quizzical, thrown off by the empathy of her question. "Wh...what do you care? I fixed it, if you must know."

Sensing Micah falter, Andrew crossed his arms and asked Diana, "If you've parted from that coven, why do you still feel like magic?"

Diana glanced up at Andrew, her expression growing thoughtful. "That...that noble faerie only has me on oath not to practice dark magic. So now I just...make intention jars, show gratitude for trees, watch the moon and stuff." She raised a brow slightly and asked, "You can feel that?"

Andrew responded with stony silence.

Diana wilted and looked away from him.

Micah said, "Who else do you know? There's the dead witch. And there's the witch with the long hair, the one who ran away."

"After you broke her arm." Diana's eyes narrowed, a storm of fury darkening her features as she continued, "That's Sophie. And Caty might have stabbed you, but you *killed* her. Sweet tea shop manager Micah, all smiles and tenderness. You *killed* someone. How does your conscience feel about that?"

Micah just stared at her, expressionless. His stomach clenched, the birchwood cuff shivering on his wrist as the memory assaulted him. Andrew had to actively resist the urge to take his hand.

Diana's resolve grew; she straightened in her seat. "And how did your faerie friends feel finding out you killed a witch? Faeries and witches have feuded since the dawn of time." Diana scoffed. "I can't believe you're half-faerie with how clueless you seem. That's why you seem so human, isn't it? You have no idea what it means to be Fae."

Andrew slapped his hand down on her closed book. He leaned close to the younger woman's face and said softly, "Watch it." Diana flinched. She inched away from him, swallowing, mercifully quiet.

Throat bobbing, Micah raced to collect himself while Andrew gave him this blessed moment to do so. Almost done. They could almost leave. Micah finally told her in a voice that did not betray his feelings, "Send a text to Sophie. Tell her you want to get dinner with her Friday night. Red Rabbit, six P.M."

Diana gave him an incredulous look. "No."

Micah invited the birchwood cuff to help him get his point across. It crawled into his palm and started to grow into a branch sharp as barbed wire, stretching across the table until its jagged end pressed into Diana's sternum

with an acid-green light. She caught her breath, lips parting, shoulders stiffening. Micah said in a quiet voice eerily
unlike himself, higher and musical and void of feeling, "Go
on then."

Diana tried to scoot her chair back to get the staff off her
chest, but Andrew stuck his boot out and wedged it against
the leg of the chair to hold her in place. She whispered
weakly, "Okay. Okay. Understood. Sirs." Hands trembling,
she picked up her phone and showed them as she pulled up
an empty text message and started typing Sophie's name.

Satisfied, Micah called the staff back into his hand. It
scuffed the table as it slithered across to him, wrapping
around his wrist and settling with the whisper of leaves in
a breeze.

Diana stared at the cuff for another moment before tapping into the messages screen on her phone while Andrew
leaned over her shoulder, watching her.

The send noise whooshed on Diana's phone, and she
swallowed visibly as she looked up.

"Who doesn't silence their phone in a library?" Andrew
asked with disgust.

Diana paused with her thumbs hovering over the screen,
giving Andrew an odd look out of the corner of her eye.

Micah held out his hand for her phone.

Diana moved to give it to him and then jolted when she
saw the twining band of his engagement ring. "O-oh. Um.
Congratulations?"

As if Micah needed her congratulations. His whole relationship almost ended because of her. Silent, Micah beckoned for her phone until she set it in his palm.

"Good girl," said Micah, and handed it back. "I'll pick you up at quarter to. Just to make sure there's no funny business." He smiled, but the expression didn't warm his eyes.

Biting her lip, Diana said urgently, "Micah, there's no reason to—"

"Bye then." He stood abruptly, thrust his hands into his coat pockets, and turned from the table. Andrew fell into step with him, hand firmly on the small of his back. He cast a single hard glance over his shoulder at the woman, who watched them leave and hunched her shoulders when she fell under his glare.

Fionna unfolded herself from the chair by the window and wedged herself between them, holding Andrew's phone between her teeth. Making a face, Andrew gently pried it free and wiped it on his coat. The three of them walked without speaking to Micah's car on the curb a block away. Micah's gaze stayed on the snowy tracks in the pavement. The clouds of his breath were staccato puffs.

Fionna glanced up at him, and then at Andrew. She dug her hand into Micah's pocket and joined their fingers, making him jump before a soft smile spread on his lips. He bumped her lightly with his hip.

A moment later, he shook his head slightly and looked up at Andrew. "You know I actually forgot I broke some random girl's arm? Just...slipped my mind. Not important, I guess." He returned his gaze to the ground.

"Adrenaline interferes with memory storage," Andrew told him softly.

Micah rolled his eyes, just slightly, just briefly, before he seemed to catch himself. He blinked hard and glared at the pavement.

Andrew's brows lowered. "What was that for?"

"Nothing," he muttered. Then he sighed heavily. "No, it's not nothing. I...I need you to tell me that I fucked up."

"Fucked up," echoed Fionna.

Indignant, Andrew replied, "What? No, thank you."

"You told me to tell Ingrid about the doll," Micah said with more heat. "I didn't listen because I thought I could handle shit myself. You get all nice, and you get all quiet, but that makes me *deeply* paranoid that you think I'm a hopeless idiot."

Andrew stopped on the sidewalk next to the car. "Micah, I get quiet because I know there's no possible way I could understand the position you're in."

"Yeah, but—"

"You're straddling two wildly different worlds. All I can do is observe." Andrew shrugged. "I'm just a guy. I have no grounds to tell you what to do or what I think of what you're doing for your people in Lilydale. I'm not one of them."

Keeping a wary eye on them, Fionna climbed onto the hood of the car, pulling her knees up to her chest.

Micah stepped into the snow, falling against the side of the car with his arms crossed. He didn't speak right away, a muscle rolling in his jaw. "But Diana said exactly what you said a month ago. Maybe I'm getting a bit more magical, but I have no idea how to manage anything about being Fae. I've spent forty years making sure that I think, act, and feel like a human."

"So are you saying being human isn't good enough?" Andrew blurted. He knew that wasn't what Micah meant, but his pounding heart spoke for him.

"No!" Micah said, impatient. He shut his eyes and said more gently, "No. Of course not."

"Here's the thing," said Andrew. "*You* get to choose what being Fae means. There's no one else like you. Not even Ingrid, even though you share the Redwood Queen in common. You are bound to be different from her. This is *your* path."

Micah's eyes were deep merlot under the powder blue winter sky. Catching his lip between his teeth, he searched Andrew's face with a slight shake of his head. He could tell by the look in Andrew's eyes, turned to that wonderful shade of antique gold under the winter sun, that Andrew believed in Micah's path with every fiber of his being. But...how could he be so confident in something Micah was so confused about?

Micah admitted softly, "But I don't know what my path is."

Andrew stepped closer to him and touched Micah's chin between his fingers. "That's okay. You're not walking it alone. And it's not a straight path."

Micah's lips screwed together and twitched as he suppressed a smirk. Losing the battle, he hiccuped, "Clearly it's not."

Andrew blinked and cocked his head.

Micah slapped a hand over his mouth and fell into a fit of giggles.

"Oh good god. Just had to get the gay joke in there, eh?"

Relaxing, Fionna slid silently off the hood of the car and started rummaging through Andrew's pockets looking for his phone. She found it easily and snapped at his fingers when he tried to intercept her. She shuffled back onto the hood, ankles hooked over each other as she tried to figure out how to get past his lock screen.

Still giggling, Micah waved his hand and said hoarsely, "Sorry. I'm sorry. Low-hanging fruit. I think this is all making me giddy, you know? Like, in a bad way."

Kissing the tip of his nose, Andrew nodded and said, "Yes. I get that. All I want to add is that the most important thing I need from you is that you not hide anything."

"Andrew, I don't think my face is capable of hiding anything from you."

"Yeah, that's true," he agreed, using the pad of his thumb to trace the curve of the dimple in Micah's cheek. Andrew grazed his lips against Micah's throat, twining his arm around his neck. He said into the smooth skin behind his ear, "I can read your face as easily as my favorite book."

Micah shut his eyes and held onto Andrew's waist as the taller man leaned over him against the car and tilted his head lightly to the side. Andrew kissed his way to Micah's mouth and nipped his lower lip.

Then with their lips still faintly touching, Andrew murmured with his eyes closed, "But if you want some feedback, what if we consider *not* Ostara for our wedding? Litha, for example. Just to give us a bit more time."

Micah growled into Andrew's mouth, "We're not doing Litha. Midsummer is trash." He moved back slightly and eyed Andrew through hooded lids. "People would think we're doing some bullshit nod to Shakespeare, and before you know it, this would all be a dream."

Andrew tilted his head. "Would they though?"

Micah scowled. "No Litha."

"Everyone loves Beltane..."

Micah drooped against the car and went limp with a mournful cry of, "You don't think we can do it!"

"So dramatic." Andrew pulled Micah off the car with his arms around his shoulders. "I think we can do anything. But if you're really set on Ostara—like, thirty-five days away—then we have a lot of work to do." Andrew kissed each of Micah's temples. "And I might go gray."

"I'm willing to chance it, Andrew the Gray."

# CHAPTER FIVE
# THE NIGHTMARE

Almost as soon as Micah fell asleep, he dreamed about women in black. Empty eyes stared through the space of his dreams. The lily wrapped with bone dangled over him, bright orange petals dripping off and turning to ash. All he could do was watch, helpless, as if the petals were his loved ones. His dream legs tried to move him, but they were paralyzed.

Hands gripped his shoulders and spun him around, making him stumble. The blue-haired witch smiled sweetly at him, cradling her broken arm—bloodied and dangling with the bone thrusting through, sharp and white.

Micah gasped and fell back, crashing into ground that felt too warm, too wet. Heart hammering, he looked down. Blood painted the limestone under him. He lifted his hands and they were smeared with it, congealing under his nails, sinking into the crevices of his ring and staining the agate black.

With a cry of horror, Micah tried to get his feet under him, tried to scramble upright. But the ground was slick, making him slip and collapse on his injured shoulder. He screamed; the eruption of pain was blinding, worse by far than when the athame had first sunk into him. Micah rolled toward his good arm and tried to push himself upright, but not fast enough. Somebody jumped on top of him, clawing for his throat and finding purchase as they pinned him to the ground, crushing his windpipe so he couldn't breathe. Vision dark with panic, Micah groped at the hands crushing his throat. He lifted his eyes toward the face looming over him.

It was Sam.

Sam's slender face was gray, his eyes sunken, black tatters of clothing draping over his shoulders. His lips pulled impossibly far back from his teeth, turning his features skeletal. Under his matted bangs, his eyes were feverish, his pupils tiny pinpricks. Micah scratched at his friend's wrists, his lungs igniting with desperation as they fought for the last wisp of breath inside. His heels scrabbled into the dirt but just kicked it loose, doing nothing to free him, leaving him to die.

In her wolfskin, Fionna jumped on top of Micah's limp, clammy body in his bedroom, clamping onto the collar of his shirt. She lifted him off his pillows and gave him a violent shake. When he didn't come to, she dropped his shirt, sprang onto his legs, and sank her teeth into his calf.

In his dream, Sam's expression blinked out as if changing channels on the television. He suddenly wasn't Sam; his face was rounder, eyes brown and smeared with dark makeup, lips making an angry red Cupid's bow. Micah shoved desperately at the stranger holding him down. As he did, a manacle of heat clamped onto his ankle and ripped him out from beneath the assailant. He woke with a hoarse scream in the dark of his bedroom in the city.

Unable to discern threat from salvation, he kicked at the stabbing pressure on his leg and struck Fionna with his heel in the side of her head. She yelped and released him, stumbling off the bed and slinking across the room with her tail tucked between her legs. Startled by her yip of fear, Micah returned to the waking world with a jolt. Pain shot through him and wrenched a cry from his chest, but it burned its way up through his throat. Was he really dying? He flailed in his sheets and fought to sit up as Andrew reached blindly toward Micah's ragged gasping, which descended into hiccuping, breathless sobs.

"Micah?" Andrew swiped his arm into the lamp at his bedside; it teetered, and he caught it just before it fell. He clicked it on to cast garish light across Micah with his knees pulled up to his chest, rocking, cradling his left arm. Unseeing, his eyes were wide and flashing blood-red in the lamplight.

"Micah? Micah. Love. Micah. Hey, you're awake. You're safe." Andrew touched Micah's shoulder and then snatched his hand back. His fingers were smeared with blood. "What the f...your back is bleeding again. What happened? Y...you were just..."

"Th-They came in my dreams," Micah whispered, frantic, still rocking as he began to whimper, touching his throat with violently trembling fingers, eyes and nose streaming.

Though the words sent a chill racing up his spine, Andrew gingerly pulled off Micah's shirt, as careful with the left arm as he had been right after his injury. The athame wound over Micah's shoulder blade was open where it had been a raised pink scar yesterday, now slowly oozing and seemingly darker around the edges, like fruit rotting after you take a bite and set it aside. Bile rose in Andrew's throat, his heart lurching in his chest.

"Honey, c'mon, breathe with me. Look at me." He leaned down to try to get into Micah's line of sight, to try to push back some of that faraway terror turning Micah's eyes into chipped rubies. Then Andrew jolted. "Shit! Your throat." He tipped back Micah's chin and brushed the column of his throat, which was dotted with faint brown bruises. "What the ever-loving f..."

He turned as Fionna's claws clicked on the floor. She emerged from under the desk, ears pinned back on her head, her haunted eyes lit from within. Before Andrew could address her, she turned away toward the windows. Throwing back her shaggy head, she loosed a low, warbling howl through her dark lips and glinting silver fangs.

Micah jumped. His first coherent thoughts shook back into his head thanks to the trembling song falling from the wolf's throat. Andrew's arms were cool and solid as they wrapped around his waist and eased his sense of terror, but as he continued to come back to his body, he realized something was horribly wrong.

"Oh my god," he cried, curling up against Andrew. "My shoulder...it's *wrong*."

Micah's blood was caked under Andrew's fingernails. It paralyzed any words of encouragement from leaving Andrew's mouth. Instead, he held onto Micah's shoulders and tried to swallow his fear.

Micah shuddered as he tasted mulberries through his slightly open mouth. He peeled open an eye and straightened to look over Andrew's shoulder, toward the windows, which then gave him such a start he almost screamed again. "I-Ingrid?"

Ingrid stood under a moonbeam, chest heaving, one foot slightly forward as if she'd arrived mid-step. Her eyes were wide, shining like pools of shed blood. She stared at them for a moment and then shifted her gaze to Fionna.

Shaking off her wolfskin, Fionna hugged herself and whimpered, "Witches."

Swiftly crossing the room, Ingrid approached Micah and began inspecting him like he was her injured pup, perched on the edge of the bed. She lightly folded him down and swiped a finger through the blood on his shoulder before touching it to the tip of her tongue. Immediately, she grimaced and spat, leaping back to her feet.

The door to Micah's room burst open to a bedraggled Julian wrapped in a crookedly tied robe. He exclaimed, "What is that wolf—"

"Dad," began Micah.

Julian froze, wide-eyed like a frightened deer. When he collected himself enough to speak, he asked in almost a whimper, "Ingrid? Wh...What did you do?"

A flash of annoyance came and went on Ingrid's features as she turned toward Julian by the door. She said with kindness belied by the look in her eyes, "I apologize for the disturbance, Mr. Stillwater. Micah—"

Micah interrupted, "I just keep getting into trouble. I'm sorry, Dad. Can we have the first aid kit and some chamomile tea?"

Julian stared at Micah and asked flatly, "What's the matter with your voice?"

"Just the usual," said Micah. "Just a nightmare."

"Was it her?" He nodded at Ingrid.

Ingrid's expression darkened.

"She came here to help," Andrew said swiftly.

"Ever since you have gotten closer to her," said Julian, voice brittle, "you keep getting hurt."

Andrew stole another glance at Ingrid, who looked to be trying very hard to keep her mouth shut. He said gently, "Julian, I know you might think it looks that way, but I promise you that she is only protecting Micah."

"Dad," said Micah, firm but quiet, his voice strained and his face contorted with pain. "Please? I need your help. Can you bring the first aid kit?" He let out a thin sigh. "And strong tea. In the pot."

Julian closed his robe over his chest, his face creased with an angry frown. He clicked his tongue and turned to leave, slamming the door behind him.

"Why don't you have more protections in this house?" Ingrid spun to face Micah, fists clenched, voice brittle as glass. "How have you lived here this long without warding it? No wonder the Redwood Queen lured Julian back!"

Micah flinched. He stared at his hands, wringing them together.

Andrew fixed Ingrid with a fearsome glare, bright with fury. She met his eyes, brows lowered. As Andrew stared her down, slowly shaking his head, Ingrid's resolve faltered.

Sighing, she sank onto the edge of the bed. "I'm sorry. I shouldn't have—"

"No," rasped Micah. "You're right." He lightly rubbed his bruised neck. "This place needs better protection."

"Yes. But you can do it. You have the power." Ingrid clasped his elbow.

"I need your help." Micah shut his eyes.

She nodded. "You have it."

Andrew slid his arm around Micah's neck and kissed his damp cheek.

Micah opened one eye and looked over at Fionna, beckoning to her with a raised hand. As a frightened little girl in heart pajamas, Fionna shuffled up to the bed and climbed onto the blankets and into Micah's outstretched arm. She tucked herself in among Andrew and Micah and bowed her head, sniffling, rubbing at her eyes. Then she pulled on Micah's pant leg to expose her bite mark, crouching over it and licking at the red indents with her little human tongue.

"Oh, oh baby girl, you're okay—stop," laughed Micah as he and Andrew gently drew the girl away from his ankle. "It hardly hurts. I bet it hurt way more when I kicked you. I'm so sorry."

Fionna's face crumpled. She threw herself around Micah's middle and squeezed him so fiercely it knocked the breath out of his lungs. Standing over them, Ingrid rubbed the girl's back with a faint smile.

Fionna rasped, "I don't want the witches to kill you."

Micah's heart sank. "Yeah," he whispered. "Same, kiddo." He took the tissues Andrew offered him and held Fionna for a few minutes until her crying abated, and then he leaned her back to clean her up as she whimpered softly.

Fionna stayed pressed to Micah's side when Julian returned with what Micah had requested. His hands trembled on the transparent teapot. The amber contents were about to slosh over the edge until Ingrid reached over his shoulder and plucked the pot from his grip. Julian jumped, shying away from her, rushing to drop the first aid kit in Andrew's lap. Micah caught Julian's hand between his own before his father could back away. Julian's breathing was shallow and his eyes were downcast.

"Dad." Micah rubbed his thumb over Julian's knuckles. "Breathe. You're safe. She was helping you. Look at me, please." When Micah met his darkened amber gaze, he smiled faintly and said, "Just take a pill and try to get some sleep. Sorry we woke you up. Fi, can you go hang out with him?"

"Sure, we can cuddle!" Fionna yipped.

Julian pried his hand free from Micah, nodded faintly, and backed toward the open door. Pulling on her wolfskin, Fionna thumped off the bed and trotted after him, licking his fingers and bumping into his knee. Julian scratched her ruff and murmured something to her as he left the room and shut the door behind him.

Frowning, Ingrid sat heavily on the bed behind Micah's back, pulling her long legs up to sit criss-cross. Andrew unzipped the medical kit and crawled across the bed to sit beside her, and in weighty silence they began tending to Micah's raw, weeping wound. Ingrid sniffed audibly several times while she swiped an antiseptic wipe; Micah hissed and clenched his fists. Once they had wiped away the tar-like blood oozing from the athame wound, Andrew carefully stuck a patch of gauze over it which Ingrid taped down with neatly torn strips of adhesive.

"Andrew..." Micah's voice was a thin, haunted whisper. "In my dream, someone was trying to kill me."

Andrew glanced up, nodding, as if he'd already reached that conclusion.

When he looked over his shoulder to meet Andrew's eyes, Micah's irises were burgundy. "It was Sam."

# CHAPTER SIX
# THE ANOINTING

BACK IN THE SLING he'd hoped he was finished using, with a large square of gauze taped to his back, Micah tried not to focus on the sharp, terrible pain that had returned to his shoulder. Or the fact that his dreams had been invaded, decimating the sense of security that the brownstone offered. And if he wasn't safe, that meant Julian wasn't either. Or Fionna. Or Andrew. Which was all the motivation he needed to find a way to guard the brownstone, to restore that sense of security, so they could all try to snatch a few more hours of sleep before dawn.

Micah left Andrew and Ingrid at the bed moments after they taped him up, heading toward the windows. He tripped on pants he'd left on the floor, making Andrew and Ingrid both suck in gasps. He ignored them, hands hovering over all the greenery thriving by his windows. Ferns and figs and stromanthes were all waiting to be called upon, but he had a specific need in mind. On his wrist, the birchwood cuff vibrated as if it were a cat hoping for a bowl of milk. He flipped through his mental encyclopedia for plants, Syabira's deep melodious voice speaking in his head, until his fingers found the enormous spikes of his aloe vera plant. He gently bent one of the stalks until it snapped off.

Delicately holding the spear with its oozing end tilting heavenward so it didn't drip, Micah turned back to Andrew and Ingrid and beckoned them with a jerk of his chin and a faint smile. His fiancé and his sister wore twin expressions of wary confusion. Micah never noticed how similar their mannerisms were, especially amusing given the pair were enemies long before Andrew even met Micah. But next to each other now, uncertainty and worry still hunching their similarly bony shoulders, it was like a fox and a wolf had reached a treaty for the sake of their wounded kin. Both creatures were lithe and sharp and easily driven away, but loyal till death. The thought warmed his heart like he was a rock in the sun. His smile broadened, and the clean syrupy smell of the aloe vera got stronger.

"All right, love," said Andrew, tracing Micah's collarbone with his thumb. "What are we doing?"

"Aloe vera symbolizes healing and protection," he said hoarsely. "Dab some on your fingertips and spread it on the lintel." As they obeyed and marked the top panel over the window pane, he called the birchwood staff from his wrist into his palm. Rather than on his blood, he focused on the leaf held between the thumb and forefinger of his injured arm, as he told its inherent power to awaken. The staff grew warm under his hand, and the aloe juice glowed softly.

"We'll go to every lintel in the house, so Andrew, if you could carry the plant with us, that would be great." He tapped the golden pot where the aloe vera was planted.

The ritual was quiet and grave. They needed no lights on in the house, as the luminous point of the birchwood staff showed the way. Cinnamon trailed after them, his tail low and his eyes reflecting alien green. With Fionna curled around him with her ears forward and alert, Julian watched them come and go from his room with just a small nightstand lamp lit. He remained still and silent, equal parts fearful and hostile when they entered until they left again. By Micah's heels, Cinnamon hissed at Fionna, who thumped her tail.

When they finished by the front door, Ingrid pushed back her shoulders and wiped her sticky fingers on her coat. She tilted back her angular face and blinked at the ceiling and the walls with eyes lit by a strawberry-hued glow. With a contented sigh, she said, "Well done."

"I'm going to talk to the plants, too," said Micah, void of irony. "But first I have to talk to my dad."

Andrew nodded and gave his arm a gentle squeeze before Micah limped up the stairs and left them. The gauze on his shoulder was already dotted with blood.

The moment Micah was out of sight, Andrew's hands started to tingle. Barefoot and shirtless, his blood kicked up a ruckus in his ears while a veil of darkness descended over his vision as a panic attack crawled into his bloodstream. His chest started heaving in tandem, but he tried to breathe through it. All he could manage was shallow hiccups. Andrew pressed his fingertips hard into his eye sockets as if he could will away the panic clawing at him every time he thought again of the fresh blood on Micah's back.

When a cool hand settled on his arm, Andrew found Ingrid's white face hanging in his vision like a beacon, and before he quite realized what was happening, the Ruby Daughter was hugging him. It was a bony and awkward thing, her inexperience with such a gesture apparent, but it was enough to shock his panic attack straight out of his body like an exorcism. With a trembling smile, he held onto her through her soft fur coat, smelling mulberries and rose hip in her burgundy curls as they tickled his nose.

When she moved back, she stared purposefully at the floor, cleared her throat, and spun toward the hall into the kitchen. Andrew remained frozen in place until she growled his name from around the corner.

Under the fluorescent lights set into the ceiling, Ingrid filled two whiskey tumblers with Jameson, fussing with her heavy mane of hair. Making her intentions very clear, she left the cap off the bottle as she held one of the crystal glasses out to him and clinked their rims together.

They both tossed back the amber contents in one gulp. Andrew focused on the rustic sweetness leftover on his throat.

"Ingrid." Andrew's voice hardly rippled the air between them as they stood over the kitchen counter casting odd silver shadows across the marble. "Tell me he's going to be all right."

Ingrid's garnet gaze remained fixed on her glass. "I have no gift of foresight, *a chara*." Her Gaelic accent was obnoxiously perfect. As was her evasive answer.

Braced over the counter, Andrew gripped the marble until it hurt his knuckles, his heart resuming its frantic pounding as he fought to keep his breathing steady. "I don't care what I have to do, Ingrid. I will chant in Latin. I will use crystals. I will dance naked under a full moon. I will fucking go to the basilica and drink holy water. I will try every single fucking thing I need to before I let this injury kill him."

"Yes." Her voice was a soft scratch of nails carving into flesh. She reached over and squeezed his hand with hers, cool and surprisingly clammy. "We will."

# CHAPTER SEVEN

# THE FATHER

JULIAN'S FACE WAS LIT only by the glow from his phone when Micah appeared in his doorway and tapped a knuckle against the wood. Julian jumped, his eyes flashing toward him like a comet trail, but he relaxed when their gazes met. Fionna opened one eye, saw Micah, and then lifted her head. Micah jutted his chin toward the door and she understood at once, standing up and pulling off her wolfskin. She gave Julian a hug around his neck and then thumped off the bed before scurrying past Micah and out of the room.

Julian leaned over to turn on the lamp on his bedside table. "Are you okay?" he asked.

Micah slipped inside the room, nodding. "Can we talk?"

"Is she still here?"

"Ingrid? Um. Yeah. She's talking to Andrew downstairs."

Julian stared at the open door, his throat bobbing as he swallowed silently. Micah suppressed a sigh, closing the door to the hall, trying to force himself into a mindset of patience. If he was going to have the conversation he wanted to have with his father, it wasn't going to help either of them if he already felt prepared to explode. When Julian's attention remained fixed on the doorknob, Micah's shoulders sagged, but he pushed in the lock. It's not like a locked door would keep Ingrid out if she wanted in, anyway.

Noticing his reaction, Julian's expression darkened. "It's the illusion of safety, Micah."

"Right." Micah nodded. "Sorry." He crossed to Julian's bed and sat down on the edge of the mattress until Julian beckoned him up to his pillows. Julian helped him with a hand on his elbow in the sling until Micah scooted his back against the headboard and let out a long sigh.

"What are we talking about?" asked Julian, plugging the charger into his phone and setting it on the table.

"Me," Micah sighed.

"What else is—" Julian cut himself off before he finished the quip. He swallowed. "And?"

"And us. And me being...not human."

"You know that isn't news to me," Julian said with a wry smile.

Micah bonked their elbows together. "That's not where I was going with this."

"All right. Enlighten me."

Micah lifted his arm out of the sling so he could lay his hand across his lap, as if somehow getting more comfortable would make this easier. He rubbed his fingers against his eyes. "Do you ever imagine that life as an architect?" Micah asked.

Julian laughed humorlessly. He didn't say anything, staring at his hands, picking at his fingernail so it snapped off past the quick, a dot of blood rising from the nailbed. "What?" Julian raised one bushy black brow as he wiped the blood off on his shirt.

"You told me when I was a kid that you wanted to be an architect."

"Did I?" Julian let out a laugh like the puff of air from a book closing. "I don't know. What's the point? That dream belonged to someone who doesn't exist anymore."

"Yeah," Micah said quietly. "That version of you has a nice boring family, too."

"Oh, come on, Micah. You're plenty boring." Julian grinned, pinching Micah's cheek when he scoffed at him.

Micah picked up his father's hand speckled with dark spots and inspected his fingers. Several more of Julian's nails were short and scabbed, and most of his cuticles were torn back. "I think you play pretend as much as I do, Dad."

Julian let him hang onto his hand for a moment before pulling it out of his grip. "What else are we supposed to do?"

"I was actually hoping we could be honest tonight," Micah said carefully. "I can't keep...I don't want to keep up this pretense anymore."

Picking at another fingernail with a shaking hand, Julian pulled his knees up toward his chest, grabbing an extra pillow from between them so he could hug it.

Taking his silence as an invitation, Micah said, "You've always treated me so kindly, Dad. But I...I wish for a life for you where you never went near the Redwoods. And I know I wouldn't exist then. And that's part of the problem. I'm an integral part of your destruction."

Julian chewed on his fingertip so hard that there was an audible *crunch.* He winced, and his eyes darted toward the bottle of pills on his nightstand, but he didn't reach for it.

When Julian was silent for long enough that he wasn't planning to reply, Micah said with a plea making his voice thinner, "Dad."

"You're the child," Julian said hurriedly, blinking against moisture that gleamed among his thick black lashes. "It's never the child's fault." He swiped the back of his hand across his nose and angled himself to face Micah. "I know they treated you poorly, too. I know they called you halfling when you're actually a prince."

Tears jumped into Micah's eyes. Julian's abrupt departure from the deflection and the avoidance caught him off guard, especially since he was exactly right. Even the Folk like Sivarthis who allowed Micah to enter their sphere of influence did so only to belittle him and to elevate themselves.

Brushing Micah's eyes dry with his knuckles, Julian said, "I know you endured their cruelty with a smile to protect me. You were always better than them. You've always been so brave."

*Better than them.* The statement triggered a long-held worry, a bitter truth between Micah and his father that finally needed to be spoken. Spoken while they were both horribly sober. He'd endured the cruelty of the Folk with a smile, but he'd endured Julian's criticism of them with a smile, too. That needed to end.

Stomach lurching, he said carefully, "I wanted to be human for you for a long time." Micah dried his eyes, swallowed thickly, and said, "I can't keep doing that. It's dangerous, to all of us. I'm not human. Not entirely. And I want to live a life where I can proudly be my whole self."

They sat facing each other, motionless, at an impasse. Experiences from their last twenty-two years living together in Minnesota crowded into the space between them. Having to choose their new name for their new life, which was demanding and terrifying and frequently one misstep away from homelessness and ruin. Yet Micah suspected that his desperation lent them a hand. How many times did he create opportunities for him and his father with the aid of a bit of unintentional Fae charm? Why else would their first landlord have let them rent an apartment with nonexistent credit, no identification, and no jobs for either of them? How else could Micah have gotten into community college with claims of "homeschooling" and absolutely no grasp on formal education? It only made sense that they limped through those first few years in Minnesota because nobody could say no to Micah. It only made sense like this when Micah finally turned his attention toward it, rather than gritting his teeth and looking away, accepting it dismissively with a comment of "I'm just glad it worked out."

And yet, during Julian's sixth, eighth, tenth hospitalization, Micah realized that he had to deny everything about his Fae nature if he was going to keep his father alive. That ended up being the only relief for Julian.

"I'm sorry," Julian said. "I know I've held you back."

Micah reached for his hand. "Dad..."

Squeezing Micah's hand and clapping it between his own, Julian said, "No, no. It's okay. I let you indulge me. That stuff has been nice, hasn't it? Decorating Christmas trees and going grocery shopping and watching baseball games."

"Well, yeah. I love our family traditions."

"We're refugees from the Redwoods but damn it if we haven't become genuine Minnesotans since then, right?"

Micah frowned. "Wait. Are you trying to say that this is some kind of trade-off? Honest discussion about what we've been through means no more...normal life?"

Julian frowned back at him. "I suppose I thought that's what you meant."

"No. Not at all." Micah shook his head hard enough that he noticed a migraine rattling behind his eye. "I don't actually want anything we do to change, Dad. Just how we acknowledge things."

"That's a relief."

"I mean, come on. Fionna's gonna *love* the State Fair."

"As long as she doesn't eat the livestock," said Julian. They both giggled, their laughter very much the same in its melodious tumble.

As the sound faded with Micah's smile, he said more seriously, "I...didn't think you'd handle this conversation as well as you are. I thought it would end in a fight or a meltdown."

Julian's throat bobbed. He thought for a few minutes, gazing toward the ceiling. His hands remained still in his lap; he left his cuticles alone. "The Redwoods feel further away tonight," said Julian, nodding toward his window smeared with aloe vera. "Whatever you did with your staff and the aloe was very soothing."

"Oh. Really?" Micah glanced dubiously at his ward. It was hardly sophisticated magic.

"Your magic always brings more beauty and life wherever you go," said Julian. "It's the complete opposite of what..." His tongue flicked over his slender red lips. "Of what your mother did with her power."

Micah felt warmth bloom behind his sternum and spread through his veins as he beamed at his father. "Dad, that means the world to me."

"But don't get me wrong. I *am* freaking out and I *will* need more Seroquel than usual after this." He laughed, the sound a little too pressured as he leaned his head against the wall and hugged the pillow tightly enough that it folded in half.

"Okay." Looping the sling back over his shoulder so he could sit criss-crossed and face Julian more fully, Micah said, "Then I'll say this next part quickly."

Julian hummed with displeasure, narrowing his eyes and glaring across the room.

"Ingrid is not the same as the Redwood Queen," Micah blurted. "You hurt me when you treat her like she is."

Unmoving, Julian didn't reply. After a moment, he lifted another finger toward his mouth, but stopped when Micah reached to intercept him. They were a tableau of a habitual exchange: Julian threatening to come apart, Micah ready with a needle and thread to sew him back up. Julian said with a tremble in his voice, "You don't understand."

"Then help me."

"I don't want to talk about her."

"Dad," Micah pressed. "She's important to me."

"I don't want to talk about her!" Julian exclaimed. He groped for his bottle of pills and spun the top off, dropping two yellow tabs into his hand. He closed them in his shaking fist without taking them, eyes gleaming, chest heaving.

"Come on!" Micah said. "It's not her fault she looks like—"

"No," interrupted Julian. "It's because I remember everything." He spoke the words with a voice as frayed as a severed electrical cord, sparking and ready to shock if you touched it. Large teardrops formed in the corners of his eyes, his lips pulled tight with grief and torment. He repeated in a whisper, "*Everything*."

Micah's mouth dropped open. He sat in stunned silence for a moment. "What? You've always said it's like trying to remember a dream."

"Because I wished that were true," Julian said around a sob. "I wish I didn't remember. But every morning in the Redwoods, I'd wake up sober with the guilt and the shame and know that the nightmare was real. My friends were murdered, and the Queen charmed me and raped me every single day. Every day." Tears dribbled down his cheeks as he rolled the pills between his fingers. "My body was in rapture," he continued quietly, "while I watched helplessly from some cognizant corner of my mind. Screaming the whole time."

"Oh my god, Dad," Micah said, crying, covering his mouth. "Why didn't you ever tell me?"

"Because we were pretending," said Julian with his cheeks soaked and his eyes filled with more and more tears.

He hiccupped and held his forehead with his bleeding fingers, plunging his hand into his hair and gripping the silky strands by the roots. "You smiled and laughed and told me we were free. I wanted that to be true so, so badly. So I told myself the Redwoods were a dream. Even when she took me back, and you and Andrew and Chamomile rescued me."

Micah's stomach flipped. "You *know* about that?"

"Of course," wept Julian, muffled as he hugged the pillow against his face. "It's what I wanted to happen. I wanted to be back there. I wanted to feel that good again."

"Dad..." Micah covered his eyes with his hand, shaking so much his shoulder ached and oozed blood that was hot and sticky under his bandaging. "I can't believe this. No...no wonder you've been so miserable for so long. I'm so sorry."

Julian stretched his hand toward Micah's, who quickly clasped their hands together, palms clammy, fingers shaking. They held hands unspeaking while Julian hid his face and cried into the pillow, but not the way he did before he lost control. It was the sound of long-held grief like a thorn embedded in his heart, piercing sinew and viscera, but now it was dislodged. It might be bleeding, but the wound was cleansed, ready to heal again.

Julian lifted his head, sniffing, his hazelnut complexion red as the skin of an apple around his puffy eyes. "Chami gave me something," he said, picking up a tissue box, pulling out a clump of tissues and then handing the box to Micah. "In the car after she got me out. I think it made the cravings more manageable. Kind of like a nicotine patch or something." He dried his face and blew his nose. "And learning about Andrew's mom, how she struggled too, that was a comfort."

Micah sat in stunned silence, eyes round and staring. He remembered their return to Andrew's Saturn in the mushroom circle, with Chamomile and the cats guarding Julian's sleeping form. She'd had plenty of time with him, and put him to sleep somehow. It was well within her capabilities to produce some kind of...remedy, and it was well within her nature to keep that information to herself. But still—she'd just let everyone quietly heal without any idea that was why Julian had been doing so much better. No more hospitalizations, no more violent outbursts. All thanks to that tricky little goblin.

"Holy shit," Micah finally said.

"Chami's one of the best unhinged psychopaths I've ever met, and I met a lot of psychopaths in the Redwoods," said Julian. "You remember Root? God, he was insane. But he would sneak me a bowl of mushroom soup every Friday because he knew I was obsessed with it."

Micah managed a hard blink. "Dad, this is blowing my mind."

Julians shrugged.

"Like, what the hell?"

"I'm surprised you thought you were the only one lying through your teeth all these years, Micah." Julian kept up his dismissive attitude, smiling faintly before he reached out to ruffle Micah's hair.

"Yeah…guess that's on me." Micah finally released a sigh. "You're something else, Dad."

Julian slung his arm around Micah's neck. "But if you're wanting me to be honest, Micah, then I need you to know that Ingrid and I might always be like this."

Disappointment settled like a stone in Micah's stomach. He shut his eyes.

"Yes, it's worse because she looks so much like her mother. Maybe I ought to work on that trauma response." His voice warbled, but he took a fortifying breath as he set the two pills back on his nightstand and pinched his nose. "But that's not all of it." His arm trembled under Micah's cheek. "It's because she was a grown adult when I was kidnapped as a teenager. She led the hunt that murdered all my friends. She looked away when they put me back in a cage after the Queen had her fill of me."

Micah cringed. He didn't even remember this version of Ingrid. When he was a child, he only remembered how she shielded him from the Queen and her court. All of her compassion went to Micah, and skipped over Julian.

"When someone is complicit in your suffering, that wound makes a very ugly scar. I am confident that she understands that. I am sure she expects nothing better than terror and resentment from me." Julian caught fresh tears on his face with a tissue.

Micah burrowed into the warmth of Julian's arm, hand over his face, his lips and cheeks trembling despite his efforts to keep his composure. "Okay," he whispered. "I understand."

Julian stroked Micah's green locks, tugging his blankets out from under them and tucking Micah in. "But we will have an armistice for your wedding, honey. I love you too much to even dare ruin that day for you."

Micah shimmied under the covers to lay on his uninjured shoulder, sniffing, dabbing at his face. "Dad?"

After switching off the lamp, Julian uncapped his pill bottle and returned the tablets, where they clacked quietly into their neighbors in the bottle. Then he rolled to face Micah and laid his hand on his cheek. "Son?"

"Thanks. For talking."

Julian snorted. Then his expression grew more serious, the lines deepening on his forehead and around his mouth as he pursed his lips. "It felt good. Being honest." He combed his fingers through Micah's soft hair like he was trying and failing to imagine him having anything but the leafy, summer hue.

Overwhelmed by the comforting gesture, and the weightlessness where their pretense and unspoken pain once dragged them down, Micah's eyes slid shut as he let out a shuddering breath. "It feels amazing, Dad."

Leaving Ingrid curled up on the couch with her cheeks rosy from the whiskey, Andrew crept up the creaky stairs to the middle landing belonging to Julian. No light showed under the crack in the door, and no voices carried out. He padded to the doorway and tried the doorknob, but it was locked. He could almost imagine Julian requesting that if he knew Ingrid was still in the house. But still, that worried part of himself needed to confirm that father and son were safe. He pulled the curl of wire off from its resting place on a framed picture of Micah in the black robes and maroon sash for his MBA graduation ceremony. Fumbling with the wire in the hole of the doorknob, Andrew listened until the lock popped open and then quietly opened the door, peering into the dimness of the bedroom. He was reassured by the two shapes in the bed, and anyway Micah's hair practically glowed in the dark. Andrew was about to close the door again when Cinnamon's billowy tail flicked against his leg as the large ginger tomcat trotted confidently into the bedroom and jumped on the bed to nestle between Julian and Micah's legs. Andrew rolled his eyes at the cat's brazen confidence and left the door cracked as he retreated to the stairs.

Up in Micah's room, Andrew turned on his laptop at the corner desk. Micah had stolen it one day last winter and plastered its hitherto tidy and stickerless surface with several Pride stickers, a To a Tea logo, and a sticker Andrew had barely allowed that said COCKNEY CODER, even though Micah knew that wasn't Andrew's accent. While he waited for it to boot, he piled his hair in a bun and secured it with Ingrid's magic black hair tie.

As a little girl, Fionna stirred in the middle of the bed and sat up. She wiped sleep from her eyes and drool from her cheek. "Safe and comfy," she said, wrapping herself in one of Micah's knit blankets.

"Yeah," said Andrew with a smile. "Is your head okay?"

"I have thick skull." She grinned.

"That was a good sentence," Andrew told her. "But don't skip your articles. I have 'a' thick skull."

"You are *a* pain."

Andrew's mouth dropped open. "I beg your pardon, little lady!"

Fionna giggled maniacally. "*The* videos on phone said that."

"Of course. I knew letting you use my phone was a mistake."

"Not *a* mistake." Fionna put Micah's blanket in her mouth before catching herself and dropping it, plucking a fuzz from her tongue. "Best choice ever."

"Uh-huh." He looked back at the computer, chewing his lip, opening a browser but not sure what he was wanting to do. It was good that Micah was back to sleep, safe with his father. It was good that the house was warded. But was it enough? These witches...the threat they posed just seemed to keep growing.

He looked sidelong at Fionna. "How come you knew the witches were in Micah's dream?"

She paused. Then she climbed off the bed and padded over to him, clambering onto the desk and plopping next to the monitor. "Different magic. Mine. Micah's like a garden. Ingrid's like stars. Yours, like library." Andrew raised an eyebrow. She shuddered. "Theirs dark, eats things. I woke up tasting it. It was like..." She blew a raspberry and pinched her nose, making a face like she smelled something foul.

"Understood," said Andrew, nodding. What an odd thought that he and a *faoladh* seemed to have the same sense for magic, that it often had a smell or taste.

Fionna picked up a stapler on the desk and shot off a few staples, eyes growing round and inquisitive. Scoffing, Andrew took it from her and set it on the other end of the desk, blocking her arm when she reached for it. He handed her a stress ball shaped like a brain instead, which she immediately put in her mouth.

"What about the girl we met at the library yesterday?" asked Andrew, getting a sudden idea.

Fionna shrugged and spat out the stress ball onto Andrew's arm. "Hers small, but white. Like the moon."

Andrew nodded, wiping off her drool and gazing thoughtfully at his screen. He tried to shift gears, pulling up some wedding sites to generate some idea of what they could do on a month's notice. He knew what he wanted to wear and that Chamomile was procuring what Micah wanted, and Andrew had already figured out what he wanted to do for the ritual during the ceremony. So many of the other details were negligible; even if they decided to get married tomorrow, they could still pull off something beautiful. But right now, it felt like he was trying to carry a bouquet in his arms while walking a tightrope over a volcano. Balancing these two polarized spaces in his head made a migraine stab through his eye.

Standing again, he went to the side of the bed closest to the bathroom. After gently setting aside the golden mulberry leaf necklace, Andrew picked up Micah's phone. He weighed it in his hand like he was weighing his options, chewing on his fingernail.

Not long before daybreak, Ingrid returned to the bluffs. "Call me back the moment something goes wrong," Ingrid told Fionna, standing back and in Micah's room as she shrugged into her black jacket. She pulled her hair out of her collar and looked over at Andrew. "Are you okay?"

Andrew blinked at her, raising an eyebrow. "Am I okay?"

Ingrid nodded with a slight sigh. "I know after Micah was stabbed while you were gone, I felt unsafe and disturbed for quite a while, especially after the initial shock wore off."

"That's so empathetic," he said warmly, even though she cut him a dirty look. Sitting back in the desk chair with a squeak, Andrew gazed out the windows, where a touch of indigo painted the sky near the horizon. "No, I suppose I'm not okay," he said. "Vengeance is all I can think about. And these dumb little bitches keep escalating, and they keep targeting Micah."

Ingrid stepped into his line of sight on silent feet. Fionna scampered across the floor to cling to her waist with fear flickering across her round, feral features. Stroking the girl's braids with her long fingers, Ingrid said softly, "This is the type of feud that made my mother what she was. Greed driving humans to try to steal our Fae magic, jealous that they themselves can't possess the wellspring of natural power that we do." She shook her head. "Micah is a far greater creature than my mother. What we must protect the most viciously from them, though, is his loving heart." Her ruby eyes flashed when she glanced sidelong at Andrew, the icy expression on her face reminiscent of the version of herself that wrought terrible fear in him for five years before they made peace. She added in a deep, expressionless whisper, "They will pay handsomely enough for making him bleed. But if they break his heart, I will raze this city to the ground." She inclined her head to him with cruel delight glowing in her gaze before she stepped out of Fionna's grasp and vanished into the shadows.

Andrew cocked his head, shuddering. "Well, that was terrifying."

Fionna stood blinking in confusion at the space Ingrid had occupied, whining. Andrew tugged her by her heart pajamas and sat her on his lap so he could hug her. "All right, little pup. We need a few hours of sleep, hm?"

She hopped off his knee, pulled on her wolfskin, and jumped on Micah's bed. The shaggy wolf turned in three full circles before curling up in a ball and shutting her eyes with a huffing sigh. Andrew tried to manifest her easy relaxation as he shut off his lamp, set an alarm on his phone that was probably earlier than it needed to be, and pulled the covers up to his chin. But the bed felt wrong without Micah, even if he was safe downstairs with his father. Andrew lay staring out the window while the wolf snored softly by his feet, every so often moving closer to him until she was nestled behind his knees.

Sleep eluded him. Every time his eyes slipped closed, it was to the image of Micah's seeping wound and the haunted look on his face. Sighing, he rolled onto his back, gazing at the pothos vines hanging from hooks across the ceiling. When dawn started to brighten the room, he surrendered the night as a failure and sat up. For a few minutes, he simply stroked Fionna's bony head and her soft furred ears, and then he climbed out of bed. He gave her a reassuring smile when she peered at him through one barely opened eye. He gathered an armful of clothes he brought with him from the wardrobe he'd forced Micah to allow him to organize. Shutting himself in the bathroom, he took a scalding hot shower that lasted mere minutes before quickly toweling off, braiding his soaked hair, and dressing in jeans and one of Micah's hooded sweatshirts inside the humid bathroom.

Back in the bedroom, he sent several texts to Sam and called him twice. Both times, the call rang once before he was sent to voicemail. Sam had been distant lately anyway, but after he appeared to murder Micah in his dream, ignoring Andrew was frustrating, and somewhat ominous. He went downstairs, checking that Micah and Julian were how he'd left them hours earlier, which they were. In the vestibule by the front door, Andrew put on an acid wash beanie also belonging to Micah and then pulled up the sweatshirt hood over it. He yanked on his winter boots, slipped into his pea coat, grabbed his keys out of the bowl where everyone kept theirs, and let himself outside. If Sam was going to ignore his messages, then Andrew was more than happy to get in his face.

He was thinking about a hot cup of tea the whole walk down Saint Claire, through the intersection bustling with weekday rush hour, and up to the black and white sign for

Magic's. He almost wiped out on a patch of ice from runoff from the red awning, making a mental note to throw some salt down on his way back to the brownstone.

Taped to the shop door was a sign that read:

CLOSED TODAY

EMAIL FOR INQUIRIES ON EXISTING ORDERS

Andrew scowled at it. He rounded to the back door in the parking lot. In front of the heavy steel outside door, he checked that his runes etched into the brick were intact. It wouldn't be a bad idea to add some Ogham symbols to the Norse marks. When he opened the door, the little bell still jingled against the metal to ward off evil. Only faintly satisfied, he let himself into the apartment at the top of the stairwell.

With his hands in his jacket pockets, he kicked off his boots. He did a superficial search of the apartment, mentally identifying and cataloging the items as Sam's, and didn't sense any festering darkness that might account for Sam murdering Micah in a dream.

Everything felt and looked normal, quiet, and underwhelming. Over the last six months, Sam had gotten more comfortable adding his own personal décor to the apartment. There was a bit more color, and a few more nerdy posters. He'd gotten a bookshelf he'd put behind the couch in the living room, and Andrew noticed proudly the abundance of coding languages and programming guides scattered among graphic novels and queer romances. A spider plant sat on a television tray by the window. And no offense to Sam's plant care, but it certainly showed the contrast between Micah's preternaturally green thumb and a normal person.

Andrew checked in with Arwen, sitting next to the cat on his couch and stroking her spine for a few minutes in silence. She purred softly, relaxed as ever, her feathery tail thumping against the couch cushion. As the thumping got louder, and she started to get up to find somewhere that she wouldn't be annoyed, Andrew left her with a muttered apology.

If Sam wasn't home, there was no reason to linger at the apartment when there were things to be done at the brownstone. He left the living room and crossed the creaky floor toward the door past the kitchen. Andrew paused, looking down at the kitchen counter. Sitting on the countertop was a scrawled note on a cat-themed notepad.

> *Impromptu road trip with some friends, gonna work extra this weekend. Sorry I*

*didn't stop by but I fig-
ured it'd be fine.*

*Sam*

Dropping onto a bar stool, Andrew groaned and rubbed his temples. Something about Sam conveniently quitting town felt more than coincidental. But Sam would never truly betray them. He hoped. He thought with a flame of guilt and anger how Sam had reacted when Andrew told him off for talking to Cirrus. Sam had kept such a strange position in their lives since he joined Andrew at Magic's, first as an assistant, then as a coworker, and now as a friend. But things shifted significantly when Andrew and Micah got together.

Andrew had hated when friends did that to him in his miserable single life. Sam dated off and on, casually, since Andrew had met him, but nothing he settled into. To not be bothered by someone vanishing into a relationship, one had to be either very apathetic, or vapidly joyful, and Sam was neither.

Andrew picked back up his phone.

> I just saw your note. Micah had an
> awful dream about you. I know
> things with you and I have been bad
> and I want to fix them. I've been
> distracted and unkind. Hope the trip
> you're on is fun.

He sighed and stood up, arms crossed, looking around the living room in silence. He refilled Arwen's food and water dish. Andrew touched his hands to Sam's books, touched the coffee-stained mug on the counter by the kitchen, and touched the doorway into Sam's room. He didn't have Micah's ability to set up wards with just a smear of aloe, but he wanted to remind the space that it was safe and belonged also to Andrew.

Disturbed, but unable to pinpoint what bothered him, Andrew locked up and headed back to the brownstone to meet his shortly arriving guest.

# Chapter Eight
## The Eschar

Coffee wafted into Micah's dreams and woke him much more pleasantly than a wolf's jaws on his ankle. He stirred and pressed his face into the pillows that smelled like the woodsy cumin Julian loved to use in his cooking.

He pushed himself up using his good arm and sat on his knees wiping sleep from his eyes. Julian snored soundly beside him, unbothered when Micah sat up. On the other hand, Cinnamon peered judgmentally at him, curled around Julian's head on his pillow with his feathery tail swishing gently. Micah reached out and cupped Cinnamon's head in his hand and smirked when the cat chirped his annoyance.

Climbing out of the bed, Micah's senses revived as sleep withdrew. He stiffened, eyes narrowing. Some presence was in the house that wasn't there when he went to sleep. He didn't recognize it, which was the biggest cause for alarm. Somebody must have welcomed it, otherwise he felt sure his aloe wards wouldn't have permitted entrance. Suspicious and curious in the manner of a doomed cat, he adjusted his sling around his neck, the muscles protesting like they did when he was first injured. Then he tried to roll back his shoulder. With a sharp gasp, he leaned against the doorway, vision blurring and head spinning.

"Micah?" Julian's voice was thick with sleep. "You okay?"

"Yeah," he hissed. Then he blinked, recalling their nocturnal conversation. "Er, no. No I'm not."

"Your shoulder?" Julian pushed Cinnamon's paw out of his ear.

"Yeah. It's bad again. Worse, I think." Micah's chest tightened. This was why he'd gotten so comfortable lying. Admitting the truth aloud like this was wretched.

"Let me know if I can help," mumbled Julian, rolling over in bed.

"I will." Calling his staff into his palm, he moved with the uneasiness of not knowing how else his body would fail him as he leaned his weight on the birchwood. The steps in the brownstone were steep and would not be forgiving if he fell. It was all exactly like his first few nights at home last month, harried and depleted by the simplest activities, frustrated by his own vulnerability. Already dour, Micah wanted nothing more than a long hug from Andrew, and some of that strong coffee he could smell. Andrew always brewed coffee like someone that didn't drink it often himself, but it tasted better for being made out of love.

"Andrew?" Micah called when he reached the living room, aimed at the hall to the kitchen rather than the couch and the sliding glass doors.

"Here," said Andrew, right when someone in the living room cleared their throat.

Micah jumped, pulled out of his fog of pain as he spun toward the couch.

Standing with a hand on the arm of his suede couch was *that* brunette with the little touch of foreign vanilla-scented magic. Diana looked supremely uncomfortable, her face pinched as if with indigestion, color rising on her cheeks as soon as he met her gaze.

Brandishing his staff with the jagged end flaring with acid-green light, Micah demanded, "What the ever-loving fuck are you doing in my goddamn house?"

"Hey, hey, hey," said Andrew placatingly. "I was on my way to wake you." He hurried over while Micah fell into a fighting crouch, knees bent, staff outstretched toward Diana, radiating a sharp cedar smell of hostility. When Andrew touched his waist, the scent evaporated almost at once as Micah tucked the staff against his chest, spinning to face Andrew with muscles rippling his back. Panting through his nostrils, Micah's wide and frightened eyes searched Andrew's face for an explanation.

"Did she bring my nightmare?" Micah asked breathlessly, clinging to Andrew's soft cable knit sweater with such urgency he almost spilled the mug of coffee between them.

Andrew shook his head quickly. His hair was half-braided and still a bit damp. "No, she can't do stuff like that," he murmured, voice soft like the sound of paging through a book, trapping a strand of Micah's hair between his fingers. "The vow she made to Ingrid was powerful magic. A Tall One like the Ruby Daughter can create the most ironclad oaths when they charm a human to follow an order. I read about them this morning before I called Diana, and I can feel it working. She can't hurt you. I promise." Andrew bent to plant a lingering kiss on Micah's cheekbone. His almond soap mingled with the strong coffee, almost making Micah's mouth water.

"I don't understand," Micah said weakly as Andrew gently turned him toward the couch and steered him onto the cushions. He lowered the birchwood staff to lay across Micah's knees so he could deposit the mug into his hands, nudging it up to his mouth until Micah obliged and took a long drink.

Fidgeting with her long, loose hair, Diana shifted her gaze to the ceiling as Micah sat down and glared at her. Somehow her cheeks colored darker. She was dressed plainly in jeans—not ripped, Micah noted with amusement—and a Fall Out Boy tee under a flannel. She mumbled, "It wasn't my idea."

"Sorry, what?" Micah exclaimed. He bugged his eyes at Andrew. "Babe, what are you—"

"Micah," Andrew interrupted. "We need her help." He sat on the center cushion next to Micah so their knees were touching. "She's our best bet."

"Oh, is she now? And how's that?"

"You were wounded with a ceremonial blade by witches who were then able to reopen the wound through a dream," Andrew said matter-of-factly.

"So you ask the person who caused it?" Micah said.

Diana bent and picked up a stack of heavy, ancient tomes from the coffee table. "I—I have several different cleansing spells we can try. Andrew requested spells that are mostly Celtic in origin, which was trickier because the Druids don't write a lot of stuff down, but during the Renaissance, more people were collecting records of...sorry, I can go on and on. Anyway, Andrew sounds more sensitive to magic than me. And...uh...the wolf, apparently. Which I would *love* to pet. But...anyway."

Fionna, laying in front of the television, woofed out a half-growled breath, her eyes fixed on Diana with her ears forward and alert.

"Don't touch her." Andrew's voice had the growl of the protective alpha male as he narrowed his dark eyes at Diana. It was a surprising comfort to Micah, who realized Diana was still in a precarious position one misstep away from being torn about by Andrew and Fionna both.

"Of course," she squeaked.

"Andrew, I don't know about this," groaned Micah. "How can you trust her?"

"I don't," Andrew assured him. "But I'm desperate. Any risk to rid you of whatever's eating your shoulder is one I'm willing to take. Especially if it's a risk with her—" He raised his voice. "—Since I feel very confident I could cut her open with a clean conscience if she wrongs us." Andrew grasped the hilt of his seax from under his collar and unsheathed it far enough for the morning light to flash across the black iron blade. Diana swallowed audibly. Satisfied, Andrew replaced the blade to its holster and nudged his arm into Micah's. "Don't trust her. Just trust me." He pressed his cool lips to Micah's feverish temple. Then he sat on the floor with his back against Micah's legs, opening the top book to the first pink sticky note in it.

Diana wasn't looking at them but she could feel the searing stare Micah fixed on her over the brim of his coffee mug. She picked up the next book and opened it and then set it beside Andrew's. She did the same for each of the five books she'd brought with her. They were all opened to variations of a cleansing spell. She reached into a canvas book bag and pulled out thick candles colored green, blue, and white.

After a long drink of coffee, Micah asked her warily, "Why are you helping?"

She glanced at him. Her eyes flicked down to his bare chest; her cheeks turned redder, and then she looked away.

Andrew raised his brows and said to her, "Down, girl."

"It's the chest piece," blurted Diana. "It's really beautiful. That looks like a bobcat skull."

Micah stared expressionlessly at her until she looked awkwardly away. Then he turned an accusatory, wide-eyed glare on Andrew. Andrew gave him a pained smile and an exaggerated shrug.

Diana said, "Anyway, I don't think I was really given a choice, for one. Your...er...fiancé is very intimidating."

"Thank you." Andrew winked at Micah, who rolled his eyes but nodded in admission.

Diana went on, "And anyway, this whole mess definitely *was* my fault. If I hadn't told the girls you were Fae, they'd have left you alone." She set a chrome lighter on the table. Then she pulled out a small booklet of blank paper and a pack of pens.

Andrew picked up the paper, glanced at the book, and picked up a green pen.

"Color symbolism is almost universal," Diana told him as he inspected the pen between his fingers. A piece of masking tape wrapped around it and said ABUNDANCE. "We don't need language in common to have a color evoke the same feeling."

They quietly went to work copying the text for the pieces of paper from the book. The page was press-printed and fuzzy with age. Andrew and Diana were head-to-head while they transcribed.

Micah leaned on his good arm on the armrest of the couch. The morning sunlight was cool and white as it slanted through the leaves of a spider plant and painted Andrew's skin with calico light. Andrew shot him a lingering glance and a steadying smile, a crinkle appearing beneath his eye. How on earth Andrew was so capable of making amends with those who threatened him—Diana, Chamomile, even Ingrid—was baffling to Micah. He had a unique ability to focus on someone's utility rather than his own ego. Dark and teasing, Andrew's gaze languished over Micah's bare chest, and he had the cheek to actually bite his lip. Micah snorted. Andrew grinned and looked back at his books while Diana cast them a brief look of confusion.

She tapped her page, "Scholars presume that this iteration of the spell focuses on the restoration nature can provide, while also using the burning of paper to symbolize the release of what bound him."

"Then I wonder why we're meant to use blue and green ink? Those are for healing. Shouldn't we burn words in orange, to dispel blockage?" said Andrew, pausing in his transcription.

Diana furrowed her brow. "I think you're right." She crumpled her paper.

Micah rolled his eyes. "Nerds."

When everything was prepared, Andrew pushed the coffee table against the balcony doors and spread a flannel blanket on the rug. He glanced up at Micah and held out his hand, and then froze. Micah's eyes were dark and frightened as he watched Diana arrange the colored candles in a large circle around the blanket.

"Hey," murmured Andrew. "We're going to make this better, okay? I won't let anything hurt you. Including Diana."

Micah held Andrew's gaze for several moments, his fear sharp as antiseptic mint and stinging Andrew's nostrils. Andrew climbed onto the cushion next to him, arm draped over the back of the couch. He leaned close so their knees touched and turned Micah's face toward him gently with his fingers.

"We have to try this," said Andrew softly. "We have to try everything to make you better." Micah searched Andrew's gold-flecked irises for courage and found it there, even though an animal fear nagged him in the pit of his stomach. Fionna approached in stealthy silence and sat on Micah's foot, leaning her head back to gaze adoringly at them with her fang snagging on her black lips. They both laughed, scratching the *faoladh*'s jowls.

Micah turned his attention back to Andrew, his belly rising with a careful breath. "I trust you."

They glanced over at the sound of one of Diana's candles clattering out of her hands. She avoided acknowledging them as she hurriedly righted the candle, tucking a loose hair behind her flushed ear.

Opting to ignore her, Andrew kissed Micah's knuckles and then carefully lifted the sling up and over his head. Micah allowed him to help him off the couch and onto the blanket on his stomach, the fleece soft and catching on his stubbly cheek.

Collecting herself with sudden efficiency, Diana moved around him and lit each of the candles, holding her hair back over her shoulder. Then she sat on Micah's right side while Andrew was on his left, on their knees, face to face. They settled into position, and everything was still for a moment.

Andrew studied Diana's expression, wetting his lips with the tip of his tongue. "You still like him," he observed tonelessly.

Micah groaned. "Andrew! So awkward. Don't do this now."

"I had to ask. Everything ought to be out in the open."

"None more than me, shirtless, on my stomach, Andrew."

"You aren't the problem, love." Andrew's glare was stony as it settled on Diana.

Diana put her face in her hands. "I'm not trying to be weird."

"We left weird ages ago." Andrew cocked an eyebrow.

Micah craned his neck to give her a dubious look. "I thought you only kissed me to test your theory."

"It was a good cover, wasn't it?" Diana's glossy hair fell over her crimson face.

"No." Andrew snorted. "No, it was not."

Micah scraped his chin with his palm. "You're giving me whiplash, woman."

She shook her head and looked at the candles. "This is not a good energy to go into this spell." She sniffed. Then she lifted gray eyes to Andrew and said determinedly, "I'm not trying to steal Micah from you. I'm not trying to hit on him. He chose you, and I knew that all along. I'm sorry," she said to Andrew. "My feelings are irrelevant."

With a pang of guilt, Micah sighed and looked down.

"It's really not a big deal." Diana swiped a ringed hand through the air, showing a glimpse of the dark lines of her tattoo sleeve. "I'm sorry it's so obvious."

Andrew inspected her face for a silent moment. Behind her, Fionna sat up and thrust her snout against Diana's neck. Diana yelped and flinched away, gawking at the wolf over her shoulder with equal parts awe and terror. Fionna swung her head over Diana's shoulder and blinked at Andrew. Diana stiffly sat under the wolf's maw, unable to suppress a goofy smile of delight.

Andrew sighed. "I don't consider you a threat to me." She was cute and intelligent but he knew Micah hadn't liked her to begin with, and liked her even less after she tried to kill him. "I need you to work with me, and you're not an idiot. But you're making Micah uncomfortable, so I need you to try to...compartmentalize, or something."

She nodded, sheepish. Fionna licked her cheek with the tip of her wide pink tongue.

Looking down, Andrew stroked Micah's cheek with the back of his fingers. Then he gently peeled the medical tape off Micah's shoulder, making him wince. He drew back the gauze pad and sucked a sharp breath through his teeth.

Blood oozed from the athame wound. The tissue bordering the bloody hole was black and raised. There were infectious red lashes spiderwebbing away from the injury over to his spine and down toward the small of his back. The smell was overwhelming.

Diana clamped her wrist over her mouth and swallowed a gag. Green tinged her complexion.

Micah remained silent, trembling visibly.

Andrew double-checked the contents of his jeans pocket for reassurance. Then he looked up at Diana. "Let's get started."

Diana nodded, taking a short breath. "Touch your first three fingertips to mine, and I'll speak the incantation. Focus your eyes on the candlelight, and on the wound being cleansed. I will let go of your hands to burn the prayers, and when I do that, keep your hands down and open toward his body." Diana was all seriousness. No trace of the awkward, smitten woman remained. She held out her three fingers face up, thumb and pinkies folded in.

Andrew touched his fingertips to hers.

Looking down at the table, she began to speak a verse.

*"Earth that birthed us*

*Sky that shrouds us*

*Water that quenches us*

*Fire within us*

*Remove the poi—"*

Eyes squeezed shut, Micah interrupted with a groan, "Ow, no, that feels very bad."

The candles guttered.

Andrew snatched his hands back, eyes growing wide.

Diana stared at the wound as it visibly throbbed. "We have to try to finish, otherwise it's worse," she said swiftly, beckoning Andrew.

"Uh-uh," Micah begged.

"It's like stopping the cycle of a day," said Diana.

Grimacing, Andrew set his fingers back on hers, his heart climbing into his throat.

*"Remove the poison*

*Remove the poison."*

Diana dropped her hands, scrabbling for the lighter and their three slips of paper. She clicked the flame to life and said as she burned the first edge,

*"Cleanse the curse."*

She burned the second edge.

*"Wash the blood."*

And the final.

*"Heal the wound."*

Teeth bared, Micah gave an animal cry of agony and curled his hands into fists. Tears soaked his cheeks, pooling on the blanket, dripping in a rush off his nose. The eschar spread around his wound.

On her belly, Fionna crawled to his head, worrying at his hair with her snout. Micah buried his face in the blanket, tense and shaking as he groaned into the floor. He clutched the wolf's cheek, fingers vanishing into her ruff.

"Shit," breathed Diana.

The candles went out. Smoke lifted into the air, curling southward on an invisible current.

"Make it stop," Micah pleaded.

Andrew dug into his pocket. He pulled out a mesh sachet and dumped the contents into his palm. Then he tipped them into his mouth. The leaves and seeds were bitter and aromatic and he fought back a gag as he ground them down between his molars.

Diana stared at him in silence, complexion gray as Micah sobbed quietly.

Andrew spat the crushed leaves onto his fingers and said as he leaned over him, "If you have any energy, send it toward your shoulder now, love." Then he packed the slurry into the wound.

"Fuck," Micah moaned, his body going rigid as Fionna curled around his head and licked his neck in small quick movements.

"C'mon, love," Andrew whispered, his thumb holding the crushed herbs inside the wound.

The birchwood cuff jumped off Micah's wrist and spun into his hand, growing into a staff, knocking into Diana's legs and forcing her quickly away. Its jagged end flared brightly, green mist rising over Andrew's thumb, the herbs underneath growing frigidly cold.

"There, that's it, love. Well done."

The change to the wound was not substantial, but at least the necrosis shrank back slightly. Micah's shoulder blades rose with several full breaths and he swallowed audibly. Andrew rubbed Micah's arms reassuringly.

"Here—" Diana dug frantically through her bag. "Ginger and willow balm." She held it out to Andrew.

Fionna shook off her wolfskin and snatched the tin out of Diana's hand. Diana yelped, falling off her knees onto her ass. She stared disbelievingly at the wolf girl, but had the wherewithal to keep her mouth clamped shut. Fionna opened the tin and sniffed deeply with her eyes flashing, licking the balm with the tip of her tongue. Seemingly approving, she tossed it to Andrew. Then she shifted her eerie wolf gaze to Diana, scowling, her jaw jumping with anxiety.

Andrew spread a generous amount onto Micah's wound as Micah gasped. Andrew included the angry red lashes and ended up with most of the skin left of Micah's spine coated and shining. He almost cleaned out Diana's tin.

Micah lifted his darkened eyes to Fionna as the girl bent over him, brushing her fingers over his eyebrow until he took her hand and grasped it in his own, managing a thin reassuring smile.

"Keep it." Diana shook her head when Andrew held out the tin to her. She climbed to her feet and began to put her candles back in her bag. "I'm really sorry. That should have worked."

"What scares me," said Andrew softly, wiping his hands on his jeans, "is that it did *something...*"

"But it felt like we walked into a trap," finished Diana. She nodded. "Whatever they did to him last night is really bad. I am in way over my head. Can't the faeries help?"

"The *Folk*," Andrew corrected absently. "And not enough. Fae magic and witchcraft are diametrically opposed. Fae magic creates, like the herbal poultice. Witchcraft takes, even in its purest form."

Diana frowned. "I'm going to go do some more research. Dinner is tomorrow night. I will come here first so you don't need to pick me up." She glanced down where Micah lay in the fetal position. "No need to have him come back to the scene of the crime."

Andrew nodded. She was owed thanks, but looking at Micah made the gratitude die in his throat. He said instead, "Two of the Folk are coming with us. Reconcile yourself to that now, as they will have no patience for your emoting."

An odd look crossed Diana's features. "That's fine. I'm used to masking." She picked up her bag. "Let me know what I can do before dinner."

He nodded and followed her to the front door so he could bolt lock it behind her. When he returned to the living room, Micah was sitting up with his forehead in his hand. Andrew sank down close to him and raised Micah's head with his hands cupping his cheeks. It took a moment before Micah could bring himself to look into Andrew's eyes; as soon as he did, he choked on a shuddering cry and leaned into Andrew. Burying his face in Andrew's fuzzy collar, he squeezed his eyes closed in silence. Andrew wrapped his arms around his waist and held him tightly, and they sat on the living room floor in an embrace for some time.

After a while Micah turned toward the nape of Andrew's neck. The question fought against his throat, fought to remain a secret fear buried in his mind, but Micah could not let it fester in silence. He swallowed the lump in his throat. "What if this kills me?"

Digging his fingers into Micah's waist, Andrew couldn't reply right away. His chest got too tight; his jaw clenched so hard he felt his teeth grind. Finally he let his hand off Micah's waist to stroke his hair as he said determinedly, "Micah, there is no way on this earth that we will let that happen. I will not lose you to this." His voice broke. "I will burn the whole world to the ground first."

Micah leaned back and sank his lips against Andrew's, left arm hanging limply but clinging to Andrew with his right. Andrew kissed him fiercely, desperate at the thought of losing him, urged on by Micah's faint moan. Micah pushed him lightly by the shoulders onto his back, following him down with whisper-soft kisses.

"Ahem. Just want coffee."

They jumped, Andrew stifling a squeak as he pushed Micah back to his knees.

"Oops." Micah grimaced, too tired to put on a show of true embarrassment like Andrew. "Sorry, Dad."

"Holy shit," said Julian, rounding the couch. "Micah, this is what your injury looks like? It's still bleeding. What the hell is wrong with it?"

Rubbing the back of his neck, Micah sighed toward the ceiling and mumbled, "I...it's..."

"It's a cursed infection," Andrew finished, pushing upright with his elbow. "Not the kind that a hospital would be able to deal with. We're working really hard to heal it, okay?"

Julian crossed his arms over his sweatshirt, face creased with worry. "I don't like this at all."

"Me neither," Micah said, face crumpling, tears welling in his eyes. He struggled back to his feet, using Andrew's shoulder and hand on his waist. Micah went toward Julian and dropped against his shoulder while Julian embraced him, giving his bloody shoulder a wide berth but paying no mind to the ointment that smeared on his sleeves.

Andrew blinked and broke into a smile as they embraced. In the time he'd spent with the family, it was usually Julian depending on Micah. Seeing Micah get to lean on his father for comfort was a tender delight. He climbed to his feet and folded up the blanket, shooing Fionna when her eyes lit up and she jumped on a fluttering corner. Fionna shuffled away and over to the father and son, leaning on the crevice between the similar shapes of their bodies. Julian dropped his hand onto the girl's head as Micah sniffled for a few more minutes before he straightened and smeared the back of his hand across his face.

Andrew set the blanket on the back of the couch and scratched Cinnamon's fluffy chest before turning to Julian. "Listen, we're going to need to take it really easy for a few days. Would you be up for helping with some wedding planning? I'm not sure what we're doing yet, but this stuff..."

"With the witches," said Micah.

"Yeah." Andrew nodded, stifling his surprise. "This stuff with the witches is urgent but distracting. Knowing you're keeping some of the wedding planning momentum would be a relief. You can assume if we need the Folk for anything, like music or floral arrangements, that they'll do it."

"Oh, yes!" exclaimed Julian, surprisingly not reacting to the mention of the Folk. "I think that's a great idea. I was hoping I would get to help, actually. Micah's little aloe ward thing has given me a lot more energy."

Andrew smiled at him, slipping his arm around Micah's waist. He thought for a moment and added, "I'd love if you could enlist Sam's help. But I think he's mad at me right now. Could you see if he talks to you?"

He nodded again. Even his complexion was brighter, closer to Micah's usual hazelnut tone, and his shoulders were less hunched. "Sure. I'll do my best." Julian looked down at Fionna, whose hands were all the way through his sweatshirt pocket. "What do you say we take a trip to the store? You're getting so polite these days, I think we can go alone."

Fionna yipped, "Yes, please, Grandpa."

Micah's mouth fell open as he looked down at the *faoladh*, then up at Julian, then up at Andrew, mouthing *Grandpa* and clutching his cheek.

"I'm grandpa?" A smile creased Julian's face and crinkled his eyes. The sparkle in his amber gaze was one rarely seen before.

Fionna spun around Julian's waist and said, "Grandpa." Then she pointed at Andrew and Micah. "Dad. Dad. Boy family who loves me."

Andrew promptly burst into tears as he stooped to whisk the girl off the ground, embracing her as Micah and Julian closed in on either side. They all formed a tight circle around her, a ring of arms linked and laughing faces and the warmth of family.

# Chapter Nine
# The Reprieve

Making it upstairs to his room left Micah damp with sweat and breathless. He leaned against the wall closest to the stairs, a blurry Andrew hurrying determinedly into the bathroom. The handles on the faucet spun with a squeak and bathwater thundered forth.

"I already changed the sheets on the bed." Andrew folded onto his knees next to the tub, picking out several containers from the cabinet under the sink. When Micah didn't reply, he glanced over his shoulder and raised an eyebrow. "You need to relax and then go to sleep. I thought that was obvious."

Micah crossed the length of his patterned rug runner and came into the bathroom, dropping to his knees next to Andrew. Gripping his neck, Micah pressed his mouth to Andrew's and swallowed Andrew's small, surprised puff of air as he slipped his tongue into his mouth in a brief swirling dance before he moved back to press their foreheads together.

Micah shook his head slightly. "You're too good to me."

Andrew cupped Micah's cheeks between his hands, the corners of his slender lips turning up in the coquettish smile that had stolen Micah's heart from the moment he first saw it. "I'll be the judge of that." He picked up a jar of dried lavender, sprinkling it in the churning water along with a generous heap of pink sea salt. Then he drew Micah back to his feet and stripped him out of his sweats and boxers with such a gentle touch Micah barely felt him. Lastly, he lifted the sling off Micah's shoulder and slid it off his forearm, hanging it on a towel hook behind them. Then he pressed his lips to each bony tip of Micah's clavicle, then the apple of his throat, all the while delicately holding his forearm immobile.

As Andrew helped Micah step into the tub, Micah said, "You don't have to—"

"Hush." Andrew's dark gaze stoically avoided Micah. "I couldn't fix your arm. I need this."

As the fragrant waters pulled Micah into their warm embrace, he loosened a heavy sigh. "Fine," he purred, eyes fluttering shut.

After the dials squeaked the tap off, Andrew's feet dipped into the bath on either side of Micah's shoulders. Soft curly leg hair tickled Micah's skin as Andrew settled onto the edge of the tub with Micah between his knees.

Micah leaned his head back to take in the hills and valleys of Andrew's lightly muscled torso, his perfectly pink nipples, his defined collarbones. The serious expression on his narrow fox-like face made Micah's breath stop in his throat. The faint pucker of his lips, the hitch in his brow, the sweep of his auburn lashes over his dark gaze...it was a look that would nestle into every bruise of fear in Micah's brain, steeped in love and tenderness.

Feeling Micah's gaze on him, Andrew's eyes flicked up from the clay mug he filled with water. He hummed a wordless question that Micah simply answered with a smile, his head growing heavier and more limp on Andrew's thigh as the fragrant water from the mug warmed his scalp and soaked his hair. Andrew flipped the cap on a beige shampoo bottle and squirted some of it into his hand. Carefully keeping Micah's shoulder dry, he worked the shampoo into a lather, fingers twined through the vines of his hair. Andrew's eyes were fixed on the muscles rippling in Micah's throat, the square edges of his jaw, the faint part between his plump lips. Having to pin his attention to the task at hand was almost impossible as Andrew rinsed out the soap with a hand cupped against the nape of his neck to stop the drips. Micah's water-bright strands looked like seagrass swaying in a coral reef. He took a small scoop of coconut oil from a jar on the sink, melted it between his fingers, and massaged it into Micah's hair.

Micah lay silently with his head back, water dripping into the tub from his hair. The bone-deep throbbing of his shoulder faded beneath Andrew's caress. It was its own kind of magic, a promise that Andrew would stop at nothing to keep Micah safe like a knight would his lord.

Drowsy with comfort, Micah blinked open one eye to peer up at Andrew, who was already gazing at him with a faint crease between his eyebrows as he tucked his hair behind his ear. Andrew used the pad of his thumb to trace the curve of Micah's lips from the dimpled corners to the philtrum below the tip of his nose.

Drawn to the coconut smell clinging to the other man's fair skin, Micah caught Andrew's wrist and brushed his lips over his palm, goosebumps rising on Andrew's creamy skin in response. He pressed a long, lingering kiss to each knuckle, and then every fingertip. Then he glanced up toward Andrew to find his eyes closed and his lower lip caught between his teeth like a ripe bite of peach. Heart somersaulting, Micah slid his hand further up Andrew's thigh, toward his groin; muscles clenched under his touch.

Turning around to kneel before Andrew with a swish of lavender, Micah fitted his shoulders between Andrew's thighs to spread his legs further. Scooping coconut oil onto the tips of two of his fingers, he used it as a lubricant and gently probed inside Andrew's warm, tight hole. He relished seeing Andrew's hands dimple his thighs, and admired his angular jaw fully displayed as his chin tipped back and he released a ragged sigh. Under the curtain of his long lashes, Micah's irises glinted silver as he took Andrew into his mouth.

When he started to feel breathless, Micah twined his arm around Andrew's hips and pulled him into the water with a splash. A surprised gasp hardly got out of Andrew's lungs before Micah sloshed them into the end of the tub, leaning back into his good shoulder and clamping Andrew onto his lap.

Grinning, Andrew melted back against Micah's chest with his legs folded to fit into the tub. Micah was all over him in an instant, lightly grazing the banded muscles of his neck with his teeth, palms flat against his pectorals. He circled each nipple with his fingernails, making Andrew shiver. When he pinched their small points, Andrew's back arched and he dug his fingers into Micah's knee as he swallowed a moan.

"Pleasuring you always takes my mind off my worries," Micah said into Andrew's ear, his voice like the lowest notes on a violin.

Twisting so their faces could meet, Andrew's dark eyes were veiled with desire before they slipped shut as he kissed Micah and teased his mouth open with his tongue. Micah's hands dipped beneath the water, Andrew tingling with anticipation as they closed around his hips.

Andrew's breath hitched and cascaded into a shuddering moan as Micah took him in his hand and entered him at once.

On fresh sheets, in fresh clothes, with fresh bandages, Micah felt deeply weary as Andrew tucked the covers up to his chin. He hated sleeping on his stomach. He thought this was over. And the ice pack on his shoulder was going to be a staple of his day; Julian had set an alarm for every two hours to rotate in a fresh one.

But when Andrew leaned in and kissed his brow, Micah's lips curved. His eyes swirled into a warm blushing lilac. "You're an admirable man." Micah's voice slurred with fatigue.

"How's that?" asked Andrew, the damp ends of his hair draped over his wrist as he propped himself on his elbow, close enough to Micah for his breath to ghost across his bangs.

"If I had to be around anyone else you've ever kissed...I'd go feral. I'd climb you like a tree and start throwing shit." Micah's eyes started sliding shut. "Probably literally. Like a monkey."

Andrew snorted. He grazed his finger over Micah's eyebrow before resting his hand against the contours of his face. "I mean, I didn't bring Diana here because I was excited to hang out with her."

"It had to be..." Micah yawned, "...*kinda* fun calling her out though."

Andrew raised his brows for a moment. "If you insist."

Dubious, Micah smirked at him.

Pinching Micah's dimpled cheek, Andrew allowed himself a satisfied grin. "She was so easily flustered."

"Literally the funniest," giggled Micah, which made Andrew laugh with him.

Andrew grew serious. "She had the knowledge I hoped she would. That degree she's working on is very tempting. I looked it up."

"I fully support it if you want to go back to school," Micah mumbled. "That's sexy."

Andrew's heart leapt. "Yeah?"

Micah hummed his assent.

"That means a lot to me, love." Andrew kissed his brow.

Eyes closed, Micah smiled warmly, his cheeks rising to create a crinkle with his eyelids.

Andrew's fingers ran over the bandages on Micah's shoulder, which was much warmer than the rest of the half-Fae's body. "I'm just sorry it didn't work. I'm sorry it made things worse." He lowered himself onto the pillows, cupping Micah's cheek. "Seeing you suffer is agonizing."

"I'm confused about it," Micah said slowly, lashes fluttering as he leaned into Andrew's caress. "Is witchcraft not real magic then?"

Andrew looked past Micah's bandaged shoulder, his gaze unfocused against the far wall near the bathroom, which still wafted the smell of lavender across the room. "I think you and the Folk can create magic. I think you're made of magic. I don't think witches are. I think they have power to some degree to harness magic, like the skills a sculptor has to make a figure out of formless clay."

Micah's lips twitched.

"What?"

"Nothing. You're just so smart. It's sexy."

Andrew rolled his eyes.

"Don't roll your eyes, sir."

"Your eyes are closed. How did you know?"

"I felt it. The sass."

With another deliberate roll of his eyes, Andrew continued, "I bet they were able to utilize your energy because they wounded you last month. It seemed like they put some kind of counter-curse on you when they cursed your wound in your dreams last night. Like a tripwire. I don't know. Mum's Druid magic isn't focused on spells and incantations like that, but this seems to be logic-based in their oldest form like the spell we were going from. *If* the curse is attempted to be lifted, *then* the wound begins to eat itself."

Micah cringed. "Very apt description. No more, please."

"Yes." Andrew slipped his arm over Micah's waist. "That's all right."

"What do we do now?" Eyes closed, Micah yawned again.

"Take the curse-giver hostage?" Andrew offered, as if he'd been thinking about it all night. He had. "Force her to lift it? If she refuses, we kill her. Presumably, then, it would lift itself, but I imagine those books Diana left here have something we could use to ensure that."

Micah's lashes flicked open. His darkened gaze accosted Andrew. "Brutal."

A muscle jumped in Andrew's jaw. "I told you, I am not losing you to this. No matter what."

Micah nodded faintly. He carded his fingers through Andrew's long hair until he saw the crease between Andrew's eyebrows soften. "Maybe Ostara's a crazy idea. Maybe we need time to...survive this."

Frowning, Andrew gave Micah a light kiss. "Hold tight. We plan for Ostara. If things fall apart, we change our plan. But I won't surrender our union for discord."

"Bet." Micah nuzzled into Andrew and released a long sigh against the nape of his neck. As usual, Andrew's warmth and softness made all Micah's worries fall away. He was safe. He was loved.

He fell asleep almost at once.

## CHAPTER TEN

# THE COVEN

INGRID AND CHAMOMILE STEPPED into the shadows with their hands clasped. The bluffs raced away at their backs, the river far beneath them as they skated over air and shadow. Micah's brownstone sped closer, and typically they aimed for his bedroom at the top. But the limestone structure seemed more solid today. It wasn't yielding to the liminal space, within which the edges of everything were soft and washed of color. A lively green sheen clung to its four stories like Micah had painted it with glitter, which wouldn't honestly be that out of character for him. Ingrid redirected them from the top story and dropped them onto the decorated balcony instead. Chamomile stumbled into her, surprised.

"Sorry," said Ingrid distractedly. She clutched a handful of shadows and tried to step herself through the balcony door, but she bumped inelegantly into the green barrier. Rubbing her nose, she mused, "Interesting."

"What is that?" Flummoxed, Chamomile flapped at the green sheen and then tried the same thing as Ingrid, staggering back with a yelp. She gaped up at Micah's fourth floor window. "Is he okay?"

Ingrid nodded, rubbing her chin. "He did this. He anointed his lintels with aloe."

Chamomile crossed her arms. Then she rapped her knuckles on the glass. "This is the second incredibly creative solution he's come up with just this week. The moss and ivy wall? Everyone in the commune loves it." She rapped again on the glass, hard enough that Cinnamon, peacefully slumbering on the couch, puffed up and then shot out of the room.

Ingrid began, "Let's go to the fro—"

"Nope!" Chamomile hooked their elbows together before Ingrid could vault over the balcony. "There's, like, three feet of snow down there. I am not in the right shoes."

Ingrid sighed noisily.

Not letting her go, Chamomile looked up at her and asked cautiously, "And anyway, doesn't this mean...?"

Ingrid looked away. She gently pulled her arm free. Chamomile's small shoulders slumped as she stared at the light-draped rafters overhead with an expression Ingrid found inscrutable—as usual.

The *faoladh* girl tore into the living room in the cat's stead followed by Micah moving slowly. Fionna flipped a switch on the glass door and flung it open with a happy yip. Her hair was neatly braided, the pink hearts on her sweatshirt were unblemished, and her glitter leggings were intact. When Ingrid picked up the girl and gave her a firm hug, notes of almond, tea, and tamarind wafted through her nose instead of wet dog or spruce forests. Fionna was domesticated, in no time at all, happy and warm and part of the family.

"You guys usually appear in my room," Micah remarked. He was freshly groomed as well, with a swipe of gold beneath his lower lashes that matched his gauges and his mulberry leaf necklace. The leather belt he was using to support his left arm almost went with his outfit, an olive green shacket over a low-cut white henley that displayed his sharp collarbone and the tips of the antlers on his bobcat skull tattoo.

"We weren't allowed." Chamomile climbed on the arm of the couch to inspect the smudge of aloe vera over the patio door. "I believe your ward works as a barrier against unexpected visitors, malicious or not."

"Yeah, Andrew doesn't like anyone dropping in." Micah laughed. "Glad it's working, but sorry for the inconvenience. We're not quite ready if you want to come up to my room." He surveyed the two Fae women and how they'd delivered on his request for them to dress in 'business casual'. Unsurprisingly, Ingrid didn't know what that meant and looked as elegant as usual in a short burgundy dress under a taupe duster jacket with sheer tights and heeled boots, her hair greased flat on top and veiling her ears with slender gold pins. Not even a date to fight witches could have kept her from her dark glossy lipstick or her sharp wingtips, brightened at the tear ducts with an opalescent gold.

Micah was more surprised by Chamomile's outfit. The goblin usually offset her sage skin with warm and feminine shades of pink or gold, but she was wearing a mint green wide-legged jumpsuit beneath a fuzzy seafoam green jacket with a matching cap pulled over her sharp ears. Her hair was loose and draped over her shoulder, and her eyes were sharp as she glared up at him with a challenge.

"Sorry." He bent and kissed her unblemished cheek. "I just don't think I've ever seen you wear green." Stairs creaked underneath their feet as the four of them made their way up, up, up the brownstone to Micah's penthouse.

Humming, Chamomile twirled her way over to his bed to make amends with Cinnamon after they scared him. "It's important that my allegiance is clear today."

Micah's lips parted. He glanced where Andrew sat in the corner on the couch. Andrew was watching Chamomile and shifted his dark eyes to meet Micah's before the crinkle of his smile appeared beneath his eye and he winked. Andrew had tried two variations of green himself, but the color didn't suit him and he'd opted for shades of russet and brown like usual, although the plaid cardigan he was wearing had been a Christmas gift from Micah last month, and his half-braid was tied with a green ribbon.

Still holding Fionna, Ingrid crossed to Micah's desk and sat in the spinning chair. "I take it from his smell that the witchcraft nonsense you tried didn't work," she said as she wheeled closer to Andrew. Climbing off her, Fionna picked up a misting bottle and started sniffing leaves and then spraying some of the plants in Micah's windows.

"You saying I stink?" Micah grumbled.

"Your back smells like ass," said Chamomile, nodding.

Micah glared at her.

Andrew twirled the pen in his fingers, casting his gaze back to Ingrid. "Can you blame me for wanting to try?"

Ingrid shook her head. "No, I don't. What else can we do?"

Pen between his teeth, Andrew turned the page in the heavy tome on his lap, scanning it in silence for a beat. He slowly lifted his gaze back to her, an animal stillness falling over his body as if the alpha wolf returned to take over. He removed the pen before calmly saying, "I have some ideas."

Ingrid raised her brows. "You're out for blood at this dinner too, I see."

Andrew shrugged.

"Speaking of blood," said Chamomile, "can I borrow your crossbow?" She grinned toothily and slid onto the couch, hip to hip with Andrew, nudging him with her elbow.

"That's a bit obtuse," he remarked, patting her head even though she snapped at his fingers.

"I brought a bag for it," she scoffed, and unfolded a large canvas sack she'd kept in an inner pocket of her coat.

Andrew shrugged. "Sure, okay."

"No!" Micah exclaimed. "We're not—"

"This is not a pacifist mission," Ingrid interrupted. "Not this time. We need to send a message that..." She trailed off suddenly, glancing at Chamomile. "I mean. Tell me what you had planned, but may I add to it?"

Micah smiled thinly at her. "You may."

Red Rabbit's industrial ceilings helped to absorb some of the ruckus of the overcrowded tables. Its wide square bar in the middle was all shiplap and shiny levers. It was the type of place that had a downtown feel but a big enough space to not rub elbows with the stranger at the table next to you. Diana wasn't entirely sure why Micah had chosen this place, given how busy it was, but then again, maybe that was what he wanted. Less isolation meant less opportunities for something to go wrong.

Wearing her hair in a loose bun, tights under a pencil skirt, and a *Howl's Moving Castle* tee with a leather jacket, Diana spotted Sophie's solitary head bowed at a small table against the far wall. Diana kept her hands in the pockets of her jacket as she sat down across from the blue-haired witch.

Sophie lifted her head and smiled faintly. Dark eyeshadow was smudged over her lids and she wore a necklace of a twisting snake. Her right forearm had a neon blue plaster cast on it, so instead of wearing long sleeves, she had a glittering black shawl draped over her shoulders. "Well, well, well. Aren't you a sight for sore eyes?"

Diana attempted an easygoing smile, propping her chin on her fist. "Yeah, ah, sorry it's been so long. Things have felt…"

"Terrifying? Yeah. I know." Sophie frowned.

"How's your arm?"

Sophie lifted the cast off the table. It was dense with signatures and a scattering of sketchy runes. "Got another month or two in this. It was pretty fucked up."

Diana winced. "That sucks."

"Good thing you got out unscathed, huh?" Venom flashed in Sophie's eyes.

Pulling a face, Diana said awkwardly, "Uh…yeah, I guess."

Primly fixing her shawl, Sophie basked in the tension between them. Finally, she cleared her throat. "What made you reach out? I thought you were done with us."

"I *have* to be done with…the dark magic," said Diana pointedly. "I told you. The woman that made me swear was definitely, like, the kind of faerie that overlaps with elves, in Tolkien and shit."

Sophie raised a painted eyebrow. "It just sounds like a convenient excuse. I just think it's because you like the guy we fucked up more than you let on."

Diana began to get up. "Look, I didn't want to come and fight with you—"

"Sorry." Sophie waved her good hand. "Sorry. I didn't mean to get spicy." She sighed and looked down. "I had to start going to therapy twice a week after that nonsense. My therapist says I have trauma."

Diana was glad Sophie was looking away so she could privately roll her eyes. Sophie was in a cast, but yesterday, Micah was reduced to tears in the fetal position, and was rotting from the inside out. She sighed. Many of her friends were the kind that would tell her not to compare people's trauma. "I bet. Are you still...doing stuff like that, then? Is there still a coven?"

Sophie smirked. "Well, duh. Actually, I hope you don't mind, but I invited some of them here tonight."

Heart lurching, Diana shifted in her seat and picked at a cuticle. She cast a surreptitious glance toward the other end of the room. From her position, the large round table under a southern facing window looked unoccupied, the light fixture hanging over it dim somehow compared to its neighbor. But she knew that's where Micah, Andrew, and the two faeries were sitting. Apparently, Folk were able to play tricks with light and shadows, falling into a liminal space and avoiding being seen by someone not looking for them. Tucked into the breast pocket of her jacket, Diana's phone was connected to an ongoing call with Micah where everyone at the table across the room listened with their heads together.

She pulled herself back to the table with Sophie and said as neutrally as she could, "Isn't that kind of a dick move to invite people without asking me?"

Sophie scrutinized Diana with a sharp glint in her eye. "Maybe I didn't feel safe being out alone with you." Her expression grew colder. "After all, you just *watched* Caty get murdered."

Ice coursed up Diana's spine and grasped the back of her neck. "Wh...What was I supposed to do? I mean, you left her there, too, so—"

Glowering, Sophie opened her mouth to reply, then her eyes slid past Diana and the storm of her expression cleared into a sunshine smile. She raised both hands to wave. Diana looked over her shoulder at a younger, curvier blonde woman with a smirk on her plump lips, which had a stud piercing below each corner. The blonde had a swagger when she walked that made her large breasts bounce under a grayscale lantern chest tattoo partly obscured by several silver necklaces. She had a hand with black nails clamped around the arm of an uncomfortable bespectacled person with a shag of brown hair tinged purple, dragging them with her over to the table. Where the blonde was wearing a skintight black dress, fishnets, and chunky boots, the person with her just wore a dark button-down under a cardigan.

The blond woman took the chair next to Diana, and her companion slid into the booth beside Sophie, scratching their cheek. Diana stared at the shaggy-haired person, brow crinkled, feeling an ambiguous tingle of familiarity at the sight of their tortoiseshell glasses and hazel eyes.

"This is Cirrus." Sophie pointed at the blonde woman, and then the person with glasses. "And this is Sam. I'm hoping the four of us can form a coven. Get some magic going again."

"I...I wouldn't go that far." Sam smiled as if biting on a lemon. "I'm actually not sure about magic."

"Don't be bashful." Cirrus elbowed them. She turned dark eyes toward Diana. "He knows a ton about magic. And I heard that you do, too."

Diana chewed on the inside of her lip before nodding. "I'm doing my Master's in folklore. I like old books."

"Ew." Cirrus gagged, looking at Sophie. "Seriously? Your amazing wellspring of knowledge is a *nerd*?"

"Excuse me." Diana erupted with indignation. "What exactly do you think you know about me?"

Smiling like a wolverine, Cirrus rested her chin on her hand. "Well, I know they're using you."

"Who's using me?" Diana asked, a little too loudly.

Cirrus cocked her head with a devilish grin. "Andrew and Micah." Her voice was false sweetness and spoiled syrup.

Diana frowned. Well, they *were* using her. But she knew that. They made no point of hiding it.

Sam shifted in his seat, eyes darting between Cirrus and Diana. "Wait, how do you know them? What...What's going on here?"

Diana blushed at the question. "Er... well...Micah was my boss."

Sam jolted, realization dawning on his features. "Oh my god! You're the bitch who kissed Micah."

Diana realized why she recognized Sam. His photo had been in Micah's living room, in a frame where he posed with Andrew, Micah, and an older man who simply had to be Micah's father. Diana was busy trying to piece it all together—why was the man who'd tried to kill Micah in his dream involved in any of this? And why did it seem like he didn't know?

"It's your fault that they almost broke up. And it's your fault Micah got stabbed," Sam added, hostility bringing a growl to his voice and a snarl to his lips.

Swallowing her bitterness, Diana said neutrally, "Didn't you just try to murder him in his dreams?"

Eyes widening, color draining from his face, Sam said, "I did...what? What happened to Micah?"

Nudging Sam's elbow, Sophie said with a sidelong smile, "*We* happened. How about that?"

Cirrus leaned across the table, high-fiving with Sophie.

Bile rose in Diana's throat. These women were triumphant about that? She was truly out of her depths with them. She cursed the moment when she'd first met Sophie and Caty and thought she could fit in with them. Wicked, wicked women.

"You two are sick," Diana spat. "How could you do that to someone?"

"Quite easily, if you know the right curses," said Sophie, flipping her hair over her shoulder.

"I bet it looked pretty nasty," said Cirrus. "Wish I could have seen that bastard bleeding."

Diana's mouth fell open.

"Cirrus!" exclaimed Sam. "What is wrong with you? What did Micah ever do to you?"

Sophie turned sharply toward him and said, "He murdered my best friend."

Sam groaned, sinking against the booth, shaking his head. "What the fuck am I in the middle of?"

"My sentiment exactly. C'mon, Sam." Diana pushed back her chair. Scheming be damned. She didn't want to sit near these women for another second.

Cirrus snatched a handful of Diana's jacket and yanked her back down with such sudden force that she successfully landed Diana's ass back in her seat. "Diana here had the right idea, trying to get some of the power Micah's wasting."

"Oh, no." Diana waved her hands. "I deeply regret that very *wrong* idea."

Cirrus ignored her. "We could do so much more with magic like that. It's time to turn the tables on that asshole and those monsters up in Lilydale."

Still shaking his head, Sam said, "Andrew was one hundred percent right about you, Cirrus. You are an absolute psychopath."

"Oh, come on, Sam." Cirrus scoffed, face contorting. "All you ever do is complain about that pompous gay string bean."

Diana's phone felt heavier in her jacket pocket as she imagined Andrew's face right now.

"Sure," admitted Sam. "Andrew and I have a lot of history. And I've been angry at him lately. But it's...like...being mad at a brother. I don't wish him harm."

Cirrus shrugged. "Too bad." Her lips twitched. "I do."

Sam started to stand up.

Sophie grabbed his arm and sat him back down. He shot Diana a pleading look.

In response, she straightened and curled her hands into fists on the tabletop. "I don't care how shitty either of those guys have been," said Diana. "Throwing around serious dark magic curses, trying to kill people, it's just wrong."

"You don't understand!" Cirrus's snarl gathered stares from nearby diners. "The Folk don't *care* about people like us. They let people die all the time. And if you get too close to their orbit, they'll shoot you down so fast you won't know what hit you. You think you're in with them, but you'll be crashing toward earth before long." Cirrus sneered. Diana wondered if the younger woman knew how her eyes were glistening. "You're not better than me, you snotty bitch."

Impatient, Sophie growled. "Show 'em what they did to you." Cirrus pulled up her sleeve on her dress to expose a scabbed red slash across her shoulder.

Diana bit back a gasp. She looked sharply toward the table in the corner, and the illusion of emptiness fell away from it. The scarlet-eyed faerie stood up from her chair, and the patrons at the nearest two tables gasped when she materialized.

Then everything happened at once.

The scarlet-eyed faerie descended on Cirrus like a heart attack. She grasped Cirrus by a handful of her hair and forced her head back, pressing an ivory-handled knife against her throat.

"You did it," Ingrid snarled. Cirrus's yelp of surprise tumbled into a strangled laugh.

"Oh, shit." Sophie shrieked, her cast knocking over her water glass.

Screams of alarm rose from the patrons on either side of the witches' table. The panic spread. Diners fled, tripping over chairs, someone knocking over a wine glass where it exploded on the floor.

"Ingrid?" Sam gasped. He looked across the table at Diana, stricken. "She's been here the whole…"

Lips spread in a too-big grin, Cirrus gazed up into Ingrid's face. "All hail the Goth Queen of Lilydale." Her brittle voice was cold and mocking.

"Any last words?" Ingrid growled.

"Oh, shit," said Diana this time.

Micah shoved his way upstream through the fleeing crowd. "Ingrid, do not shed blood!" He threw himself over her arm and upset her stance with her knife as she fought to regain her balance. "This is not how we do things!"

With a grip still tight on Cirrus's hair, Ingrid shook her like a dog toy while she fought with Micah. Cirrus tried to pry herself loose, tried to press her iron necklaces into Ingrid's hand, but Ingrid didn't even notice the sting under the heat of her rage. The girl dangled helplessly from Ingrid's grip, cheeks flushed and tears jumping in her eyes despite her stoic expression.

Sophie glared at Ingrid with narrowed, hateful eyes. That had to be the faerie that had murdered Caty. And right now, she wasn't paying attention. Sophie launched out of the booth and onto the table, scattering their silverware and glasses onto the floor. Brandishing a pocket knife, she lunged toward the tall female faerie.

"Ingrid!" Sam screamed. He grabbed the dangling ends of Sophie's shawl and yanked her back; she screeched, the pocket knife in her hand arcing off its path. Sam scrabbled for Sophie, who yelled and clawed at his face as they fell back into the booth in a tangle of limbs.

Ingrid snarled and stumbled back, running into Micah, who caught her with both hands. She clutched her bicep, the sleeve of her coat fluttering open. Blood ribboned from a finger-length cut which blistered and smoked.

The restaurant, Diana realized in the sudden silence, was now empty. Passersby stopped and stared as the restaurant patrons and staff flooded the sidewalk. Andrew and Chamomile tore across the room; Andrew's hair stuck out from his braid and the short faerie's hat was askew as if they'd been scuffling.

Andrew snarled at Chamomile, "You shouldn't have held me back! Ingrid's blood is on your hands." He climbed onto the booth, confidently prying apart Sam and Sophie and pushing himself between them with a hand on Sam's stomach. Sophie lost her balance and fell onto the bench on her casted arm before quickly lunging at Andrew. He pulled out his ankle knife and held it out in warning, eyes flinty, making Sophie stop fast and sit back, picking her mussed blue hair out of her mouth. She had a trail of bright red fingernail scratches on her cheek. Andrew kept his dagger extended as he checked on Sam, who clung to Andrew's collar and wiped his bleeding nose with shock warping his expression and making his hazel eyes too bright.

Micah pulled back on Ingrid's thumb to make her release Cirrus, who dropped heavily back to the table with a cry of relief. He pushed Ingrid behind himself, and she was distracted enough with her hand clutched over her bleeding arm to let him. Opening his palm, Micah drew the birchwood cuff into his hand where it sprouted into his staff. He touched Ingrid's wound and then the staff flashed with spring green light; his hand glowed, and Ingrid sucked in a gasp and bent her arm to inspect the hole in her jacket—and the unblemished flesh beneath.

Micah turned back to Cirrus and Sophie, stoic. "This ends now."

Hand on her scalp, Cirrus grinned, tearful but delighted. "It does." She clambered up to her feet. Raising her arm, she threw something at the flagstones under them and then stomped it under her heel. A blast of red light and heat consumed the room, lightning streaking across the ceiling, sulfur crowding mouths and noses.

Micah screamed.

When the air cleared, he was on the floor, facedown and writhing on his knees, shirt drenched in blood. The birchwood staff rolled silently away from his right hand which was curled into a fist.

Cirrus was gone.

Ingrid yelled and dropped to her hands and knees, slipping in blood that was already pooling under Micah.

When Andrew's attention snapped to Micah, Sophie scrambled off the booth with eyes wide, staring at the puddle of blood beneath Micah's limp form. In the chaos, nobody paid her any mind, and she knew for the moment there was nothing more to be done. She backed away and fled toward the deserted front doors.

Something twanged into the door frame a few inches from Sophie's face. She yelped. It looked like a short, metal arrow. Sophie stole a glance over her shoulder. The small blue-eyed faerie had a crossbow raised at her. Her stony expression and her narrowed eyes told Sophie she had missed on purpose.

It was a warning. Sophie sprinted out the door.

Lamely, Diana unrolled the napkins from the silverware left on the tables. But uncertainty paralyzed her—frankly, so did the terror of watching a man die.

"Micah—" Andrew's knees cracked against flagstones. Shaking, he lifted Micah by the chest. He was dead weight, limp and silent as Andrew cradled him against his chest. Ingrid's long fingers tapped desperately against Micah's cheeks, trying to provoke a response. But Micah's skin was drained of color, slick with sweat, his eyes glassy and unseeing. He rested unmoving against Andrew, blood pumping from the wound in his back with each sluggish beat of his heart. Andrew fumbled for the birchwood staff, slotting it between Micah's knees, begging the conduit to come to their aid.

"No, no, no, no," pleaded Andrew, tears leaping into his eyes. "You're fine. You're okay. Stay with me. We've got you, okay? Can you feel me? Don't…" His voice broke. "Don't go to sleep."

Chamomile squatted to determine what Cirrus had stepped on. She picked up the copper-wrapped vial, jagged and in pieces. She recognized it—she'd helped Micah make it so Andrew could wear it as a ward. "Where did she...?" With a jolt of realization, Chamomile's eyes narrowed and slid toward Sam.

Tears welled in Sam's eyes as he clapped his hands over his mouth.

Pocketing the shattered vial, Chamomile turned resolutely back toward them. "Go get more Folk," she ordered to Ingrid. She slung her canvas bag around and dug inside. "We need more energy." She withdrew three packs and spread them over the flagstones, unrolling them to sachets of herbs, small silver scissors, thread, and gauze. She was prepared for this, but only in the event that all else turned to ashes—and now it had.

"I am not leaving him," Ingrid snarled back, holding Micah's hand between both of her own.

"Ingrid, do as I say!" Chamomile said. She added, desperation making her voice break, "*Please!*"

Ingrid's resolve crumbled. She let go of Micah's hand, rose to a crouch, and then melted into a shadow.

"Diana," said Chamomile, "I need your hands. Take off your jacket, take a deep breath, and get down here." She reached for the napkins Diana had grabbed and used them like a dam around the blood gushing from the angry dark wound near his shoulder blade. "Cut his shirt back. Fast, not neatly."

As the cold metal scissors slid against Micah's skin, his green lashes fluttered. Cradled against Andrew's chest, Micah gazed up at him with glassy, unfocused blood-red eyes. "Andrew." The name fell from his lips like the last curling leaf from a tree branch falling loose in autumn.

"Hush, don't say anything," Andrew said, fingers tangled in Micah's hair. "You will not start giving me your last words. Just hold on, okay?"

"I'm sorry we...tried to wait till Ostara," he said faintly. "I sh...should have married you the second you asked..."

"Please stop," sobbed Andrew, not budging as Diana took Chamomile's scissors and started cutting through Micah's shirt and rolling it toward his armpits to keep it out of the way. "Please don't. Please." Andrew's words dissolved into weeping, shoulders heaving, his features creased and warped and soaked with tears.

Micah let go a small sigh as Chamomile pressed a sharply odorous pad of tea tree oil to his shoulder as hard as she could. Labored, he went on shakily, "I...tried to..."

Footsteps clattered across the bricks from the main doors. A woman Diana didn't recognize ran up to them, clutching a large carpet bag. She wore jeans and large boots and a heavy hunter jacket, with a thick gold band around her neck. Surveying the situation with sharp brown eyes, she shook her head with a faint *tsk* as she slipped a

Y-shaped dowsing rod into the deep pocket of her jacket. The woman reached out a thin hand and touched the back of Andrew's head.

Andrew jumped. He wiped his eyes with his shoulder and looked up. Then he jolted, mouth going slack. Hope lit up his face, despairing as it was, like the first brush of dawn on a darkened sky.

"Mother?"

# CHAPTER ELEVEN
# THE HONEYSUCKLE

LIATH RYAN LOWERED HERSELF to her knees at Andrew's elbow. Chamomile, Diana, and Sam stared at her like she was a valkyrie: hair and skin shining under the can lights, cheeks bright from the cold, eyes alight with the fury of a frightened mother.

Andrew shuddered and sobbed, "Mum? Oh. My god. Mum. I'm...how did you..."

"I can help him," said Liath. "May I?"

On the tip of her tongue, Chamomile had a rebuttal about Liath's action with Micah's blood ward. But she swallowed it with one more glance at Micah's blood-stained back and the taste of copper and tears souring her tongue.

"Please," Andrew begged, turning toward Liath. He curled up into her shoulder while she put an arm around him, holding him while he gulped in several fractured gasps, tears streaking through the blood smeared on his face. "Help. Help him. I can't...I can't lose him..." He sobbed, "Please."

She leaned over Micah. "Tell me what I'm looking at." Her brogue tugged on her gravel and bracken voice. She lifted a pair of cat-eye glasses up from a chain around her neck and perched them on her nose.

Andrew glanced pleadingly at Chamomile, stroking Micah's head, leaving streaks of red in his hair.

Eyes on her work, Chamomile explained steadily, "A month ago he was stabbed with an athame by a powerful old witch." Diana continued to wipe the blood from the wound while Chamomile covered it with herbs. The blood rushing out made it impossible to pack anything inside, so Chamomile held them in with her slick stained hands. "Two nights ago, they attacked him in a dream and woke a curse in the wound. The spell these two tried to use to lift it—"

"That's enough," said Liath. She picked up Andrew's hand, lifted it to her mouth, and bit down hard on his palm. Blood spurted under her teeth.

Andrew snarled and thrashed, trying to pull away from her, but Liath held tight, folding his arm into her chest. Shooing Diana and Chamomile out of the way—Chamomile gave her a nasty look—she pressed Andrew's hand to Micah's shoulder. Blood seeped around his fingers into the jagged tear in Micah's skin. Between them, the birchwood staff shivered and writhed, creaking as if being rocked by a storm. Green roots wriggled out of the bark and climbed onto Andrew and Micah, becoming fuzzy flecks of light that faded like the afterimage of a firework. Micah groaned softly, but otherwise remained as he was.

Ingrid reappeared in the restaurant with half a dozen Folk holding hands behind her. She jolted when she saw Liath, but then her eyes settled on the golden necklace she wore and wonder parted her lips and pushed up her slender eyebrows.

Still holding Andrew's hand against the wound, Liath looked up and said with relief, "Good, madame. We need all of you. I need a faerie circle around this pair, please, and everyone, including you three—" She nodded to Ingrid, Chamomile, and Diana. "—Hand-in-hand round about us."

A short woman with dark skin and hair under a silk wrap reached into deep pockets on an apron. She withdrew handfuls of red-capped toadstools, which a winged man with blue skin and yellow hair picked out of her hands and arranged in a careful circle. A fawn placed a small round pebble between each of the mushrooms.

Diana grabbed the nearest two salt shakers, spun off their caps, and drew a large circle that encompassed those kneeling around Micah and all the Folk that had appeared and linked hands in a circle. Inside the salt circle were the toadstools and stones, and inside those were the circle of people.

Ingrid and Chamomile, now on their feet, glanced back at Diana and both held out a hand. Diana didn't even have time to acknowledge the marvel of the act; she clutched both their fingers and squeezed a bit tighter than she meant to. But they squeezed back.

As soon as the circle was complete, Micah groaned again, eyes closed. His hand twitched on the birchwood staff.

Andrew glanced at his mother, who pulled out a white stick of chalk and bent over the floor. She began scratching thick, powdery lines at Micah's feet, resembling a tree and something more, slashed through and dotted in a furious, confident way as if she were making it all up to suit her needs at this very moment.

"Love is the most powerful curse-breaker," said Liath as she continued to draw. "It flows strongest in your blood, Andrew Phalen, to banish the death in his."

Andrew curled Micah's body into his own, leaning his head down onto Micah's clammy shoulder and squeezing his eyes shut. Blood soaked Andrew's clothes, and his face, the rancid smell so overwhelming that his stomach churned. Staring down the violent possibility that Micah was about to...about to die, Andrew knew without a doubt that he could not survive his absence. Such was the powerful press of his love, so true were Liath's words that Andrew felt the ache of them.

"Love binds the wound that hate created. In this circle, death and fear are cast out to be filled instead with healing and renewal. We have all the power at our fingertips, and those who wish to harm us have none." She slashed one final line of chalk on the flagstones.

For a beat, nothing happened. But something stirred invisible beneath their feet, in the sky overhead, in the heat of their blood. All the power in the earth converged, sensing the need of Lord Heartwood and his mate, acknowledging the desperate need to remain tangibly joined as one.

Wet, red leaves sprouted between Andrew's fingers. They unfurled and then withered and fell. Disbelief made Andrew's mouth fall open as he snatched back his hand and leaned to inspect the athame wound, which wept fertile vegetation.

More small leaves grew beneath those that fell, the red stains progressively fading into green, still withering and rolling down Micah's back and piling on the flagstones beneath him. Trembling, Andrew's bloody fingers curled over the healing injury. The cascade of leaves slowed. Slower. One final leaf sprouted, withered, and drifted off Micah's back. Tar-black necrosis flaked off to reveal pink, new flesh like charred earth after a fire, and the red slash of the athame wound thinned, thinned, and sealed up into a pointed, scaly scab. Andrew touched it lightly with a finger. Crusty scales crumbled off. Silky petals unfurled beneath and a delicate pink honeysuckle blossomed, only its shivering stamen were blood-red instead of yellow.

Micah moaned, his brow creasing, his lips regaining a rosy hue as he fought to form words. A shudder shook his core, goosebumps rising on his skin. The birchwood staff trembled where it leaned against his chest, glowing softly like a firefly blinking on a summer afternoon. Sage eyebrows lowered in consternation and bewilderment as Micah reached a heavy hand toward his shoulder. "Huh?"

Ingrid swallowed a small sob of relief.

"Don't move—there's a flower." Andrew plucked at the honeysuckle, but it was fused into the shiny pink scar. A green sunburst radiated from it, as if the infectious red lashes had inverted themselves and left a tattoo. Twisting it gently, Andrew nipped the bud off Micah's skin and cupped it in his hand as Micah gave a sighing, garbled exclamation and opened one eye, a plum-purple iris glittering like a gemstone beneath the can lights. He blinked several times, shifting against Andrew's arm, reaching up to touch the Auburn Knight's cheek.

"Micah." Andrew's voice was muffled by disbelief and exhaustion. "You're alive."

"'Course I am." Micah beamed. "I had you protecting me."

Fresh tears burst from Andrew's eyes as at last he allowed himself to feel relief. At last he allowed himself the thought: Micah was alive.

The ring of Folk released each other's hands and erupted into cheers and applause. Ingrid peeled free of Diana's hand and dropped to her knees, throwing her arms around Micah and crushing him to her chest, showering the sweaty crown of his head with kisses.

He groaned and tried to escape as a child would, an arm flapping over hers as he wheezed, "Red! Can't breathe! Red! Leggo!"

Andrew sat back hiccuping on shallow breaths, trying to wipe the blood off his hands using his jeans. He watched Micah move and laugh and paw at the draft blowing across his bare back, but some petrified part still didn't believe it. Andrew swiped his cleaner sleeve across his face, lifting his eyes. Liath stood on the perimeter of her blessed circle, wringing her hands, her jaw working as she ground her teeth. She looked up, and suddenly their eyes were locked.

Gulping, Andrew clambered to his feet like a fawn standing for the first time. The honeysuckle was still safe in his cupped hand as he reached for Liath and crushed her in his arms. He thought they were through, and he thought he'd been happy with that. But Micah would be dead if he'd been right. "You saved him," Andrew whispered into her hair. "You saved me. I owe you everything."

"You owe me nothing," hiccupped Liath, gripping him so tightly he could feel her bony fingers in his ribs. "I'm your mother."

Andrew moved her back, his hands on her shoulders bloodying her jacket. "How the devil did you find us?"

She pointed toward Micah and said, "He kept calling me. Every day. He…he asked me to come. For—for your wedding."

"He…he did what?" Andrew turned to pass his incredulity toward his fiancé, who was buried on the flagstones beneath the Folk, Ingrid at their core with her arms stubbornly around Micah's neck. Exhausted though he looked, Micah's eyes glittered as he patted Ingrid's elbow under his chin, gazing up at Andrew with a faint smile. Noticing their attention, Ingrid released Micah with a dignified sniff as she wiped at her damp cheeks. She tousled his sweaty hair and then rose to her feet, approaching Liath with a regal nod.

"Your reputation precedes you," said Ingrid softly, making Liath flinch. "But what a wonder you performed today. You saved my brother's life. I owe you a debt of gratitude."

Liath didn't trust herself to speak, managing a simple weak-kneed bob as the Ruby Daughter named her debt.

The other Folk around Micah helped him rise unsteadily to his feet, small hands on his hips and elbows, helping him use his staff to stabilize himself. Andrew peeled away from Ingrid and his mother. Micah opened his arms, and Andrew curled into him like a wayward knight finding his way home. Gathering him up against his chest, Micah held Andrew's head against his shoulder as he felt skinny arms slide around his waist and grip him with a ferocity that made him catch his breath.

"I almost lost you," whimpered Andrew. He let Micah hold him until he could breathe again, until his heart stopped quavering like a leaf clinging to its branches during a tornado.

"I'm okay. We're all right, babe," said Micah, leaning Andrew back with a gentle grip on his chin. "Look at me." He wiped away Andrew's tears, smiling gently, taking the honeysuckle from Andrew's fingers. "Wow. Look at you. Look at the magic you performed."

Andrew hiccuped. "I didn't—"

"Babe. Your love brought me back to life." Micah shook his head patiently. "I'm back. It's okay."

As hard as logic and reason fought Micah's words when they burrowed into Andrew's ears, his eyes were on Micah's side. A rosy glow had returned to Micah's apple cheeks; his eyes were bright and warm. His grip on Andrew's shoulders was firm—with his left hand, the one that couldn't so much as hold a coffee cup that morning. Andrew allowed himself an unsteady but deep breath, swallowing, nodding faintly.

Wrapping his arms around Andrew's neck, Micah pressed his lips against Andrew's and kissed him until all the fear was gone.

"It looks deserted inside," said the sergeant. "You sure you saw a woman with a knife?"

Red Rabbit's manager was dressed in black and had streaks of mascara running down her cheeks. "Yes, sir. She was holding a girl by the hair."

Three squad cars lined up on the curb, red and blue lights flashing. Saint Paul police officers conferred with heads bowed; one man, a sergeant with bright blue eyes rubbed his chin and peered through the windows. Enormous next to the small manager, the sergeant turned toward the dark doors of the restaurant as they silently slid open.

A woman with burgundy hair pinned over her ears met the sergeant's gaze with unsettling eyes red as a stoplight, raising her chin—which was smeared with blood, he realized with alarm—and shaking her head. He'd seen her before, a few times, and the old woman Eda had warned him about her. The scarlet-eyed woman was...not to be trifled with, and not to be ignored.

As her gaze pinned him in place, the sergeant felt his muscles grow warm for a moment as he cleared his throat and drew the attention of the other officers. "I'm sure there's no threat," he told the manager, who blinked in surprise. "You know how paranoid people are these days.

We'll clear the scene and catalog the damage, but I'm sure the restaurant can reopen in...a few hours, don't you think? You can make sure the staff that decides to stay will be compensated for the trouble."

The officers raised eyebrows at him and muttered into radios clipped to their shoulders. The burgundy-haired woman led her group onto the sidewalk, away from the restaurant, confidently not looking back. Two men coated in shining, fresh blood followed her. The shorter of the men wore no shirt, and his back was marred with some strange green sunray scar on his shoulder. The taller man shrugged out of his pea coat and draped it over his companion.

As they departed, the group drew no attention from the lingering diners or wait staff. As if they stepped into some pocket only the sergeant was allowed to see. Abruptly he knew they were being cloaked in magic. He also knew he'd seen something like it before...but he couldn't remember right now. As if they were spelled to avoid curious eyes, stepping into the shadows beyond streetlamps and dissipating into nothingness.

Sam skulked by himself behind Andrew, Micah, Liath, and the faerie women. He tucked his jacket tighter around himself, glancing up as Diana split off from the group. She slipped past a stop sign and opened the door of a black pickup truck idling at the corner, a small man with glasses and a beanie behind the wheel leaning over and kissing Diana's cheek. Then the truck raced off, and Sam looked back at his sneakers.

Green Uggs came into his line of sight. He snapped his head up just as the goblin Chamomile snatched his elbow and twisted it behind his back. Yelping, Sam folded into some perverse yoga pose with spine curled and knees bent. Her fair heart-shaped face drew close to his, their noses touching as fury creased her features, violence flashing in her eyes.

"The only reason I'm not going to slit your throat right now," growled Chamomile, "is because I don't want to argue with Andrew about it."

Sam gulped.

"You are a traitor, no matter the details," Chamomile went on, still with her small nose hot against Sam's. "You are the only one who could have gotten Micah's blood ward to that blonde bitch."

He stammered, "I'm s—"

Reaching into the bag on her shoulder, Chamomile pulled out Andrew's crossbow and stuck the cold loaded bolt into the flesh of his chin. Her green fingertip curled around the trigger as her eyes lit up with wicked antic-ipation.

Sam's knees buckled, but Chamomile held him up by his elbow.

She said, "I'd love nothing more than to murder you and make it look like you killed yourself. Slit open your wrists. Fling your limp body into your bathtub." She bared her serrated teeth past rosy pink lips. "Nobody would question it. It would be delightful."

Tears sprang into his eyes at the gruesome picture.

"That's enough."

Sam stole a glance to the side. Andrew hadn't moved from the middle of the sidewalk, his arm around Micah's shoulders, his expression carved into cold indifference as he gazed back at Sam and Chamomile.

Andrew said, "Leave the stranger here, Chamomile. Let's go."

Snapping her teeth, Chamomile let go of Sam's elbow. She slammed the shaft of the crossbow into his chest and shoved him. With a cry, Sam landed in a snowbank, arms and legs splayed, glasses falling off the tip of his nose.

Fixing his glasses, shaking snow off his palms, Sam lifted his head just in time to see Andrew turn and walk away.

# Chapter Twelve
## The Balance

Carrying two hot toddies, Micah stuck his foot first through his tent flap. He left behind a blazing fire ringed in by Folk dancing to ukulele and piccolo music. He didn't have to duck when inside the tent anymore, and their limestone walls were almost complete. There were now multiple jars of faerie lights hanging from wire hooks across the thatched ceiling, casting a warm flickering glow inside.

Andrew sat in the middle of all their blankets in sweatpants and a sweatshirt, hugging his knees to his chest with his head down.

"Andrew? What's wrong?" Micah set the mugs on the stump they used as a nightstand. Next to the mugs was the honeysuckle delicately placed under a bell jar in a tiny vial of water.

Clambering through the blankets, he lowered Andrew's knees so he could see his face. A blank expression cloaked

Andrew's features as he limply allowed Micah to shift his body.

"Sorry. I'm fine," Andrew said quietly.

Micah sat cross-legged with his knees pressed against Andrew's. "Liar. I know your face when you're dissociating. Everything goes slack."

Andrew dropped his forehead on the heel of his hand. "It would be better if I didn't talk about it."

"Oh, you think so?" Micah tipped Andrew's chin up with one finger. "Did that help this summer, when you started getting suicidal and didn't tell anyone?"

A growl rumbled from Andrew's chest as he moved his chin. "Leave it."

"I can't. I'm entering my era of annoying you into talking about your feelings." Micah folded himself sideways to catch Andrew's eye again. Annoyance was evident in the crease in Andrew's brow, but that was better than no expression at all. It brought a smile to Micah's face as he took Andrew's hand in his and traced his nails along the skin of Andrew's wrist.

Then Micah frowned, spreading Andrew's fingers on his palm. "Wait. Why are your hands all chapped? They weren't like this earlier today."

Andrew tried to pull his hands away but Micah held on. His chest labored as Micah's grip thawed him out and all the images started flashing in his mind again. "I still see all your blood. I feel it on my hands. I've been washing them and washing them, and yet..." He started to curl up again, but Micah climbed onto his lap so he couldn't. The pressure on his legs helped, actually, and he started to be able to feel his skin again as he clutched Micah's shoulders. Face pressed to Micah's neck, Andrew breathed in the scent of somber spruce and twilit meadows. His senses told him Micah was still alive, but... "I still feel like you're dying."

Micah's stomach flipped with unease. "I'm so sorry."

"How am I supposed to get over that? It's such a relief we saved you. But...you were almost dead in my arms." As if to reassure himself, he flattened his hands against Micah's shoulder blades so he could feel the healthy rise and fall of his lungs and the thumping of his heart.

Micah stroked Andrew's hair and kissed the crown of his head. "I guess on the dying end I don't know how scary it all was. I got...really calm. Kind of felt like I was floating."

Cringing, Andrew blinked back tears and shook his head. "It was horrid. It was a nightmare but it was really happening and I...it keeps replaying in my head."

Micah ran a strand of Andrew's hair between his fingers. The caress softened the intensity of Andrew's panic, bringing down his heart rate. When Micah noticed it working, he used both hands to smooth Andrew's hair, pressing his lips to the hinge of his jaw, sliding Andrew's hands beneath his sweatshirt against bare flesh.

"Did you know," said Micah, voice gentle, "that honeysuckles stand for undying true love?"

Andrew snorted as he gripped Micah's warm hips. He leaned their foreheads together. "Of course they do." With a faint smile, Andrew glanced over at the stump and saw the mug. "Is this a hot toddy?"

"Yeah. I sent Gwynn down the street for some whiskey. You like Jameson, right?" Micah climbed partway out of Andrew's lap as he struggled out of his sweatshirt. He tipped himself off balance and flopped onto the bed with his arms stuck over his head. Laughing, Andrew helped free him from his shirt. Micah sat back up, blushing, and Andrew stuck his hand in Micah's hair and messed it up a bit more.

Picking up the mug and wrapping both hands around the warm clear crystal, Andrew took a careful sip and sighed as it burned down his throat. "Splendid." He offered it to Micah, who took a drink himself.

"Mm, splendid." Micah faked an accent, and Andrew pinched his nose in response.

They sipped quietly for a few minutes, listening to the revelry outside the tent, faint as it was becoming as the limestone walls blocked most of it out. Soon enough, their shelter in Lilydale was going to be a substantial little home, albeit very different from the brownstone on Saint Claire.

When Cirrus shattered the wall, that sense of safety was shattered with it. For more than just him and Micah, Andrew suspected. No paranoia could stop the Folk from song and dance and feasting, but whenever a hush fell over them, it was tense and watchful.

"Here's the problem." Andrew's voice was raw. "We set out on this doomed meeting with the witches to identify who broke the wall. Right?"

"Yes. And Cirrus made the mistake of bragging about it and showing where Chami's arrow hit her. She also had to have gotten my blood ward from your apartment when she was hanging out with Sam."

"Right," said Andrew, "and she and Sophie were obviously the ones who invaded your dreams."

"Yeah. Fortunately Sam didn't seem involved. They must have just used his image." Micah's fingers ghosted over his neck as he remembered the ghastly version of Sam in his nightmare.

"Right. That's a conversation with him and I for later."

"Sure."

Andrew continued, "So, at this doomed meeting, we determined it's Cirrus who has been targeting us. Now, yes, your back is healed. But who escaped the restaurant unscathed, without consequence, very much with the upper hand?"

Silent, Micah blew steam off his cup, eyes downcast.

"Cirrus is an evil little girl." Andrew's chapped hands curled into fists. "She's an evil girl who wants to take everything that's not hers and bring us all down with her. She deserves to die." He paused. "I want to kill her, Micah."

Micah winced. "C'mon, babe…"

"This isn't just your choice." Anger seeped through the cracks in Andrew's voice. "I can't bring back the part of me that died today when I thought I was going to lose you."

Still staring at the knitting in the blanket under them, Micah started to say something.

Andrew didn't let him. He said sharply, "I think you should have let Ingrid kill her."

Micah's eyes flashed. "You're wrong."

Indignant, Andrew began, "But if—"

Micah raised his hand. "No, listen to me, Andrew."

Offended, Andrew immediately clamped his mouth shut. His cheeks flamed red.

"I let Ingrid kill someone not even six weeks ago," Micah said, firm but calm. "It's what got us into this feud with the witches in the first place. Ingrid thinks I'm being a 'pacifist' relative to her, and my mother. But I'm not, actually."

Andrew remained silent, staring at his drink.

"And if your instinct is always going to be to wreck shit and get revenge, Andrew, then you and I are going to struggle over that," Micah added frankly. "That simply isn't an option for me."

"What's wrong with wanting to fight for you?" The fire in Andrew's voice softened to glowing coals.

Quieter, Micah said, "I know in your case you're being protective, and passionate, and I like that. I don't want you to care less." Micah squeezed Andrew's fingers, successfully smoothing over Andrew's wounded spirit. "But I'm trying to be strategic. I'm trying to be balanced. If we take life that we shouldn't, then things tip against us. It's the only truth I've ever known. Okay?"

Andrew nodded, silent. Liath had told him the same thing last month. He just didn't like it.

Micah finished, "So, no, I shouldn't have let Ingrid kill Cirrus."

Andrew mustered a soft, "I'm sorry." He ran his tongue over his lips. "You're right, about balance. And I knew that. I just...got so scared."

Frowning, Micah sipped his drink before swallowing audibly. "Ingrid is hot-headed. She steps into violence immediately, and that might be fine in a domain like my mother's was, but we don't have the luxury to cut everyone down here. There's houses not even half a mile east of us. We're small and we have to play nice with the powers around us." He set his mug back on the stump. "But you are right. Nothing regarding Lilydale is just my choice. Not if we're going to keep our tiny slice of magic on the bluffs alive."

"We will. It's survived here this long."

Looking down, Micah opened and closed his mouth. He swirled a finger around the rim of his teacup.

"What is it?"

"I'm going to give my notice at To a Tea tomorrow."

"Wow." Andrew's eyebrows shot up. "Really?"

Micah said with some bitterness, "The more I come into my magic, the more magic I'll attract. It isn't fair to keep playing pretend, showing up to make bubble tea when I'm not busy with whatever madness is going on up here."

Andrew said nothing for a moment, nodding faintly and pursing his lips. "You just seemed to like it there."

Micah nodded. "I do. I'll stay on part time to train my replacement and make sure I can cover bills for the brownstone."

"There isn't a mortgage?"

He grinned sidelong at Andrew and scraped his fingers through his hair. "Chami actually paid it off for me last week. Apparently she hoards currency too."

Andrew snorted. "Naturally."

"But be warned, because she claims the trade-off is that she can show up whenever she wants and cause mischief. She says there's some buttons of yours she's been eyeing."

Andrew groaned.

Grinning, Micah kissed Andrew lightly until he made him smile.

"I had a wedding idea," said Andrew. "When you said this little slice of magic. Why don't we have the ceremony in Cherokee? It'll be cold, but...Folk can come and go discreetly. We don't have to rent out a space, because parks only require a fee in the summer. And we can come back here for a...whatever idea of a reception we want."

Micah didn't hesitate or break eye contact. "Yes. It's perfect." The corner of his lips quirked, dimpling his cheek.

"Cool." Andrew grinned.

"It is cool, babe." Micah crawled across the blankets and kissed the column of Andrew's neck, pulling down his sweatshirt collar to nip at his collarbone.

"I had another thing," Andrew said as Micah pushed him down onto the blankets so his red hair spread beneath him like a corona. His hand sliding up under Andrew's sweatshirt, Micah pressed a kiss to the corner of Andrew's lips with a distracted hum. Andrew's firm stomach shivered under Micah's roaming hand.

"I want to take your last name," Andrew said, gasping softly.

Micah froze. Pulling back to survey Andrew's intensely dark gaze, the words settled like a warm and cozy rabbit in his heart. "Aw." Micah bit his lip. "Really?"

Nodding, Andrew traced his fingers over Micah's shoulder blade, the faint impressions left on Micah's skin from his magically healed wound. "I want to be free of the last thing I have in common with my father. I want to be Andrew Stillwater."

Letting out a breath that descended into a ragged growl, Micah gripped Andrew's hips with both hands. "Yes, please."

# CHAPTER THIRTEEN
# THE BREAKFAST

UNDER A LIGHTLY FALLING snow, Sam knocked on the door to Micah's brownstone, shivering. He was still wearing the oversized tee he slept in under a school sweatshirt and a fleece jacket over sweatpants, his hair hidden beneath a fair isle patterned hat. Exhaustion showed in heavy smudges of darkness under his eyes. Snowflakes clung to the lenses of his glasses. Four steaming coffees in a drink carrier hung from one hand.

After one more knock, Julian opened the door with bedraggled hair and a sleepy squint. "Hi, Sam." He finished pulling a sweatshirt over his head, his wire glasses tipping off his nose. Fixing them, he added helpfully, "You look terrible."

"Thanks, Julian." Sam rubbed his eyes with his fingers behind his glasses.

The little wolf girl leapt down the stairs with a *thud* and clung to Julian's waist. Her hair was a scraggly mane over a gray tee that looked like it belonged to Julian, hanging down to her knees. She saw Sam and growled, an unnervingly frightening sound from a girl's throat, like she was in an exorcism movie.

"Oh. Uh. Hi, Fionna." Sam avoided meeting her eyes, since he'd read somewhere that wolves considered that a challenge. Weird to be trying not to dominate a four-foot-tall girl, but he knew she had the tendency to bite no matter which form she wore. "Is Andrew here?"

"No, I only have the wolf. Andrew is up in Lilydale with Micah. His mom's with a sponsor in Eagan, I guess."

"Oh...shoot. I really needed to talk to him."

Julian paused. "Yeah. I heard you blew it yesterday." He glanced at the coffees. "Apology caffeine isn't gonna cut it, kiddo."

Sam pulled out a chai and handed it to him. "I know. I'm going to try anyway."

"Andrew and Micah are fairly forgiving men," Julian told him. "But make sure you earn it."

Sam nodded. "Yeah. Okay. Can you give me a call when they're back?"

Fionna gave him a long, serious look and then said, "Go up there."

Julian frowned at her. "Sweetie, Lilydale isn't meant for humans."

She lifted her uncanny golden eyes and frowned back at him. "I love Lilydale." Fionna gave Sam a bit of a challenging smirk. "You scared?"

"Er." Sam gazed down at her. She was so short, her face so pudgy and young, drowning in an adult man's shirt. But fearless. Totally, completely fearless. Unlike Sam. "I am scared of Lilydale," he said, nodding. "And I hurt Andrew and Micah, so..."

"I know." Fionna's bristly eyebrows lowering. "Dads are sad."

Sam's stomach dropped into his boots. He sighed and handed Julian the drink carrier. "All right, fine. I'll go talk to him at Lilydale. I just have to go get my car, and...hope that I won't get lost in the bluffs, or slip, or get charmed..."

Julian grimaced. "Sam, just—it's fine if you wait."

"Fionna will guide you." The *faoladh* puffed out her chest.

With a loud sigh, Julian set the drinks inside on the table with their keys tray. He sat on the bottom step leading to the living room and pulled on his snow boots. "Oh, let me drive you to Cherokee at least."

"Are you sure?" Sam blinked. "But...you and...that stuff..."

Julian shrugged. He pulled his jacket out of a slim and shallow closet and zipped it up to his chin. Fionna hopped around him with excitement, already in her boots and jacket because she'd been told so many times she couldn't leave the house in the winter without being properly dressed.

Julian explained, "From what I understand, Micah's been making some pretty positive changes up there. Besides, I'm not getting out of the car. I've got some shopping I can do up in that direction."

Fionna pulled on her wolfskin, making Sam sneeze so hard his hat fell below his eyes. The wolf heaved back and put her paws on Sam's shoulders, giving his cheek a wet kiss. Julian pocketed his wallet and then locked the brownstone behind them. Sam climbed into the passenger seat of Micah's fancy Audi, which still smelled like new car with a touch of stale brown sugar from the bubble tea shop. Fionna hopped into the backseat and snuffled around on the floor.

"Fionna," Julian said sternly. "Girl with seatbelt. Plus, Micah will kill us if his car smells like wet dog."

The wolf huffed, her tail thumping on the back of Julian's seat. Then she climbed out of her wolfskin and flopped onto the bench behind Sam, fumbling with her seatbelt until she got it to click. She kicked the back of Sam's seat a few times until Julian reached back and stilled her with a hand on her ankle. Fionna bent and licked his knuckle.

With a patient sigh, Julian reversed out of the spot in the lot behind the brownstones. They were past the Smith

Avenue bridge before Sam would have wished it, fidgeting with the snap on his jacket sleeve.

Idling in the deserted park near the start of the Brickyard Trail, Julian glanced sidelong at Sam. "You almost got my son killed, Sam."

Tears came immediately. "I'm so sorry, Mr. Stillwater."

"Yeah, I know." Julian stared out the windshield, the wipers sweeping away the light fluffy snowflakes coming down. "You're a good kid. But as a human, it's very easy to make the wrong move when you're messing with all this magic stuff. You have to be a hundred times more careful than someone who's made of magic. Just keep that in mind."

"I don't even wanna be involved," he whispered.

Julian sighed, squeezing Sam's shoulder. "But you care about someone who is. I know how that goes."

"Thanks, Julian," murmured Sam, using his sleeve to dry his eyes.

"Just text me when you're back here and I can come and grab you."

Fionna threw open her door, pulled on her wolfskin, and leapt out with a happy yip before appearing at Sam's door with her tail wagging. Sam reluctantly climbed out of the car, waving at Julian as he drove away before awkwardly turning to the wolf. Fionna trotted off toward the trail, but Sam stayed where he was, wondering if it was too late to just go back and wait for the next time Andrew stopped in at Magic's.

Fionna stopped, tail down, ears back, eyes narrowed with annoyance. Her yellow gaze inspected him carefully. Then she ran behind him and shot between his legs so he fell forward and hit her shoulders, landing awkwardly across her back. She was barely big enough to hold him; he bent his knees and hooked his ankles together quite on instinct, desperate not to fall off or hurt the young creature. He had no time to hang onto more than a handful of her scruff before she split between the trees and took off into the woods with a happy growl rumbling between Sam's thighs. Hollering in disbelief and horror, Sam shortly decided to close his eyes.

When he peeked again, they were on no path, whipping through barren trees with startled deer bounding away from them. Fionna's head tracked the fleeing deer and Sam screeched, "*St...stad!* Or something!"

It seemed to be enough, and she turned her snout back toward the way ahead. In a moment, a large wall of ice smooth and almost as clear as glass rose above them. Sam gasped, head tilted back, squinting against the white sky. It looked like there was something growing along one top edge of the wall, impossibly leafy and green in the frozen depths of winter.

Fionna slipped through an arched opening in the wall, but Sam didn't come with her and crashed into the seemingly empty space. He yelped and tumbled off her back. It felt like he'd hit hard enough to make his nose bleed—more—but nothing came out on his jacket sleeve. He rubbed his face and sat at the gateway into Lilydale, completely alone, shivering on his ass in the snow.

Pulling on a sweatshirt, Micah knelt on their futon in Lilydale and brushed his lips against his fiancé's temple. Andrew sighed and tucked the blankets under his chin.

"I'm gonna put together a family meal," Micah murmured.

"Wake me up when I can eat," said Andrew, muffled against his pillow as he rolled onto his stomach. The blankets fell below his sharp shoulder blades and gentle curve of his spine. If Micah's resolve was even slightly shakier, he'd have slid those blankets down and followed the slope of Andrew's back with his mouth.

With a shake of his head, Micah grinned, kissed the ridge of Andrew's shoulder, and tucked him back in. There was nothing surprising about Andrew's reluctance to get up at dawn. They'd stayed up late the night before and Andrew had still kept Micah awake for a few hours with his restlessness.

Barefooted, Micah stepped into the gray light and took a deep breath. He was truly unscathed, feeling better than he had since before he'd been stabbed outside Diana's house. Maybe the best ever. Whole, and hopeful, and home.

He went behind their shelter and up the crest of the hill over the kiln throne. Built over the kitchen structure was a triple bunk bed where the goblin triplets slept. Micah climbed into the low branches of the maple tree next to it until he could see their three bark-brown heads of hair poking out from their pillows and piles of blankets.

"Psst, Brynn. Uh, or Gwynn. Whoever's on the bottom bunk there." None of the goblins moved. "Gwynn! Spinn?" Frowning, Micah unwound his birchwood staff from his wrist and into his hand, sending the staff out to bridge the gap to the bunk bed until he gave the goblin on the bottom bunk a light poke. With a snort, the bottom goblin lifted their head. It wasn't Spinn, but Micah wasn't sure if it was Gwynn or Brynn. He had to figure out some distinguishing characteristic for the longer-haired siblings...

"Lord Heartwood?" mumbled the goblin. Their voice was high like a larksong, and made Micah think this was Brynn. The two beds above them creaked as they woke their siblings. "What's wrong?"

Micah pulled his staff back into his hand, which shifted his weight unexpectedly on the branch between his thigh and made him start to tip. He yelped; Brynn shot out of her bed toward him, but he spun his staff to his opposite side and caught his balance. Brynn slapped her hands over her face with a heavy sigh. Her siblings climbed down the posts of the bed like lizards and onto the branches of the oak. Spinn was still naked, but Gwynn wore a child's bikini. The triplets pinned him under their springtime-green gazes fresh as sprouts in soil.

"I have a favor to ask," Micah told them, dropping down from the oak tree and brushing bark and crispy moss off his legs. "I know it's early by Lilydale standards, but I'd like to put together a bit of a...communal breakfast for everyone."

"Maybe in four hours," Spinn grumbled, his lisp more pronounced in his sleep-slurred words. Brynn pushed him out of the tree with a vicious shove. He thumped onto his back in the dirt with a wail of protest.

"He doesn't speak for us, Lord Heartwood," Gwynn said hurriedly. He noticed a little scar over her lip when she spoke. "We should have an adequate selection put together within an hour." She bobbed in a little curtsey. Her hair was a bit longer than Brynn's, who climbed down to stand next to her and grabbed her hand. Brynn the Lark. Gwynn the Scar.

"No, no," said Micah. "You misunderstand. *I* want to prepare it. But I don't want to barge into your kitchen and start fucking things up without your knowledge."

"So I can go back to bed?" asked Spinn hopefully.

"You bloody little git!" Brynn squawked. She picked up a rock and was about to throw it at him but Micah blocked her hand and lowered it.

"Let him, that's fine," Micah laughed. "Are you guys from the British Isles?"

"Many years ago, when we were children. Like the Auburn Knight," Gwynn said, nodding. Micah loved that the Folk were all calling Andrew that now since their engagement. "Will you permit us to help you, Lord Heartwood?"

"If you insist," Micah said with a patient smile. "But Spinn really doesn't..." He glanced up past the oak, but the male goblin was already burrowing back into his bunk, his toes the last thing to vanish. Micah grinned, shaking his head as he ducked into the kitchen. He'd prepare Andrew's food last from the selection in the mini fridge labeled with a crude, but not inaccurate drawing of him as a fox that Spinn had drawn. The goblins put it up a year or so ago for storing human groceries for Andrew's consumption.

The goblin sisters lit the fire under the cauldron and began moving through cupboards and drawers with practiced ease, making it so Micah had to hurry in and focus so they didn't put him out of the job. By the time they had trays and platters filling the counters, Micah had cast off his sweatshirt and was damp with sweat from the heat of the cauldron.

He was frying two eggs and brewing tea for Andrew when Gwynn gasped and Brynn shushed her hurriedly.

Micah glanced over his shoulder. Both goblins quickly looked away. "Sup?" He raised an eyebrow.

"Sorry, Lord Heartwood," squeaked Gwynn. "We'd heard you were left with a mark when you were resurrected, but it's more beautiful than I could have imagined."

"Oh?" He strained to peer at the green sunbeam veins that remained radiating from the pale pink athame scar. "All right then. You guys must have all been up late if you've already heard what happened."

"The Ruby Daughter came and went so fast when she was retrieving people that most of us who didn't go with her regret it deeply," said Brynn. She peeled another orange skin back with her sharp nails and pressed it into the orange squeeze so the pulpy liquid trickled into the mostly full pitcher underneath.

"Noted," Micah said with a slight smile. "Well, my gratitude is for all of you, not just the people who showed up at the restaurant. Hence, the breakfast." He finished Andrew's tray and then turned his attention to the coffee presses, picking up the large clay pot that stored the coffee beans. "Speaking of, could one of you get these beans ground for the presses? I think I should wake everyone."

Brynn and Gwynn nodded, elbowing each other to try to get to the pot first. Micah left them to fight with a smile and went back to the oak tree, peering past the roof of the kitchen toward the grove of trees where most of the Folk slept. He didn't want to fall all over himself trying to get to everybody's hammocks. But his idea was likely to work just as well. Focusing on his birchwood cuff and on the bark of the oak tree under his hands, he asked for the tree to wake up and gift him some leaves. The oak tree must only have been dozing, since the branches shivered almost at once, sprouting buds that unfurled into delicate, jeweled leaves that came off with a *snick* and floated down to orbit around Micah with a whisper-quiet breeze. Brynn and Gwynn froze amidst their fragrant billow of coffee grounds to stare at him with glittering eyes. Even Spinn reappeared from the bunk bed to stare at him.

"Breakfast is in twenty minutes, if you would be so kind as to wake the residents," he murmured to the leaves, which flitted off like butterflies to complete their task. A couple faeries sneezed, and several more squeaked in surprise. He wasn't sure this was going to be a wakeup style he could utilize twice, but it was worth a shot.

He and the goblin girls set out their meal swiftly on a flannel tablecloth laid over the log table near the fire pit. Not long after, Spinn deigned to join them. The table started to fill with sleepy-eyed sprites, yawning pixies, quiet gnomes, and nixies from the stream looking irritated, and Andrew, creeping up without a sound and startling Micah with lips on the back of his neck.

"I just woke up with a leaf up my nose, and I feel like that's your doing," Andrew said in a gravelly whisper, leaning against him, still radiating the warmth of slumber like a stone baking in the sun.

Turning to face Andrew and wrap his arms around his neck, Micah laughed and kissed the corner of Andrew's mouth apologetically. "It was an experiment, and like, it got results." He poked his thumb over his shoulder to the table, where every stump and toadstool was now almost occupied. Micah dropped his arms so he could give Andrew his cup of tea and sit him on a stump near the end of the table. He also leaned over and smoothed Andrew's bedraggled hair.

Ingrid slipped into the seat next to Andrew looking equally unkempt and bleary-eyed, swinging back her head with an accusatory glare at Micah as she fought her frizzy curls into a thick plait. But then she seemed to realize she couldn't fix it with anything, looking helplessly around the table with both hands on her hair, groaning wordlessly. Andrew slipped his hair tie off his wrist and held it out to her. She took it with a sigh of relief, secured her hair, and then glared at Micah again.

"God, all right," said Micah with a laugh as he put his hands up. Addressing the whole table of sleepy, quiet Folk, he said, "Not so early next time, I get it. But I'll be damned if I don't make communal breakfasts a thing. Breakfast food is the best."

"Here here," said Syabira, sounding very deeply sarcastic.

Armed with the two coffee presses, Micah went around the table filling the mismatched novelty mugs nestled among the plates of sweet rolls, eggs, fruit, and meat. Spirulina and Leif, more chipper than most of their neighbors, both held their mugs over their shoulders while humming their appreciation. When he felt there was adequate coffee available, he set down the presses and took the only remaining seat, which happened to be at the head of the table.

As he sat, Andrew took his hand and laced their fingers together with affection warming his mahogany eyes.

"I'm glad you're alive," Andrew said softly.

Throat tightening, Micah nodded and kissed the back of Andrew's hand. On his other side, Chamomile socked Micah in the shoulder before pouring half a bottle of champagne into her orange juice. The champagne wasn't included in the selection Micah and the goblins had brought down; she must have brought it from her hut.

"Sorry!" cried blue-skinned pixie, Thorn, buzzing over the kiln throne toward the table. "Sorry I'm late. I had to get this thing out of bed." Dangling from his hand by their collar was the chalky-skinned sprite, Wex, flailing their limbs futilely until Thorn dropped them near the table and they landed with a thud. Thorn pushed himself into a spot between the goblin triplets and goat-eyed Nox, immediately picking up a handful of strawberries and popping them into his mouth. Wex sat up with a scowl, slinking around the far end of the table, where some other pixies begrudgingly scooted to make a spot for the sprite.

"All good." Micah amicably raised his coffee mug toward Thorn. "I'm just happy to be around a table with all of you. Especially when my life came so close to ending last night." He smiled easily, though Andrew and Ingrid swallowed and stared at the table in the shared trauma of the memory. Micah glanced their way, his smile faltering. "I just want to make sure that the version of events you all collectively assembled includes Andrew and his mother as the corner-stone of the whole...uh, ritual?"

"We know," chirped Lina. "Don't worry, Lord Heart-wood. Leif and I are already working on some songs about the Auburn Knight and his Druid Ma." She winked a bright, silver eye at Andrew. Leif started tapping a rhythm on the table and humming a low, serious tune.

Andrew straightened, blinking, a crease appearing be-tween his slender red eyebrows. He glanced in their direc-tion, held his breath puffed in his cheeks before letting it out in a pursed-lip sigh. Speechless.

Grasping Andrew's hand, Micah grinned widely. "I can't wait to hear it."

Fionna exploded into the northern end of the compound. She zagged through the grove of trees with excessively tight turns, kicking up snow and dirt with her tongue lolling out in delight.

"Fionna!" cried Leif, waving with both hands at the wolf. Beside him, Fionna's self-proclaimed Auntie, Cosmos, started to clap with excitement.

Heaving back onto her hind legs, Fionna scooped a full tray of bacon into her mouth and chomped messily, spraying bits and grease onto Chamomile and moth-winged Reave. The goblin triplets tittered. White-haired, charcoal-skinned Nox smiled patiently at her.

"Ew!" Chamomile gave her a shove. "Table manners, you beast!"

"Fionna, what are you doing here?" Andrew set down his teacup. "You were supposed to be with Julian."

When she finished chomping on the bacon and swallowed with satisfaction, Fionna pulled back her wolfskin. Dressed in a shirt belonging to Julian with her hair in desperate need of braiding, she picked up a pear and took an enormous bite out of it. Juice running down her chin, she said with the fruit stuffed in her cheek, "Brought Sam. So much fancy food! I want it all."

"You brought *Sam*?" exclaimed Andrew and Micah at once.

"He can't get in," Fionna added. She climbed onto Chamomile's lap despite the goblin's squawk of protest. Fionna made a grab for the mimosa flute and Chamomile snatched it out of her reach with a slap to her hand. Fionna whined mournfully, and Chamomile *tsk*ed and then gave her a glass without champagne in it.

"He can't get in?" Micah made a face. "I didn't do any-thing formal to the wall. Would it turn him away?"

"Did you want to see him?" asked Ingrid.

"Absolutely not." Micah sniffed and picked at a straw-berry.

"Well, that's enough then." Ingrid shrugged with a sat-isfied smile.

Dropping his head, Andrew sighed and pushed to his feet. He glanced at Micah. "I won't bring him in, if that's what you want. But I would like to talk to him."

Micah took a slow sip of coffee and then added a drizzle of honey to his cup. "I don't know what I want. So I trust your judgment."

Leaning down with a hand on Micah's shoulder, Andrew kissed his temple and then his lips when Micah turned to him. "All right." Then he sank his hands into the pocket of his sweatshirt as he picked his way toward the perimeter of the compound.

Micah glanced at Ingrid. "Can you help me with a project today?"

She shrugged. "If it's interesting enough."

He glared at her.

Meticulously spreading jam on a roll, Ingrid avoided looking at him as a corner of her lips quirked in a smirk.

Sam was still on the ground, feeling the snow seep into his pants and thinking it was a good metaphor for his current predicament. Then he heard footsteps crunch in the snow and he tensed up, wincing, waiting to be...charmed, or something, and taken in to be humiliated. Or beaten up by Chamomile, probably.

But he looked up, and it was Andrew. He still, oddly, looked more or less at home coming out of Lilydale, though he looked more stoic than usual. His sweatshirt hood obscured most of his hair except for a stray strand falling across his face. He was only wearing jeans and moccasins, which surprised Sam given the snowy weather.

Andrew didn't cross the threshold, standing inside the perimeter as if he knew Sam couldn't cross over. Gazing cooly down at him, Andrew punished Sam by remaining impassively silent.

"H...Hey." Sam managed an uncomfortable smile. "I went to the brownstone with coffee for you guys, and...since you weren't there, and Fionna was really pushy..." He trailed off, rubbing the back of his neck. "Look, Andrew, I..."

"Don't," Andrew said, sharply raising his hand. "If you try to justify yourself, I'm walking away."

"But I..."

Andrew squatted in front of him. "You blew it," he said. "I want to make that very clear. It all worked out, no thanks to you. But this will be difficult to forget. Especially for Micah."

Tearfully, Sam nodded. "I know."

"But since you're here...I'd like you to clarify some things."

He nodded again. "Anything."

"What exactly was your role in nearly murdering the love of my life?" The ice wall and Andrew were one and the same—cold, closed off, insurmountable. "For example, we know Cirrus got the vial from you."

Sam rose off the snow enough to brush off his soaked butt and wrap his arms around his knees. "The vial had been sitting in the apartment since you came home from up north. She saw it when she was hanging out up there with me. It was right after you yelled at me, and I was really angry. So I gave it to her." He dropped his head, swallowing an apology. "She said she wanted it for witchy shit. I figured she'd put it on a necklace to look cool or something stupid. I thought witches were fake."

As if it wasn't the first time he'd heard that recently, Andrew shook his head with annoyance. "Why? The Folk are real. Why would witchcraft be fake?"

Sam shrugged. "'Cause girls like Cirrus do it." He gave a faint and halfhearted smile.

"My mum was doing small magic my whole life, so I guess I just don't understand the assumption." Andrew thought about Micah asking the same question earlier this week, and then it had come from someone who'd grown up with magical beings. So maybe people just assumed magic was sparse, or something. But even Lilydale thrived with magic, though within sight of the sprawl of the city. It was proof there was magic everywhere. He rose from his crouch and looked over the whitened sky and barren trees. Within the next month, buds would appear on the branches, and the river would thaw and swell and flood the plains. After all of the dread and darkness the winter had brought him, Andrew was more excited than normal for the warmer months ahead.

"Andrew," said Sam, gentle, as he stood up as well and hugged his arms to his chest. "You really aren't a normal guy."

Incredulously waving a hand, Andrew scowled. "I swear—"

"That was the first thing I realized about you." Sam smiled. "You have a certain air about you. You always feel a bit blurred around the edges. You move a bit more gracefully than other people."

Andrew shifted uncomfortably. "Anyway."

"Right."

"Micah said you could come in if I wanted you to. What do you say?"

Sam looked down, thrusting his hands into his coat pockets. "That's the other thing. I...don't think I want anything to do with magic anymore, to be honest."

Andrew raised his slender red brows.

"I'm sorry," Sam murmured. "I still want to be friends. I still love Magic's, linguistically confusing as that is at the moment. There's so many ways we can grow the company. But...uh...I just...I miss the days of you and me being boring nerds. I know that's not your life anymore, but I want it to be mine."

Andrew's brows rose higher. He remained in stunned silence.

"I have a programming friend who wants to work on some freelance projects with me, and I was wondering if we could work out a schedule so they can work in the shop with me if you're not going to be in."

Andrew leaned his head back against the ice archway and sighed through his nostrils. "You're breaking up with me," he deadpanned. It was only a very small quirk of his lip that gave him away.

Sam said, "I just get the feeling that Cirrus won't be the last person who tries to use me to get to you guys. So the less I know, the better."

Andrew met his eyes with some sadness in his own walnut-brown gaze. Anxiously, he took a small step forward over the boundary out of Lilydale as he asked, "W...Will you still come to my wedding?"

Sam socked his shoulder. "Duh."

"I was hoping you'd be my Best Man."

"I assumed so, since you don't have any other friends."

Andrew looked away with a bland frown. "Nevermind. I take it back."

Sam giggled. "I missed your neverending fountain of dry wit."

Snow fell gently on their shoulders and a soft breeze rustled the dry branches over them. Chickadees pecked at seed pods in a cluster of dead reeds. Weekend traffic was slow across the interstate bridge south of them, but the roads that wound around Pickerel far below were deserted. Sam marveled at the natural beauty of this sweet little spot, so wild, yet so close to humanity.

His thoughts drawn back to the approaching wedding, Sam asked suddenly with a tremor of guilt, "Does Micah even want me there? At your wedding. Around, in general. Or, just...alive."

"Not really." Andrew never danced around his point. "But you know him. He'll be very polite regardless. Nothing like me."

"I...I don't want to make him uncomfortable."

Andrew smiled faintly, but Sam wasn't entirely sure why.

Sam offered, "Maybe I can cook dinner next weekend. Get some time between us and this whole thing."

Andrew nodded. "Sure. That could be good. He wouldn't want to get between you and Julian, anyway. We know you've been a great support for him."

After a moment, Sam said, "Thanks for giving me the chance to talk."

Looking down at him as he nodded slightly, Andrew said softly, "Thanks for talking honestly."

Sam suddenly understood why sentimentality made Andrew so awkward. It took all his self-control not to clear his throat or comment on the weather under the intensity of Andrew's scrutiny.

Eyes glittering as if he knew it, Andrew said, "Well, I can walk you back to the road."

Chamomile appeared at Andrew's side.

Sam jumped. He felt his cheeks heat up. "Look...Chamomile. Hi. I...uh..."

Arms crossed, she interrupted, "Don't trouble yourself, Andrew. I can drop him back off at the brownstone. Don't want him to trip and fall in with any witches on the way back."

Sam grimaced. "Deserved."

"That was impressive wordplay," said Andrew with admiration.

Chamomile shot him a proud smile. "I thought you would like that." She took a viciously tight hold of Sam's hand, and then pulled him into the shadows with her.

When Chamomile and Andrew returned to the table, Micah poked the goblin's shoulder. "Found something out recently," he said.

"Good for you," said Chamomile around an enormous bite of omelet.

"My dad said you gave him something in the Redwoods that made his cravings more manageable." Micah took a sip of coffee.

Andrew straightened. "Hold on, what? He knows that wasn't a dream?"

Micah shook his head. "Yeah. He dropped that on me the night I slept in his room. Apparently he remembers everything about...everything."

Ingrid and Chamomile exchanged a look.

"Well," said Chamomile, "I didn't know if that remedy would do anything. There was no need to get your hopes up that it would. I think it brought him relief partly because it was immediately after he'd consumed Fae-spelled foods."

Micah could feel everyone's eyes on him, but his focus was fixed on Chamomile. "Well, whatever you did worked. So thank you. He's much better off without such an enormous addiction."

The table of Folk fell silent but for Spirulina's uncomfortable cough. Near her, Wex let out a conspicuous groan. The goblin triplets nudged shoulders and elbows into each other. Nox widened their goat eyes, and Leif stared pointedly at Wex.

"This again?" growled Wex. "I'm trying to enjoy my meal."

Andrew's eyes narrowed, shifting down toward the opposite end of the table as he lifted his teacup to his lips.

"Sorry, what part of this conversation makes you so sick?" Micah's voice was steady enough to thread through the eye of a needle.

The atmosphere of the table shifted. Fionna whimpered and slipped under the log, jostling Andrew's ankles as she sat on his feet in her wolfskin.

Wex muttered something and glared at their knees.

"I asked you a question." Micah narrowed his eyes. The bark along the sides of the log table trembled, sharp twigs sprouting forth with an audible snap. Fear rippled through the Folk around it. Spinn fell off his toadstool, Thorn catching him by the scruff of his collar.

"Your obsession with the wellbeing of humans is nauseating," Wex exclaimed, their eyes flashing.

Andrew started to rise, hand going to the hilt of his seax. Micah pressed on Andrew's shoulder and got to his feet himself.

"I am half-human," Micah said, rolling back his shoulders, his mulberry leaf necklace slipping out from the collar of his fleece pullover. "I will always concern myself with humanity."

"Then maybe you don't belong here," Wex spat. They hunched over their plate, curling their spindly fingers into fists so their knuckles poked out like spikes.

Micah hummed curiously, scrutinizing the Folk at the table with their colorful faces and diverse features. Few looked alike, and none looked like Micah, not even Ingrid. In that sense, Wex was correct. Micah stuck out. But everyone was looking at Wex and him in such a way that it left no doubt in Micah's chest as he said with a slight smile, "Actually, Wex, I think you'll find *you* no longer belong here."

Wex's green eyes snapped to Micah's face. A red grape flew across the table and struck them in the cheek so they yelped in alarm. Across from them, Syabira made no attempt to disguise herself as the perpetrator. Thorn followed suit, pelting Wex with a bread roll, which Spinn picked up, tore into pieces, and distributed to his siblings to throw at Wex again.

"You need to leave," said Micah. "You and whomever else intends to continue distributing our foods to humans no longer have a place within the walls of Lilydale."

Wex's mouth dropped open. "But you can't—" Their head swung toward Chamomile, but her face was impassive. Their head swung toward Ingrid, whose squared shoulders and low eyebrows were completed by the deep frown on her mahogany lips. Fear opened Wex's features as they began to argue again. But then Brynn struck them with a sweet roll. Syabira threw an apple, hitting their sternum with a *thwack*. Leif picked up a goblet of honey mead and splashed its contents over the sprite so they screeched and jumped to their feet.

"Bye," said Micah brightly. "Hey, Fionna? Andrew? Why don't you see that they cross the threshold."

Fionna shot out from under the log table with a snarl, making more than one faerie squawk in terror as she snapped at Wex's ankles. Wex took off, a streak of white painting its way toward the cobblestone fence with Fionna in pursuit and Andrew stalking after them with his black iron blade drawn.

Micah watched them disappear past a naked lilac bush with his lips quirked in a satisfied smirk as he sat back at the head of the table. "Boy. Issuing decrees sure dries out the mouth, huh?" He plucked Chamomile's mimosa from her fingers and downed it in one gulp while she stared at him with her pink lips parted in an awestruck grin.

He glanced at Ingrid. "What's that look for?"

Shaking off her stunned paralysis, Ingrid lifted her fruit-dappled wine and called to the table, "To Lord Heartwood!"

Calls of, "Here, here!" echoed down the table, and then the usual chatter of the Folk resumed.

# Chapter Fourteen
# The News

Behind the kiln throne and the kitchen stood a sizable plywood shack with a brick-laid deck beside it under the open air. It was brimming with supplies of all sorts for creative projects. Textiles; all manner of marking utensils including natural dyed paints, powders, and saps as well as several boxes of craft brushes from an art store; tools for leather work; small and large torches; papers both hand-made and bleached from the store. Set up to make ceramics were two foot-pedaled pottery wheels, a tub for glazing, and a small firing kiln, all which ran manually.

Ingrid and Micah sat over a small table with their heads together, a small brush in Ingrid's hand as Micah held onto a pair of tweezers while she worked. With her curls loose around her shoulders, Ingrid was in a cozy cropped sweater with her white belly pure as untouched snow rolling in and out as she breathed slowly. The leggings she wore were slightly sheer from her thighs down, with criss-crossed panels of mahogany. Micah knew this was the equivalent of her lounge wear, but he still felt shabby in a sweatshirt with a low ripped collar exposing his bare chest, and distressed joggers he saved for Lilydale since they were so flexible.

"Micah," Ingrid said after about twenty minutes of companionable silence. "I need to tell you something."

He lifted his eyes with sudden unease in the pit of his stomach. "Ingrid, it's a universal truth that 'I need to tell you something' is deeply ominous."

Brush pausing over the object in Micah's tweezers, Ingrid glanced up at him with a dubious look.

"It *is*," he insisted.

"Well, I...feel...awkward. I believe. That's a word you like." She dabbed carefully with her brush, and then sat back in satisfaction. She shifted her attention while he held the tweezers and started to put together a complicated electroforming setup with multiple jars, one dark blue and two clear.

Micah found out when he moved to Minnesota that humans needed precise electric currents to transform metallic ions into atoms. An organic substance would be painted with a fixative, and then the jars would conduct electricity which would coat the organic in layers of metal until Ingrid was pleased with the result. For all of his childhood, unwittingly, he'd been watching Ingrid do alchemy by hand. The mulberry leaf he was currently wearing was one such example she'd made for him when he was barely old enough to speak.

A gold rod was fixed in place with a pair of clamps in the blue liquid. Ingrid touched two other rods of metal together, and sparks zapped out of them. She concentrated in silence for a moment, the point of her pink tongue sticking out between her lips, and electricity seemingly flowing from her fingertips. She transferred the white crawling light from her fingers into the rods, and then moved her hand back. She nodded in satisfaction as the light kept dancing over the touching rods, flowing down a thin wire into the blue jar where Micah's ring was submerged.

"I am awkward, all of the time," Micah agreed, chin in his hand. "Also, I haven't seen you do this since I was twelve. You're so gifted. It seems like your magic is only made to make beauty."

Ingrid glanced anxiously at him, thrusting a stray curl behind her pointed ear. "Micah, I'm..." She trailed off and shook her head. She turned a thin gold loop downwards and hooked the ring in Micah's tweezers, using steady hands to lower it into the blue liquid. Then she tapped the metal rods together and looked back at the blue jar, peering into it, sniffing it. She straightened, and then looked at Micah with a pained expression.

"Go ahead," Micah prompted. "I'm currently emotionally stable."

Ingrid closed her eyes and blurted tonelessly, "I'm returning to the Redwoods after your wedding."

Lightning struck inside Micah's body. His hands went clammy. For a moment, swallowing an influx of saliva, he was afraid he would vomit.

Pressing her hands over her face, Ingrid hunched her shoulders and sat in silence for a moment. She finally looked at him, tearful. "I'm so sorry to leave you."

"I...Ingrid, I...I don't understand." He wasn't going to cry. He would *not* cry. "Why—why do you want to leave?"

"I don't *want* to leave you, I assure you." Ingrid took his hand. "I care more about you than all the stars in the sky, Micah."

Damn it all. He started to cry. "But then...why would you go back there?" He wiped at his eyes with the heel of his hand. "I don't understand. Don't leave me."

She pressed her fingers into her eyes and took a long breath without saying anything. Finally she sniffed and scooted closer, taking both his hands and leaning toward him as she said seriously, "Lilydale is yours, Micah."

Sniffling, balking, Micah tried and failed to pull his hands from her.

"Since we came back from the Redwoods, I've known I would need to do this. I didn't know if it would take a month, or thirty years. I've been waiting and watching as you've grown into your own, with a powerful and sensible man by your side to stay your hand or urge you on. And I felt that it was close."

"N-ot that close! I...I don't know what I'm doing!" Micah's voice broke, petulant, insistent.

She smiled. "Micah."

"No." He buried his face in his sleeve.

"You've fearlessly challenged me during this last month in a way not even my peers in the Redwoods would have. You know what you're worth, and you know when you're right. It's been...honestly deeply refreshing. I've been here twenty-two years with only Chamomile occasionally standing up to me."

"B...But Chamomile—she leads these guys." Maybe that would change her mind. If he had nothing to lead, she'd have to stay.

Ingrid shook her head. "She doesn't want to. She never has. Why do you think it was so effortless for me to step in here as leader so quickly after we arrived? I didn't contest leadership with her. She thrust it upon me." She straightened, running her fingernail over her lower lip. "But I am not suited for this place." She glanced back at Micah, some sorrow on her features turning her eyes dark merlot. "I'm sure you've noted that."

For a moment he caught his breath, the words he'd spoken just the previous night burning in the pit of his stomach. Maybe she'd heard him. "It doesn't matter," he insisted. "You can't leave. And...back *there*? Start somewhere new, or something. Why the Redwoods?"

Ingrid fussed with the tweezers, pressing her lips together. "For one, I...deserve it. I'm heir to the Redwood Throne, and it is mighty, in a vast and magic-drenched land. Next, I...I can do better with it than our mother." She lifted her gaze to Micah and told him with a slight tremble in her voice, "Especially since you have taught me so much about compassion."

Micah swallowed painfully. "Shut up," he whispered.

"And finally, I will ruin Lilydale if I remain here." Wistfully, she touched her electroforming cups with her fingertip. "I am all sharp edges and extremes."

"No! You...you won't!" He felt like a boy, trying to deny a truth he felt in his bones because it didn't suit him.

Ingrid took Micah's face between her hands, tender, smiling sweetly. "You're going to be amazing. With Andrew, and Chamomile, the three of you will help Lilydale thrive for years to come. You have a long, happy life ahead of you. Do not let me turn this place to stone."

"Why do you think about yourself like that?" he demanded, shaking her off, rejecting the affection that was so out of character for her. "You let me become who I am. You protected me so I *could* be so much softer than you. Twenty years in the Redwoods would have been more than enough to ruin me, if not for you."

"I will make it better there for you. I will make it safer, just like I did this place. For you. It's always for you, Nightshade Boy." She traced his brow with her long fingers.

"Ingrid," he pleaded.

"And I'll come back as often as I can. Nothing could keep me away. And when it is time, come and visit with your husband." She smiled softly, and a tear finally escaped her lashes and trailed prettily down her cheek.

Micah recognized the finality. This was something that was already happening. He didn't want to keep begging. He didn't want to make her feel worse. Micah caught her tear on the pad of his thumb and smiled tremulously. "We will." When he hugged her, he clung to her as a child would, with the crushing realization that she'd been a mother to him all along.

# CHAPTER FIFTEEN
# THE CRASH

AFTERNOON SUN MELTED THE snow from the limestone steps in Lilydale. Micah trudged down from the east end of the commune scraping his fingers through his hair. Ingrid's news sat in the pit of his stomach like sour milk.

Outside their tent, Andrew stared contemplatively over the valley. He was still in the cozy kind of sweats they wore while in the bluffs, his hair up in a bun. Micah wolf whistled him, drawing a smirk to his lips and a gleam to his eyes. He wished that Andrew's lovely face could cut through some of the fog in his thoughts, but since it didn't, he doubted anything could. He descended the last few steps that separated him from Andrew and then dropped his cheek onto Andrew's head. They both staggered while Andrew got his footing and threw an arm around Micah's waist. Micah draped himself around Andrew's shoulders, sighing until his lungs were empty so he could fill up on the almond-laced smell of campfire and sweat clinging to Andrew's soft skin.

"All right, love?" Andrew rubbed a circle in Micah's back. Micah's sadness felt like a cold puddle of rainwater in autumn.

"I'll tell you later," Micah rasped. "You're supposed to go meet your mum."

"Ah, you must be upset. You said 'mum' with a straight face." Andrew squeezed Micah's waist and nudged his chin with his nose. He stepped onto the next highest stair so he could cover Micah's mouth with his own, kissing him until some of the petrichor faded from Micah's scent. Then he moved back and asked, "Can you come with me?"

Micah blinked, looking up at him and searching his face. "Really? Yeah. Of course."

"Splendid." Andrew kissed his cheek. "Let's get to the brownstone. Shadows, right?" He clasped their hands.

"Oh, Andrew, I'm sorry but I don't think I can risk folding shadows. I think we'll have to walk." He grimaced. "We should really figure out a better way in and out of here...maybe get a snowmobile..."

Andrew's heart sank. "Oh." He rubbed his brow. "All right. I...guess if that's our only choice."

The tragic slump of his shoulders and the way the spirit sank out of Andrew's voice dragged a sigh out of Micah's throat. "Ah, no. I can manage. You're right."

"Are you sure?" Andrew asked, grazing his lips over Micah's knuckles.

"Yeah, what the hell. How bad could it go?" Micah turned them toward the river valley. "Ready?"

When Andrew nodded and twined their arms together, Micah reached an empty hand toward the river. He pulled them into a shadow shafting across the bluffs from the branches of an enormous pine. The curtain of liminal space yanked them in, bucking and jerking like driving a car bottoming out on a gravel road. Despite this, Micah felt sure-footed for a few beats, carrying them down the hills and out onto the river, almost like flying. Maybe he was going to make it to the brownstone. Then he felt his shoe slip and plunge through shadows as unstable as broken planks on a bridge. Gasping, he hung tightly onto Andrew and pulled himself back in, staggering half a dozen steps as the frozen river raced up to meet them. Swearing and tripping, Micah dragged them forward, but the shadows rejected his efforts and spat him out.

They crashed into a switchyard west of the riverbank, breaking apart from each other, tumbling over the unforgiving steel tracks and into the wooden beams between. The rasping snarl of metal on metal pummeled the air, too loud, and growing louder.

Micah jammed both forearms into the gravel and jerked his head up. Monstrous headlights like wide staring eyes swallowed his vision. Flying straight toward them. The deafening horn of a freight train rattled his teeth. Too terrified to make a sound, Micah grabbed handfuls of Andrew's sweatshirt and folded him into his arms before somersaulting them off the tracks. The tornadic force of the engine roaring past sent them tumbling again before they rolled into a deep muddy ditch. The train cars rumbled past with merciless ignorance, twigs and gravel raining down on them.

Groaning, Andrew rolled onto his back. He stared at the cheerful blue sky while he sucked in ragged gasps of air. "Bad listening, Andy," he moaned. Then he lurched upright, twisted, and vomited into the gravel. Andrew didn't move, curled up, coughing quietly.

Numb with dread, Micah grabbed Andrew's arm and helped him sit up. "Shit! Andrew, I'm so sorry. You okay, babe?"

Dusty and stamped with grease from the tracks, his elbow bleeding through a tear in his sleeve and his forehead scraped open, Andrew swayed unsteadily with a pained smile. He wiped his mouth with the back of his sleeve. "I'm...er, fine?"

"I can't believe I almost got you hit by a train!" cried Micah, digging his nails into the soft underside of his forearms. The guilt was enormous, temporarily paralyzing him as he tried to plan their recovery, pulling up nothing but self-loathing.

Andrew stared up as the caboose of the train rattled away from them, barking a laugh and blinking in expressionless shock. "All right, pip pip, let's try again." He tried to get up, lost his balance, and fell into Micah.

"Like hell I will!" said Micah. "I don't know how that could go any worse, but it could, and I'm not going to find out how."

"Oh, *tush*. I'll just help you." Andrew squinted at the sky with a smile.

Perplexed by his dismissiveness, Micah pulled Andrew closer and peered seriously at him. "I...I think you have a concussion."

Andrew looked at Micah like he was speaking French. "What'd I hit?"

Micah gripped Andrew's chin and turned his face toward him, but he didn't actually know what he was looking for. He'd heard that mismatched pupils didn't always occur with a concussion. Micah dabbed at the pricks of blood on the scrape on Andrew's forehead. The sight made him ill, and he had suddenly more understanding of how Andrew had felt the day before, after Red Rabbit.

"Look at the sun for me." Micah pointed to the sky.

"You're the sun." Andrew giggled.

"Andrew."

Huffing, Andrew blinked his eyes toward the midmorning sun. His pupils were difficult to see in the depths of his dark irises, but they were undoubtedly *way* too big.

Micah held his hand up to cast a shadow over Andrew, his nose almost touching Andrew's cheek. But when the light should have changed Andrew's pupils again, nothing happened.

"Fuck," Micah whispered. "Okay, we were on our way home to the brownstone. I need to get us there right away and...er...figure out what to do with you."

Andrew sat in silence, swaying slightly, staring at the tracks over them with his lips parted quizzically. Micah looked westward. They had fallen near the sharp escarpment that rose up toward Cliff Street, right beyond which was his brownstone. He'd literally almost made it. Kicking himself mentally, he knew with certainty he couldn't trust himself to fold shadows the rest of the way home. It was too bad Ingrid had stopped tailing him since Andrew had come home. Maybe if she'd witnessed this disaster, she would rethink leaving Lilydale for the Redwoods.

But...the escarpment was all rough limestone under a scraggly line of barren trees. *That* he could work with. He hyped himself up with one more look at Andrew's blank expression and bleeding forehead. Making the terrain work for him was not an option. It was a necessity.

"I'm not going to fold shadows," said Micah, "but I think I can get us home in one piece." He stood up and brushed off gravel dust from his pants and elbows, and then he reached down for Andrew, who tried to grab his hand but missed.

"I'm so sorry, babe." He miserably rubbed Andrew's arms. "I really messed you up."

"I'm fine." Andrew squinted, his brow furrowing. "Just feels like I got hit by a train." He froze for a moment before the pun dawned on him and he tumbled into childish laughter. With a beleaguered groan, Micah summoned the birchwood staff and hauled Andrew to his feet.

Andrew slapped his hand over his mouth, gagging so hard his shoulders heaved. Micah cringed involuntarily, shutting his eyes, braced to be covered in vomit.

Swallowing and smacking his lips, Andrew shook his head slightly and said, "Got 'er down. Sorry." He hooked the staff under his armpit like a crutch.

"Okay, babe. Hold tight." Micah shifted his attention to the escarpment. Rather than relying on petulant shadows, Micah asked for help from the roots and the stones. The roots grew down toward him at once, like a giant's tangled hair, slithering over the limestone. The limestone was a new friend formed by his kinship to Lilydale, ever more familiar, ever more willing to work with him. The stones groaned, waking up. And as Micah fed the stone and the roots with the lively energy from his staff, a ragged and wild staircase formed, steep and uneven but functional. Micah breathed a sigh of relief and gratitude.

"Feels like my arm is falling asleep." Andrew hiccuped with laughter.

Micah dropped to a squat and leaned back between Andrew's thighs before rising sharply and throwing the taller man completely off balance. As Andrew fell forward with a gasp, Micah used his momentum to wrap Andrew's arms and legs around him.

"Hold on, okay?" said Micah. "Just squeeze me for all you're worth."

Andrew hummed happily. "Okay, Micah." Andrew was
actually very slight on his back, his thighs and arms clench-

ing so tightly that his muscles trembled. Micah fought for purchase on the rough stairway, pretending he was just scaling the familiar cliff outside Lilydale. But his fingers quickly became sore with cold, and Andrew didn't feel light for very long. Panic jangled like alarm bells in his ears, knowing how easily he could lose his grip and his fiancé if he failed. He climbed frantically until at last he grasped the wrought iron railing next to the sidewalk and sent a final burst of energy into the staff, which vaulted them up onto the pavement. To safety.

Tripping onto one knee, Micah let go of the birchwood staff and shook out his numb red fingers. Andrew dropped off his back, landing heavily on his ass with a groan. Micah turned toward him as Andrew's head swung down between his shoulders, and he dropped his forehead onto his scraped up palm.

Andrew groaned. "I'm gonna barf." He heaved, and then swallowed, saliva pooling in his mouth. Swallowing again, he took a deep breath. "No. I'm okay."

"All right," said Micah. "Just gotta make it down the block. Easy, right?" He stood up with the staff grinding into the pavement and closed Andrew's hands around it. "Come on, then. Hang onto my staff, okay?"

"I'll hold onto your staff any day." Andrew tried to wink, but he shut both his eyes. He climbed the length of the birchwood staff and got shakily to his feet.

Micah sighed. "Come on, big boy." They moved like an enfeebled old couple down the street, Andrew becoming slightly steadier as he went but keeping an arm around Micah's shoulders and a hand on the staff. The brownstone had never looked more inviting than now with its safe aloe ward, solid brick walls, heated interior, and running water. Andrew's boots scuffed on the iron steps as Micah got them to the front door, fumbled with his keys, and let them inside.

He called, "Dad? Fi? Can I have a hand?"

"Handful of that ass," slurred Andrew, and groped Micah's ass just as Julian came around to the vestibule.

"Uh." Julian turned around to go back up the stairs. "Can't unsee that."

Blushing, Micah hollered wordlessly before he managed, "Dad! Wait!"

Micah's tone made Julian turn back around. "What's the matter?"

Andrew stood over Micah, grooming his hair with his fingers. Making a face, Micah clung to Andrew's waist. "I...I was trying to get us home from Lilydale, and I messed up and dropped us on the switchyard off Shepard. Andrew has a concussion."

Julian *tsked*. He ushered the two of them further inside and shut the door behind them. "You need to be careful with him, Micah. Andrew is more mortal than you."

Micah's cheeks burned. His scalp tickled as Andrew braided his hair until Micah shooed him away. Andrew whined and dropped his hands, dejected. To Julian, Micah said, "I have to get him to see his mom in, like, thirty minutes. I need to get him cleaned up and changed and...I need help."

Julian nodded. "Tell me what you need."

"I can fun...function," stammered Andrew, grabbing the railing before the stairs that led to the living room. He tripped over the first two steps and made it up the rest with Julian and Micah herding him with hands on his arm and waist. Embarrassment heated to frustration in Micah's belly. Frustration and regret and a deep, deep sense of shame. At least when Micah had been shuffling around earlier in the week, it was because of evil mystical forces working against him. Andrew was tripping over himself—truly an unsettling sight with how graceful he usually was—because Micah couldn't successfully utilize one of the *first* skills Folk learned when they were children. He'd seen faerie children that were mere months old slip into the shadows when they tantrumed. Micah was *forty-two* and couldn't even travel a mile without almost getting hit by a train.

And what was worse: Andrew was in no condition to discuss this with him. The isolation was insurmountable, and it made Micah's eyes burn with the threat of tears.

In the bathroom on Julian's level, Micah peeled off Andrew's sweatshirt, wiping off the dust from the railway using a damp cloth before cleaning Andrew's bloody scrapes, while Andrew remained pliable but pale and clammy. Disappearing up the stairs, Julian retrieved a change of clothes for both of them from Micah's room before returning to his bathroom. Fionna trailed after him without her wolf-skin, clinging to Julian's shirttails, whimpering when she saw the blood on Andrew before Micah bandaged him up. Andrew was quiet and distant when Micah closed the bathroom door to change Andrew and himself into clean clothes. Julian must have had the same sense as Micah, giving them nicer button-downs and sweaters so they'd look presentable for Liath.

"I'm so sorry," Micah said to him as he fixed Andrew's collar and brushed his long red hair.

"I'll be okay," Andrew assured him softly, still with a distant gaze and white lips, and a steady pounding in his forehead so thunderous that he felt the pain in his ears.

Micah opened the door to Julian and Fionna waiting anxiously.

"Thanks," Andrew said to the pair. He reached out to try to pat Fionna's head, but he missed twice before he managed to touch her.

"I'm coming with," said Fionna. "I want to help Dad-Andy. And see Liath."

"Oh." Micah blinked. "Yeah. I guess you lived with her."

"*Around* her," Fionna corrected. "Not allowed inside."

Julian frowned. "That's sad. You were very easy to housebreak."

She looked up, confused.

"The toilet," Julian clarified.

"Oh." She nodded knowingly. "Toilet much better than going in cold."

Julian held up a finger. "In *the* cold."

Fionna butted her forehead into Julian's elbow and scampered away.

"Or just be a barbarian!" Julian called after her with a roll of his eyes. "See if I care!"

Next to the bathroom, there was another spare room which Julian had converted into a bedroom for the wolf girl two weeks ago. He took pleasure in making the room cozy and childlike, with lacy white curtains and a silky purple bedspread. Fionna took pleasure in slamming her own door, frequently, like now.

While they were waiting, Andrew leaned against the wall, arms crossed over his stomach and chin on his chest.

"Drink some water," Julian said, pulling Andrew's wrist and setting a cup in his hand, hanging on so he couldn't spill. "Careful." He glanced at Micah, taking in his son's anxious hand-wringing and how he gnawed on his lip. "Hey, I know this sucks, kiddo, but it's not the worst thing that's happened this week," Julian remarked with a slight glare of his amber eyes. "I'm still very, very upset about how you almost died last night."

Andrew flung the glass into the air and showered all three of them with water as he exclaimed, "Same *here*, Julian!" Micah and Julian gave identical cries of protest as Micah caught the glass and held it out of Andrew's reach. Julian sucked his teeth, ripping his spectacles off his face and shaking them dry.

Fionna galloped out from the bedroom next to the bathroom, tamping down her wild hair with her hands. She eyed the three of them and demanded, "Why you wet?"

Micah closed his eyes and gritted his teeth. "Never mind. We gotta go, Fi. Give me a hand with him."

Fionna held out her hand for Micah to shake.

Julian smothered a snort of amusement.

Micah didn't relax until Andrew was safely buckled into the leather passenger seat in Micah's car. About halfway through the twenty minute drive, Andrew's complexion greened. Over his shoulder, Fionna stretched around the seat and opened the paper bag Julian had sent with them, just in time for Andrew to vomit into it.

"Dreadful," Andrew muttered.

Micah groaned. "Oh, babe. I'm so sorry."

"Quit apologizing." Andrew wiped his mouth with the back of his hand, leaning back against the headrest. "Just turn the air up for me or I'll be sick again."

Though Micah started to shiver, he obeyed, blasting air conditioning and pointing the vents at Andrew's pallid face. Andrew's long fingers touched the bandage on his forehead, exploring the extent of the injury, which caused him a wince and a long sigh.

Fionna plucked the bag out of Andrew's hand and crumpled the mouth of it so the smell was sealed inside. She replaced the bag with a water bottle, twisting off the cap, and nudged Andrew's wrist till he lifted it to his lips.

Micah looked back at the road, chewing hard on the inside of his cheek, gripping the wheel more tightly. He followed the console map's directive off the highway and idled at a red light. While he waited, he ordered the birchwood staff to grow. "Here. Maybe this'll help."

As Micah seized Andrew's wrist, the bark flaked off Micah and onto Andrew's bony wrist, reshaping itself into a bulky bracelet.

Andrew blinked. His vision was blurred, but the wooden bracelet was quite clear, and warm around his wrist. When the car lurched back into motion, he felt less sick than in the moments before.

"It did," agreed Andrew. "Are you sure I should wear it?"

Micah shrugged. "Why not? If it helps, that's that."

Relaxing into the cocoon of Micah's magic, Andrew rested his hand on Micah's knee and shut his eyes for the remainder of the drive winding through wide suburban streets past red and white drive-thrus and upscale grocery stores.

It had been some time since Micah had driven out of the city into the suburbs. It had been some time since he'd been even this far away from Lilydale. It felt foreign, like he was a bit empty. Like some pit in his stomach opened up with longing to be back. The address Andrew had for where his mum was staying led to a house in a generic neighborhood belonging to a wide but old rambler with a well-groomed lawn and a steep driveway that had a red truck parked in it.

Fionna unbuckled herself from the backseat and hurried over to the passenger door to let Andrew out. She took Andrew's hand and helped him to his feet. He looked almost as green as Chamomile standing outside the car wrapped in his tartan scarf.

When he caught Micah staring at him, he tapped the birchwood bracelet on his skinny wrist and managed a thin smile. Micah and Fionna mirrored Andrew's uncertain pace as they went up to the door, crunching over a healthy layer of salt on the slushy chunks of ice on the driveway. There was a trellis that had dried up roses clinging to it, and a doormat that said SPEAK FRIEND AND ENTER. Micah rang the doorbell.

A short, round old woman opened the door. She had wisps of white hair, enormously thick red glasses, and an equally enormous mole on her nose. Some kind of crocheted shawl hung over a black dress that was too tight for her. Maybe he was being a little paranoid, but Micah's heart flipped in his chest. She looked like a witch.

She eyed him up and down. "Lord Heartwood, I presume."

Expression carefully blank, Micah said, "Beg your pardon?"

She snorted. "Mm-hm."

In a buttoned flannel and worn jeans, Liath appeared at the woman's elbow. Her short, faded auburn hair was streaked with white and partially obscured by a cream-colored beanie. She might have been Irish, but she looked like an archetypical Minnesotan.

When Fionna danced from foot to foot and squeaked excitedly, Liath smiled and held her fingers out to the girl. Delighted to be acknowledged, Fionna bumped into Liath's chest and nuzzled her shirt while keeping her hand tightly clamped on Andrew's.

"Come on, then, you lot," said the old woman, receding into the shadowy house which wafted the stale scent of incense out into the mild air.

As he stepped over the threshold and into the house, Micah already had regrets. Before he could bite his tongue, he said flippantly as he passed Liath, "If anyone tries to kill me in here, so help me, I will go feral."

"Me too!" Fionna chomped her white teeth. She put Andrew's hand on her head and led him inside.

Guilt sank into the crease of Liath's frown as she looked away. "I vouch for your safety on my own life, for whatever that's worth," she told him quietly. She glanced up as Andrew passed her and caught his elbow immediately. "Andrew?" She touched the bandage on his forehead. "Are you all right?"

"Totally," Andrew mumbled, leaning a hand on the door jamb.

Liath's dark gaze turned to Micah for an answer.

"Well, ma'am, I'm afraid I gave your son a concussion." Micah's neck prickled with the heat of shame, back with a vengeance. His first real conversation with Andrew's mother and he had to confess to stupidly injuring her child.

Liath stiffened.

"Mum, it's no big deal," Andrew said seriously, talking to the door frame two feet to Liath's left.

Clicking her tongue, she muttered a profanity. "Come on, then. We'll have to take care of that if we expect him to remember why he needed me."

Micah slid out of his sneakers and adjusted the peeking hem of his striped dress shirt beneath his cardigan. "Ma'am, don't you think maybe he just wanted to see you?"

Liath smiled ruefully. She led him out of the vestibule into a sitting room with a bay window which allowed in cheerful afternoon sunlight. "You overestimate his affection for me." She sat in a floral upholstered chair adjacent to the window and cast a serious glance at the ceiling in a way that Andrew did when he was anxious.

Fionna yelped; in the vestibule, she was crouched helping Andrew get his shoes off, but he'd lost his balance and was leaning his elbow on her head. Micah hurried back to help as Andrew muttered defensively, "I *almost* made it." Micah held onto his waist and finished pulling off his boots, kissing his jaw when they were steady.

When the three of them turned back to the living room, Liath's eyes were fixed on them with thoughtful intensity. She looked away when Micah noticed her.

Nosing Andrew's elbow, Fionna led him into the living room and pushed him down onto a yellow velvet couch opposite Liath. It reminded Micah of a service dog attending to an owner in distress.

With Andrew situated, Fionna turned to Liath and said as she rocked on her heels, "Hi, Liath." Her little voice was a tentative petition for attention.

Rising from her chair, Liath reached for Fionna and pulled her onto her lap. "Oh, little one. I'm so happy to see you again."

Fionna squeaked joyously, squirming in the woman's arms. "I missed your smell. Like candles and ginger."

Eyebrows raising, Liath said, "Listen to those sentences. You've learned so much English."

Beaming, Fionna nodded. "Grandpa Jule teaches nicer than Dad-Andy. So does this." Fionna pulled Andrew's phone out of the pocket of her sweatshirt. Across the room, Andrew hummed in protest.

"I bet you know how to use that better than me," remarked Liath.

The old woman hobbled into the room with a decorated tray that Micah politely took from her and placed on a low oak table in the center of the room.

Liath looked down as Fionna hovered over the carpet bag by her feet, her tongue poking out of her lips. Giving Fionna a slightly exasperated look, Liath picked up the bag and fished out a shortbread cookie, dropping into Fionna's outstretched palms. Micah grinned despite himself.

Liath extracted a red square tin with a lid from her bag, glancing up at Micah's curious expression. "I always have the supplies for concussion relief. It's an old habit."

"Concussion relief?" he repeated.

"Aye. Part naturopathic—willow bark and ginger—and part enchantment."

"Andrew's been doing a lot of that herb mixing since he came back," said Micah. "Mostly on my account, trying to help my shoulder. But you should be proud to know that his concoctions were frequently effective."

"I am proudly not surprised," Liath replied. The old woman noisily cleared her throat, which Liath ignored with a frown until she did it a second time.

The women regarded each other in silence, making Micah feel like he was intruding on a private conversation. He backed up to the yellow couch and lowered himself to the cushion beside Andrew, sliding his arm around Andrew's small waist like he was holding onto a buoy in angry waters. Between Ingrid's announcement, Andrew's injury, the complex relationship Micah understood Andrew and Liath had, and this...witchy-looking woman, Micah's stomach was in knots and his blood pounded in his ears. He hoped this healing concoction worked for Andrew *fast*.

Shaking her head slightly as the old woman sat in the twin to Liath's chair, Liath returned her attention to her tea. She shuffled through plastic packets in the tin and then sprinkled several different colored herbs into the teacup. Her lips moved inaudibly while she cocked her head and studied her tin of ingredients. Then she filled the cup with steaming water and stirred for several quiet minutes, her eyes barely open.

The old woman smoothed her shirt and fixed her necklace before eyeing Micah without speaking. It felt like she was either reading his mind, or setting another curse on him. He stiffened, moving a bit closer to Andrew. The woman sniffed and said, "My name is Eda."

Swallowing, Micah said, "You already know me, apparently. But you can call me Micah."

The woman nodded. Her jaw worked for a moment and then she said, "I heard what those young girls did, and I'm personally concerned."

It took Micah a beat to realize she meant the witches. He flexed his shoulder, the thought of them bringing back a phantom pain to his sunburst scar. "All right," he said warily.

"Those girls violated a very old treaty," she went on. "And then so did the Ruby Daughter."

Clinking the spoon gently against the teacup, Liath handed it to Fionna, who hurried over to the couch and gave the cup and saucer to Micah. She sniffed Andrew's forehead, pawed at his cheek, and then returned to Liath. The cup wafted a stinging, heavily grassy fragrance into Micah's face that made his head briefly spin. He hoped this wasn't dangerous to feed to Andrew, but Andrew confidently reached for the saucer.

Helping Andrew get the cup to his lips, Micah kept his sights dubiously on this strange old woman sitting with Liath. He weighed his words carefully. "I'm sure Liath told you some of what happened, but I have a suspicion that you have other sources of information as well. I'm curious what your part is in all this."

"Yes, of course. I'm a witch," answered Eda calmly.

A growl rose in Fionna's throat and she edged further from Eda into the space between Liath's calves.

Eda waved dismissively at Fionna and said, "Peace, little *faoladh.* I have no interest in you."

"Sorry, but she's not the only one of us with a sour opinion on witches," Micah remarked.

The woman gave a long sigh.

Stroking Fionna's hair to soothe the girl, Liath said gently, "This is neutral ground. We needn't be dichotomous here. We meet in the gray areas."

Eda glanced at Liath, shuffling in her seat, and then shook her head slightly and slumped her shoulders. "Fine, fine." She pointed at Micah and explained, "Those girls—the ones who were there yesterday, who used your blood as a weapon—they are dabbling in dangerous magic with no respect for the context of any of it." Eda held him in suspense as she leaned forward and prepared herself a cup of hot water shot with honey, dropping a tea bag into it before sitting back in her chair. She blew gently on the cup. "I should know. I've been practicing witchcraft in Saint Paul for fifty years."

"That's an impressive resume," Micah admitted.

She nodded. "I helped write the treaty between the witches and the Folk in Lilydale with the goblin Chamomile."

Jaw dropping, Micah stared at her.

"What the fuck," Andrew muttered between sips.

"You haven't heard of it?" Eda quirked a brow.

"She was holding out on me," Micah remarked in wonder.

Eda shrugged. "The city creates many secrets as the decades pass. Those of us who hold them tend to preserve them."

"Apparently." Micah raised his eyebrows. This reframed many of the comments from Syabira and Nox about witches. They must have all known that Chamomile's treaty was falling apart.

"Tricky goblin," said Andrew, taking a deep drink from the teacup. He glanced at Micah and said, "She's always got something up her metaphorical sleeve."

Micah touched his hand. "You sound better."

He raised the teacup toward Liath. "She knows what she's doing."

Smiling uneasily, Liath gently pulled the bands for Fionna's pigtails out. She began a complicated braid with the wolf's silver-brown hair, slightly wild and very intricate. With a glance back up at Micah, she said, "I came up with that tonic when Andrew was a boy. I was able to perfect the recipe since his dad gave me quite a few concussions," she told him. "The drink will help him feel like himself—but he will need plenty of rest for the next week."

Micah grimaced, glancing from her to Andrew to ensure he didn't spill. "You two didn't deserve all that."

Liath shrugged. "We're safe now." She eyed Andrew. "Relatively."

Micah covered his face with his hands. "I'm sorry, Miss Ryan."

With a trace of a laugh, Liath said, "I'm only slagging you. Call me Liath." Her eyes crinkled the same way Andrew's did when he was teasing Micah, which was the only reason Micah knew what the hell she was saying.

"It was my idea that landed us on the train tracks," Andrew argued, his words slurring together.

"Did you say train tracks? Blimey," exclaimed Liath. "You two attract trouble, don't you?"

"Yes," they said together.

"So—" Andrew set the teacup and saucer on a rickety antique table on his side of the couch. He gestured to Eda. "What kind of 'sponsor' is this woman, exactly?"

"Hmph," grunted Eda.

Liath shot him a very faint smile. "The kind of sponsor someone needs when they're addicted to magic."

"Is it her cabin you're living in?" asked Andrew.

"Aye, that it is."

"Liath told me about your involvement yesterday, as well, curse-breaker." Eda wagged a finger at Andrew. "You have an aptitude for magic, especially given your bloodline."

Micah quirked an eyebrow. "Bloodline?"

Giving Eda a sharp look, Liath said hurriedly, "Andrew, love, do you know what you needed from me today? You said yesterday you had something to discuss."

Andrew started to nod, which made his head swim until he stopped. He took another long drink from the tea cup and picked off a flower petal that stuck to his lip. He glanced at Micah and then leaned into him, taking comfort in the way Micah's thumb traced circles on his forearm. "I'll be in Lilydale too much for the hassle of getting in and out on foot or making Micah risk the shadows."

Micah looked down, shame heating up his cheeks.

Catching his look, Eda snorted derisively. "What do you expect, child? You are still a bit human."

Annoyance prickled Micah's skin. Why did this witch know so much about him?

Andrew glanced between him and Eda, his eyes slow to track and shift, his vision flipping upside-down. It made him nauseous, so he took another sip of the drink from his mum. Scooting into Micah's hip and pulling Micah's arm further around his waist, Andrew said to the women, "I...I was thinking, like, can we...er, Cirrus could just...disappear out of the restaurant. Can I find a way to disappear between Lilydale and the city and back?" He wrinkled his brow. "Does that make any sense?"

"Genuine curiosity here," said Micah, "but how do you know she didn't just sneak out the kitchen door when I was dying?"

"Could we make a waypoint?" asked Andrew, still watching Liath. "Like a—a video game?"

Liath and Eda traded a thoughtful look. Liath shrugged, but Eda nodded.

"But for whom?"

"At first I thought just for me, but maybe it's for anyone with a pee." Andrew blinked. "Key. Anyone with a key."

"It would certainly reduce careless access to Lilydale," said Liath.

Andrew nodded slightly.

Micah leaned his chin on his fist and asked Eda, "What did you mean, ma'am, about Andrew's bloodline?"

Eda looked at Liath, who widened her dark eyes with a silent plea.

Eda turned her watery blue eyes back between Andrew and Micah. She said with some scorn, "Don't you know where Druid magic came from, Lord Heartwood?"

Andrew kept his eyes on Liath.

Frustration boiled forth from Micah's carefully preserved calm, his palms going sweaty, blood pounding in his ears. "Look, Eda," Micah snapped, "I don't know what you think I'm supposed to know, but if you could cool it on the condescension, I would appreciate it. I came with my fiancé to support him, not to get lectured. Mind your own business."

Casting an uneasy glance between the women across from them and back to Micah, Andrew gripped Micah's knee, to comfort and to caution. Taking a breath, Micah leaned back with his arms crossed and narrowed his eyes, silent.

"I think you could use a pair of twin objects to make something function like a door for you, child," said Liath as Eda glared back at Micah and sipped her tea.

Faintly incredulous, Andrew told her, "I can't do anything like that without your help."

Liath grimaced. "Andrew, I...I don't know if setting foot in Lilydale is a good idea for me. For people in recovery..."

Andrew's shoulders slumped, almost imperceptibly, his sweater rustling enough to catch Micah's attention.

Micah said with sudden conviction, "I can ensure you have no access to anything with intoxicating properties. I don't like the idea of any humans accessing Fae-spelled foods. Folk don't even spell their food on purpose. It just happens. But now more than ever, most of the Folk in Lilydale would prefer just to be left alone, mind their own business, make simple foods to share with each other."

Eda raised her eyebrows.

Liath paused. "The Ruby Daughter has never restricted access to Lilydale. She's too ambivalent."

Andrew thought back to what Ingrid told him when they first met and he injured her. She couldn't be bothered. That had always been her stance; it was what Chamomile stated about her, as well. Ingrid couldn't be bothered. It was a significant obstacle even now for improving the safety of humans who meddled with the Folk. At least Micah had cast out Wex today, which would make the other Folk pause before distributing Fae-spelled foods outside the commune.

"The Ruby Daughter will be back in the Redwoods after Ostara," Micah told her firmly.

Andrew's jaw dropped. He suddenly felt like he was disoriented again, like someone gave him a violent shake just after his head began to clear. Ingrid was leaving? He turned to Micah. "Hold on. Ingrid is leaving?"

Micah glanced guiltily at him. "Sorry. That was why I was all out of sorts. She told me just before we came here, and..."

"Holy shit." Andrew leaned back and steepled his fingers over his mouth. "Oh, that's depressing."

"Fascinating," remarked Eda, sipping her tea.

"What happens then?" asked Liath.

Andrew looked over at Micah, silent, lips slightly parted.

Micah rolled his shoulders and squared his chin. "Lilydale is mine."

# Chapter Sixteen
# The Redwood

BATHED IN CREAMY ORANGE afternoon sun and framed by the blue-gray band of the Mississippi, Micah vibrated with anxiety as he stepped barefooted into the fire pit in the heart of Lilydale. His dark green corduroys were cuffed above his ankles beneath an open flannel shacket. Intricate lines of his chest tattoo peeked out beneath the slouchy collar of his shirt underneath, his mulberry necklace glinting with the same gold glow as the loops of metal through his stretched earlobes.

Andrew reveled in watching Micah work, in the smudge of dirt across Micah's squared chin which was dusted with green stubble, in the lively flush in his cheeks. It made Micah look like he was returning to the earth to join the twelve saplings he'd planted in a ring around the perimeter of Lilydale.

In order to ensure that his trees would be an effective ward, Micah wanted all other barriers around Lilydale taken down. Over the last two weeks, the Folk had dismantled the crumbling cobblestone fence left there from ages past. Ingrid had allowed the Agassiz ice wall to melt away with the warming of the air indicating oncoming spring. Even though the ice wall had only turned to water that morning, its sudden absence made Lilydale look undressed and vulnerable over the limestone cliff that dropped down toward Pickerel Lake.

Standing in the center of the fire pit, Micah tamped down his birchwood staff until it remained erect in the soot and soil between his feet. He glanced to his right where Syabira knelt with a mound of dirt in her cupped hands with twelve neatly clipped buds vividly green against the darkness of the soil, each leaf erected like a flag and creating the impression of a microcosmic forest. Delicately, with his right hand curled around his staff, Micah plucked the serrated rowan leaf from Syabira's collection and held it near his lips.

"*Luis*," he whispered, marking the Ogham symbol for rowan in the soot beneath his feet. "Will you bring your protection to Lilydale?" His nightshade gaze flicked toward his one o'clock. Northwest, the rowan sapling was planted within a circle of red-capped mushrooms, and it reached for the leaf between Micah's fingers only to find his magic and the magic of the land urging it to *grow*, to thrive. Happy to oblige, the tree of protection reared toward the sky with a creaking, growling rumble. Fanned out on the amphitheater steps leading to the kiln throne, several of the Folk squeaked and gasped in alarm, pointing at the rapidly growing rowan tree. Others happily sipped honey mead or clapped in quiet admiration. When it settled, the rowan stood taller and fuller than most of its naturally growing counterparts, settling at about forty feet tall and framed by a puff of soft white clouds. Its branches were overflowing with the early arrival of rustling leaves where the surrounding trees were just beginning to bud. Around it, the forest grew quiet, curious, attention turning to this impressive display of natural power. Deer in their hidden beds lifted velvety heads to peer at the rowan tree through dark glassy eyes.

"Well?" Andrew stepped closer to the fire pit, reaching a nervous hand out to grasp Micah's wrist. "Do you feel all right?"

Micah smiled. Soft green highlights shimmered on his skin—his brow and cheekbones and clavicle—as he was trading magic back and forth with his staff. "Better than all right. That was thrilling." He set the rowan leaf in Andrew's outstretched hand, and Andrew placed it carefully inside the clay pot they would use to preserve each leaf from the tree ring. "Chamomile?"

"I'm ready!" Her voice drifted across the compound as she waved an enormous spear of aloe vera over her head.

"Go ahead and use the gel to mark a ring around the trunk. Tell me when it's whole!"

Barefooted, Chamomile danced lightly around the rowan, its heavy red berries brushing the crown of her loose silver hair as aloe dripped down her wrist. She whistled a high, pure note when she'd completed the line of syrupy green.

Micah smiled, glancing toward the tall stump where his sister watched him, her eyes a warm rosy pink as she sipped from a goblet of wine. Both her legs were bare beneath an oversized sweater that slouched off one shoulder. Crossed over her left leg, her right foot bobbed softly.

The second leaf he picked up had the smooth spikes of a bur oak. Giving the stem a twirl, he breathed on the oak leaf. Then with a slender charcoal stick, he made a mark on its pale underbelly.

"*Dair*—join with us by offering your strength." At Micah's two o'clock, the oak as much as the rowan was ready to grow in thunderous spurts, bark snapping as it slotted together so loudly that it echoed over the river plain. Soaring to its full, magicked height, it dwarfed the rowan tree and truly the other trees in the area, only coming to settle when it was at least a hundred feet tall. Its spreading branches brushed its neighbors but kindly respected the space they took up, weaving between but not butting up into them. Nearby, a barred owl blinked from the burrow in its own oak tree to assess just how soon it could move into the protection of this new, holy tree. Chamomile marked its enormous trunk and whistled when she was done, and so Micah moved on.

Three o'clock was an alder tree, *fern*, to promote spiritual health and creativity. Tiny brown cones hung among its leaves; one jiggled so much it snapped free and plunked on Chamomile's head as she marked its trunk with aloe. She yelped, but picked up the cone and slipped it into the pocket of her white velvet dress before whistling.

*Ceirt*, an apple tree, grew luscious First Kiss apples Syabira procured from the University of Minnesota. The apple tree would encourage rest and mental wellness, continuing the feelings Micah had over the last six weeks he'd spent recovering. Several of the Folk bounded over to pick off a few of the fruits, laughter like a sweet breeze in the afternoon air.

Next at five o'clock was *coll*, a hazel tree for enlightenment, not growing tall but full and almost fluffy with leaves. Chamomile's whistle came, and Micah moved on to the sixth, then seventh, then eighth and ninth and tenth trees. A white fir, a willow, an ash, an aspen, and a heather tree now hemmed in Lilydale, dense branches touching in at least one place and creating an uninterrupted loop with only two trees left to close the gap. Much like the enchanting effects of a ring of Folk, of mushrooms, of a marriage band, the twelve guardians would stand watch and turn away the eyes and the curiosity of wayward humans. Even those hiking off the path and brushing the boundaries of the trees would be turned around, disoriented by the impression that maybe they saw something between the trees, but unable to grasp the thought for long enough to glimpse the faerie compound.

Hands on his hips, Andrew balked at the newborn trees as his precious gravelly chuckle tumbled from his lips. Fionna in her wolf form was by his calves, her big gray-brown tail thumping against the limestone. She opened her jaws and lolled out her tongue as if to taste all the new sharp, sweet fragrances from the ten trees.

"Micah—" Andrew laughed again, swiping his hand through his windswept hair. He looked handsome in a maroon cardigan over a cream-colored turtleneck that was tucked into his black jeans he wore over tan chelsea boots. "When I met you, *one* tree was a feat—now a whole army!" Heedless of the soot, Andrew stepped into the fire pit to throw his arms around Micah's shoulders, squeezing him tightly until Micah couldn't help but laugh with him. Even though the ritual was yet to be complete, the tense anticipation in Lilydale had eased. In its place was a wooly sense of safety like that of a swaddled baby, the brittle winter air warming to

"I'm not done, babe." Micah gave Andrew's waist a squeeze and used it as an anchor as he stepped out of the fire pit with his staff and moved toward the eleventh mushroom ring. The turned soil within did not have a sapling. With barely more than a passing thought, Micah grew a twig from his sturdy birchwood staff. He gently snapped it off before he knelt and pushed it into the patch of dirt, building it up around the stick into a mound. Micah had hardly pulled his hands back before the white birch eagerly wriggled roots into the soil, the sensation making Micah's nose tickle so strongly that he gasped and sneezed. Promptly, as if in some sort of call and response, the birch twig cast off its diminutive size and erupted. Micah fell back and landed on his ass, laughing, cradling his birchwood staff against his chest. The creamy white trunk was as wide as his thigh in a matter of seconds.

It broke into three mighty channels as it went, becoming an enormous birch tree with the golden sunlight shafting through it and turning their heart-shaped leaves into precious emeralds.

Micah, humming happily, leaned forward to hug the trunk of the birchwood and pressed his cheek to the curling bark while he frowned at the twelfth spot. A wave of anxiety rolled over him, turning his stomach into a painful knot. He clung desperately to the birch as if it could save him from the demand of the final sapling.

"I can't grow a redwood here." Micah's voice warbled, a thin and childish plea to be rescued. "What about a—a maple? Or even a cedar." Andrew's fingers brushed along the nape of Micah's neck and shot fireworks beneath his skin. He swallowed. "I—I know Ingrid went through the trouble of going out to Washington to get the sapling, but...I just can't bear the constant reminder."

"Of what?" Andrew knew what Micah meant. He remembered his hours in the Redwoods vividly. The sharp, earthen smell. The mossy, deep orange bark wrapped around the eldritch giants made Andrew feel smaller than anything else ever had. Andrew knew Micah wasn't talking about the trees themselves. Andrew had been on his knees before the Redwood Queen and felt the terror her horrible presence inflicted. It would be a lie to pretend as if the sight of a redwood tree here in Minnesota wouldn't also make him think of that wicked Queen.

Micah blinked hard, shifting so his forehead pressed against the tree instead, taking a shuddering breath. "I came to Lilydale to escape that place. And now I want to erect an enormous monolith that will remind me of my mother every day I'm here?"

"The Redwoods are in your blood," Andrew reminded him.

Revulsion made Micah twitch violently as bile rose in his throat. Darkness swirled into his eyes. A muscle jumped in his jaw. Feeling like he couldn't avoid it, he scooted himself on his knees over to the little redwood sapling. It sort of looked like a pipe cleaner. Small enough to fit between his palms, pliable, innocent. Like Micah had been as a child among the savage Folk of the Redwoods. But those monsters had made a sport of his humiliation and fear. His stomach knotted again and saliva flooded his mouth.

"Micah." Andrew brushed his lips against the smooth divot behind Micah's ear, smelling the tang from his gold earring. "You're in Lilydale. You're safe. And you came up with this plan to keep this place safer."

"I can't do this." Micah reached around to grip Andrew's elbow until Andrew slid both arms around his waist. The warmth was welcome, the smell of almond and honey soothing as a cup of tea. "I should have dealt with all that trauma sooner." Tears stung his eyes, turning them into glistening amethysts. "Twenty-two years trying to escape it, and that's what it comes down to, huh? Can't even bear the smell of the magic I grew up around. Can't do what my people need from me because I'm stunted."

"Micah!" Andrew pressed his palm flat into Micah's chest as if in this way he could steady the wildly hammering heart within. "People try to avoid their painful pasts for good reason. It's never too late to deal with it, but being angry at yourself right now as you're trying to finish this ritual is just cruel." Andrew's left hand massaged Micah's stomach until there was at last a shift in his breathing, a steady slow down.

Micah was only getting his shit together for Andrew's sake. His body was so accustomed to running from the Redwoods that he vividly imagined leaping off the cliff even if it meant tumbling into the Mississippi. His body was desperate to continue the denial, to bury the Redwoods in that shallow grave in the corner of his mind. But his dumb ass had planted this sapling right outside of Lilydale thinking it would be some sort of full circle exercise. And maybe it would be, but he hadn't anticipated the sheer emotional havoc that would accompany it. Of course he hadn't. For as much work as Andrew had done reconciling with his past, Micah had sat on his ass and let him do it without sparing a single thought to his own ghosts.

So now, on this afternoon two weeks before his wedding, Micah allowed himself to focus on the deep and tender touch of Andrew's hand on his stomach. "Pickerel. Saint Paul. Minneapolis. That eagle's nest across the river." He lifted his left hand. "My engagement ring." Micah laid one hand on the soil and the other over Andrew's. "Soil. Your knuckles, and the tiny hairs there. My flannel, and your wool cardigan." He ran his fingers through Andrew's loose red hair. "Your silky hair."

Andrew realized what he was doing. He nuzzled into Micah's neck and grew quiet. "And what do you hear?"

Micah smiled faintly. "Your accent. A delightful combination of Minnesotan, Londoner, and Irish. You've literally made it up. You've decided how people will hear you and trained yourself to talk like that."

"I don't know what you're talking about." Andrew smirked against Micah's neck.

"Traffic on 35." Micah glanced at the highway crossing over the river toward the south. "And the wind in the trees, which are getting ready for spring and sounding like grumpy old men about it." Andrew chuckled. Micah didn't need to count the sound for his grounding exercise, but truthfully Andrew's joy was hard-earned and moved Micah deeply. "I smell you—almonds, honey, and lemon balm tea. I smell this little redwood, which didn't do anything wrong, did it? It's just starting out. Its future is yet to unfold."

"That's right." Andrew brushed the chilled skin of Micah's jaw with his lips before twisting around his square shoulders. He used cold fingers to turn up Micah's chin. "And what do I taste like?"

A thrill of warmth bloomed between them as their lips met and Andrew teased open Micah's mouth with his tongue. Micah could taste the baklava Julian had served them earlier, as well as bittersweet notes of tea. Andrew settled himself across Micah's lap, arms around his neck, lapping up the mulberry taste rolling off Lord Heartwood that had started it all.

He untangled their mouths and pulled back, a gleaming thread of moisture stretching between their slick lips. "Can you focus your power to grow the redwood while you kiss me? I want to see if I can feel it."

Micah gave him a crooked smile. "If you insist." Leaning them both forward, Micah buried the root of the birchwood staff between his knees and pressed his palms into the damp soil on either side of the redwood sapling. With a hum of delight, Andrew sank once more against Micah's mouth, while Micah tried very hard to think about what it would be like to have his own solitary redwood standing over Lilydale. His own mother watching coldly over him. Andrew felt the change in Micah's thoughts as a subtle clench of teeth, and in response, Andrew insistently drummed his fingers on Micah's shoulders and squirmed until Micah resumed a more languid kiss. It was a few more breaths before the redwood sapling even budged, and when it did, it barely grew more than an inch. Micah could feel how pitifully it changed, but Andrew clutched his face with both hands.

"Let it choose its pace. Nobody wants to be rushed."

"I need it for the—"

But Andrew stopped Micah's words with another kiss even though it provoked a moan of protest. Teasing him was making Andrew fight to keep a grin from stretching over his cheeks. Micah got the redwood to grow by about a foot before he fell onto his back with an enormous groan.

"I give up! I'm done." He scowled at the navy sky just beginning to be touched by the gold and magenta shades of a sunset. Ingrid's white legs stepped into his line of sight. "You do it, Red!"

"No."

He whined.

"You are too impatient."

Andrew waved a hand, sitting with knees up and the birchwood staff cradled in his arm. "That's what I'm saying!"

"Oh, yes, please. Gang up on me. That's exactly what I need." Micah glared at the three foot tall redwood, its trunk about the thickness of his wrist. The problem wasn't the tree. It was his fear of it looming over him. It was his fear that he wouldn't be able to look at it without his past tearing at his throat like one of his mother's red hounds. He found it painfully difficult to imagine a scenario where a redwood tree here could simply live in the present. Micah sighed. "I don't think I need it to be...you know, three hundred feet tall to use it in my ward."

"Obviously." Ingrid spoke with a snide lilt to her words, but her eyes danced as she crouched near his head and hugged her legs.

"But I'm not sure a three foot tree is gonna offer much protection." He sat up and patted the wobbly trunk. "Let's get you to twenty feet, all right? That's nothing." He gently took his staff from Andrew and tapped the conduit against the redwood, and, after a moment, he asked the roots from the neighboring birch tree to come over. Then the rowan tree, just as young as the redwood but happy in its new heights. Not understanding, Andrew yelped and scrambled toward Ingrid and Micah as the barren ground bucked and rumbled. He clung to Micah's arm as the neighboring roots pitched in to encourage the little redwood, so it wasn't even

Micah directing the growth anymore, but rather the other members of his ward, speaking for him when the trust between him and this little sapling was so tenuous.

A contented smile curved on Micah's lips as he let the power of the trees surge over him, like static dancing between his hand and a wool coat on the driest days of winter, like the pleasure of his favorite zucchini dish coating his tongue in flavor. Andrew leaned his cheek against Micah's shoulder, Ingrid propping her elbow on his other shoulder.

"The most natural of Micah solutions," said Ingrid. "Teamwork."

Eyes burning, Micah put his arms around both of them, crossed his legs, and tracked the progress of the timid redwood. Twenty feet arrived, and was surpassed. Thirty feet arrived before the redwood slowly creaked to a halt. A halo of spiky branches fanned out far above them, gilded gold by the sunset which limned the three foot wide trunk and cast a stripe of aubergine shadow across its dark side.

Micah and Andrew jumped as Chamomile twirled forth from the trunk's shadow. The aloe spear in her arms splattered thick green juice over all three of them sitting on the ground as she hummed and marked the tree with a wide, goopy line.

Andrew gasped, harmonized by a croon of delight from Micah. Her aloe mark lit up like a sparkler. Rustling like a downpour in a jungle rose to a nearly deafening volume, as all around them the ring of trees came to life like they were going to grow legs and become shepherds. Though the twelve anointed trees stayed where they'd been planted, their leaves roiled and multiplied and formed a solid hedge as the trunks became fence posts between which a spring-green film shimmered. Andrew reached out to brush his fingertips over it. As he suspected, the film vibrated like Micah's heartbeat. Sturdy and joyful, youthful and spry.

Micah eyed the forcefield with a skeptical raise of his brow. "So, the aloe marks need to be renewed on every new moon, and this guy—" He climbed to his feet and patted the redwood tree, trying to push away the memories that its remarkable smell kicked up in his olfactory. "I'll have to check him everyday as he grows to make sure the ring remains unbroken. But now that you're big enough to work with the others, we need to start implementing phase two."

# Chapter Seventeen
## The Curse

The woodsy ward didn't help the temperature in Lilydale as much as the Agassiz wall had, but it was still milder than without it, especially with the kiss of springtime. There was an impression of excitement about the new tree ward, if the general conversation and wary investigation was any indicator.

Hands gray and dusty, Micah had a smear of soot across his nose as he finished planting the seed for the hawthorn tree in the eye of the fire pit. Unlike the other twelve trees which grew from preexisting saplings, Micah wanted this thirteenth tree to exist in its embryonic form until he needed it.

He stood up when it was hidden beneath the soot and blackened soil, accepting the scrap of terrycloth that Nox held out for him and scrubbing clean his hands. Nox blinked their goat eyes up at him and tapped their wide nose; understanding, Micah folded the cloth to a clean side and swiped it over his whole face, feeling it lift a sheen of sweat he didn't know was there.

Micah turned to face his assembled team seated on the amphitheater stairs. Liath occupied the rapt attention of Chamomile and Andrew as she showed them an intricate braid on Fionna's hair; the girl sat with eyes closed and a lazy smile on her face between Liath's knees as the older woman worked.

Ingrid prowled a few steps away from him, hair in a severe braid, draped in a black shawl and wearing a slender black choker. When their eyes met, she gave him a fortifying smile. Micah mustered a wobbly grin in return before he resumed his preparation of the fire pit. He adjusted his grip on his birchwood staff as he gazed down at the ring, checking in with the roots which crawled beneath the limestone bedrock of Lilydale to see what they were willing to do.

"I'm going to need a lot of help tonight," he whispered.

"You talking to me, or the trees?" Andrew's gravelly purr slipped into Micah's ear at the same time as the arms around his waist.

With a chill racing up the nape of his neck, Micah squirmed against Andrew's chest. "Uh...both?"

"Liar." Andrew stooped to press his lips to the hollow behind Micah's ear.

Shaking off Liath and Chamomile, Fionna pulled on her wolfskin and hurried over to the couple. She rooted around by their legs as the soil began to churn. Sleepily, roots and branches laden with worms and centipedes prodded forth, gasping as they stretched toward the heavens. Andrew's skin tingled at the sight of the roots doing Micah's bidding, reaching up to cup the fire pit like a richly scented rib cage.

"What if I got everyone here and it takes them like, three days to find her?" Micah glanced up at Andrew.

Andrew scoffed, nuzzling into Micah's jaw. "*I* could find her sooner than that. Just breathe, darling." He spread his hand over Micah's belly. "I can feel that you're not."

Before Micah could draw in the sort of full restorative breath Andrew requested, an anxious buzzing cut through the quiet. The yellow-haired pixie Thorn, wearing a halter dress with an open back, winked back out of the shadows and flitted down on iridescent wings. Fionna flinched before her tail started to wag as she shuffled over to nudge Thorn's hand. He absently scratched the wolf's cheek, but his cat-slit pupils remained enlarged with obvious irritation.

"What's wrong?" Micah tripped over the question. "Can't you find Cirrus?"

"We found her," Thorn said carefully. "But we can't get inside. Her room is warded and smells of iron."

Frustrated, Micah stamped his staff. Fingers dug into the meat of his shoulder as if he was caught in the talons of a hawk; Micah looked up as a feral grin broke through Andrew's features. White teeth glinted in the torchlight.

Andrew's voice was a rumble of distant thunder. "Now that—" Thorn turned his face up to balk. "—I can help with."

The chilling edge to Andrew's words made a shiver race up Micah's spine. He grimaced. Perhaps part of him wanted to urge Andrew to swallow his thirst for blood. But the feeling that won out spoke for him. "Hey, just...don't kill her, all right?"

Unsheathing his black seax and crossing it over his chest, Andrew swept back his knee in a bow. "You have my word, milord."

Micah's cheeks blazed with color. A crinkle appeared beneath Andrew's eye before he winked. He reached for Thorn, who clasped their hands and flicked his iridescent wings. With Andrew in tow, Thorn got back into the shadows in a blink. Thorn was like a hummingbird as they raced through darkness over streetlights and interstate exits. When they emerged, it was onto the slope of a steep gabled roof outside a small window. Andrew tripped to one knee on the shingles. As if surprised Andrew couldn't fly, Thorn gasped and clutched his hand while Andrew caught his balance and braced himself in a deep lunge.

"Sorry, Sir Andrew."

The other Folk flocked on the roof like a murder of crows. Some watched the two of them with vague amusement, but most had their eyes on the curtained dormer window. It belonged to a small house tucked into a crowded street on the opposite side of the river from Lilydale, somewhere off Snelling and Grand, Andrew guessed.

Andrew pulled his iron dagger from his ankle holster. As soon as he did, the Folk crowding near him edged back a bit, although he had no ill will toward any of them anymore. Wedging the blade into the window frame, he pried it open. The wood grumbled softly, but the sound was indistinct, just as easily mistaken for a creak in the pipes or a car door slamming somewhere below. He quickly stuck his boots through the crack and slipped inside, his narrow hips and slim chest posing no obstacle as he dropped softly to his feet.

Straightening, Andrew inspected the window. He reached up and used his dagger to scratch out two protective runes that were drawn into the wood. Then he used two fingers to dislodge a bundle of rowan leaves and berries from a hook on the wall. He dropped it into his palm, crumpling it as he thrust the bundle into his pocket. That seemed to be it except for a small pile of salt on the window sill. Andrew bent and blew it away. As he padded further into the room, nearly choking on the stench of cheap incense, a floorboard creaked under his weight.

Traced by the white light of a phone screen, a shape in the bed jolted at the sound. "H...Hello?" A young blonde woman rolled over and sat up, dazzled and blinded by her screen. She blinked a few times, squinting as a specter emerged in her vision.

A tall wisp of a man stepped toward her, haloed by the acid-orange light shining through the window. Behind him, Folk spilled into her room, their movements irregular, animalistic. Eyes reflected blood-red, murky green, tail-light yellow. Teeth glinted sharp and silver in stretched, sneering smiles.

"Good evening, Cirrus." The man stepped into a beam of streetlight which illuminated his fox-like features and glinted in his brown eyes like primordial fire.

"A-Andrew..." After she shattered the vial of Micah's blood and left him to die, she was expecting Folk—she was ready for Folk. But none of her protections would work on *him.* And he'd...he'd let them all in. "You're t-trespassing." Her voice was thin beneath the cinder blocks of her terror. She started to tap the power button on her phone to dial 911, but Andrew was faster.

In one long stride he closed the distance to her bed and slapped her phone out of her clammy hand. Andrew stopped it with his boot, holding her gaze while he ground her phone beneath his heel. As the screen crunched and went dark, he gave her a wolfish smile ripe with satisfaction.

Feral as a cornered cat, Cirrus dove at his face with her fingers crooked into claws. He back-stepped, and she lost her balance and fell over the edge of her bed. Her knees and elbows smarted, wrenching a yelp out of her and leaving her stunned and disoriented. Before she gathered her senses, Andrew used his boot to roll her onto her back, pinning her down with his foot on her stomach.

Cirrus held her hands up, gasping. "Let me go. I promise, you'll never see or hear from me again." Her eyes filled with tears.

Andrew laughed, the sound like snapping fangs. Behind him, the Folk jeered and tittered. Lifting his foot off her, he dropped to a crouch. "Oh, no, little blight. We're way past that." He flipped a dagger into his hand, which flashed as he gave it an artful spin.

Cirrus screamed and squirmed, but despite this he hooked the tip of the knife under her necklaces and yanked sharply. The three chains snapped, scattering across the floorboards.

A tear dribbled off her round face as she cowered under Andrew. Coursing with savage delight, he stroked her cheek with the flat side of his dagger, relishing how her eyes went round with horror. He wanted to do more, to taunt and terrorize the woman who had wrought so much misery on Micah. He wanted to paint his face with her blood while she screamed. But it was for the same person he wanted vengeance that he stayed his hand. With a regretful sigh, Andrew stood up. Cirrus released a ragged sob of relief.

"Take her to Lord Heartwood." Andrew's order was soft and mild, like a poisonous flower.

Hungrily, the Folk descended upon Cirrus, clawing at her with outstretched hands like ghouls dragging her into the darkness. She screamed, but she was powerless against the swarm of them. As they pulled her into the shadows, she was convinced she'd never see daylight again. She was convinced this was the last night she'd even know her name.

The Folk spilled back into Lilydale. Leif and Thorn held Cirrus under her armpits, with Cosmos on her feet, and the goblin triplets bracing her in the middle to be sure she couldn't twist or wouldn't fall before they were ready. Cirrus gasped and panted, sobbing quietly, her face bright red. They dumped her into the fire pit and she landed on her stomach in a dirty soot cloud.

Spitting out a mouthful of ash, she wiped her lips, smearing darkness across her cheeks. For as much as she'd flaunted her knowledge that Lilydale existed as a hideout for wicked and greedy Folk, Cirrus had never been within its walls. The air tasted like hazelnut, heavy and warm in an unnatural way. As she steadied herself and tried not to vomit, roots wormed from the ground, rising up, turning to sharp sticks and a tangle of brambles which created a barbed wire fence around her. Not too tall to jump if she were desperate, but discouraging, toothy.

Framed by the crumbling arch of a massive brick kiln, a man descended shallow limestone stairs toward her. Antlers rose above his brow, crystals winking and flashing in the shaky torchlight that dappled Lilydale. A feline skull was framed by two violet blossoms, neon yellow in the middle. Nightshade.

"M-Micah?" Her mouth dropped open. "You're—alive?"

"Disappointed?" Micah's lips formed a sardonic smile around the word. He'd never looked so...Fae. Barefooted, in an animal skull crown, with a tattoo visible below the slope of his shirt, holding a long branch of birch with a jagged, luminescent tip, he was formidable in every sense of the word. The Folk that had brought her here flowed behind him to form a crescent of shadowy bodies, shining eyes, and wicked smiles. Over his shoulder, the Ruby Daughter materialized, made of shadows and moonbeams and narrowed crimson eyes.

"Y-you kidnapped me." Cirrus's mouth was too wet with nausea and tears, and it made her words sound pathetic. She sucked in a trembling breath and lifted her chin like there was any way she could pull off haughtiness dressed in pajamas and coated in tears and snot. "I thought you were benevolent."

"You changed the game, busting up my sister's wall. You threatened my people then."

Cirrus snorted. "*Your* people? Dude, you're a *half-breed*." Bolstered by the way Micah failed to hide his flinch, she sat up on her knees, wiping her arm across her face. "You don't belong here any more than I do."

An arrow whistled through the darkness. Shrieking, Cirrus's head whipped to the side, a comet tail of blood arcing after her from a slash across her cheek.

Chamomile had moved in a flash to Micah's side; the string of her bow still vibrated. "Watch it, you stupid little girl. That's Lord Heartwood you're speaking to. You will address him with respect."

A hysterical chortle fell from Cirrus's mouth. "Are you for real? This...this place is such a joke!"

"Cirrus." Micah crouched before her, his amethyst gaze grave. "Cooperating with me will be for your own benefit."

"Fuck you, Micah!" Despite the vitriol of her snarl, fresh tears streamed down her cheeks. "Fuck your stupid elitist fake nice bullshit. I wish I'd killed you!"

Hostility rose like hackles among the gathering; Andrew's seax crossed slightly over Lord Heartwood. Fiona growled, the sound so low that it rumbled the silt beneath Cirrus. The Folk bared serrated, silver teeth and hisses caught on the wind, swirling with the firelight until it felt like Cirrus was in a vacuum with the unsettling sounds.

Micah sighed through his nostrils, brow pinched with pity. "When I met you, you just wanted to live in a fairytale. You were so whimsical and passionate. I refuse to believe this was all some long con designed to get close to me so you could fuck me up."

Cirrus snorted. There was a strangled hiccup caught in the derisive sound. "Like I'm gonna tell you anything!"

Amused, Micah's lips twitched. He tilted his head so the undying nightshade blossoms fixed to the bobcat skull in his crown fluttered in the low light. "You misunderstand. I'm not asking for your sob story because I care. But it will help determine your fate tonight."

The girl jerked back as if he'd struck her. "You—You wouldn't kill me..."

Micah tipped his chin down, causing the firelight to flash through his eyes like chips of molten jewels. "Have you no imagination?"

Cirrus shuddered. "What?"

"Death is nowhere near the worst thing we can do to you." He smiled. No trace of humanity warmed his features. The streak of his lips were more like blood.

An animal terror gripped Cirrus down to the marrow in her bones. Her power was slipping through her fingers. She wanted—needed to keep it. Her power was all she had left. All that made her important.

The wolf. *The wolf.* Cirrus locked eyes with the wolf at the Druid woman's heels. She reached into her desperation and her fear and demanded aid from the shifter wolf. She reached into the dark pit of her heart and gave the wolf no other option.

Fionna cringed away from the pulsing brown gaze of the girl in the fire pit. She whimpered and resisted, but the puppet strings yanked taut. Her golden eyes flickered and lost their luster, replaced by rings of darkness that glinted blood-red. Ingrid felt the shift happen, but not quickly enough. Fionna's body became a puppet, and her vision tunneled till all she could see was the pale delicate flesh of a man's wrist. Her little girl's heart cried out in horror as her powerful wolf jaws wrenched open of their own accord.

Fionna's maw snapped shut on Andrew's left wrist, tearing a scream from his throat. The pain stabbed bone-deep as the sharp wolf fangs sank through his skin and tore into tendon. She fought and fought the darkness choking her, but all she managed to do was to weaken the vise of her jaw, just a little.

Andrew started to pull back but stopped, trying instead to get his fingers deep in her molars as he cried, "Fi! *Stad! Scaoil sé!* Fionna! Don't give in...gah!"

But the tunnel of her vision narrowed and her muscles told her *thrash!* So she clamped down harder and shook her head. Andrew lost his footing and fell to his knees in front of her. Blood ran from the punctures in his wrist and splattered the firelit air as she shook his arm as if to kill her prey. The little girl inside her wailed and reached for him, but the sinister blood rings remained around her eyes.

Arms grabbed her barrel chest and hands yanked on her scruff and fists beat her skull. Fionna desperately hoped they could overpower her, but all she could see was the agony on Andrew's features, the tears staining his cheeks as he struggled with her jaws. His fingers dug into her cheek, but as she shook his arm, his grip slackened.

Liath threw an arm toward the fire pit. "Micah—" The urgency in Liath's tone snapped Micah's attention to her. Both of them could see the crimson rings around Cirrus's eyes.

With his staff gripped in both hands, Micah leapt toward the fire pit and swung toward Cirrus's head. Like a crack of thunder, wood met skull. Cirrus shrieked. Her eyes widened and then rolled back beneath her slackening lids as her body went limp.

Gold flooded back into Fionna's eyes. Howling, she released Andrew and leapt back, tail between her legs. Andrew dropped into the muddy snow, groaning, blank with shock. Liath grabbed Fionna by her scruff and pulled her away, the girl releasing her wolfskin and scrabbling to climb into Liath's arms. Fionna wailed, piercing, loud enough that the residents in the houses above along Highway 13 paused what they were doing, frowning, shivering.

Wordlessly, Micah used the end of his staff and scratched the Ogham mark for *huath*, hawthorn, by the unconscious girl's hip. He allowed the hawthorn seed underneath her to do what it needed to do before he dropped the root fence. She'd need no fence to restrain her as Lord Heartwood's intentions joined with the hawthorn. Gnarled arms like twisted sentient prison guards came down as the hawthorn grew rapidly, six feet tall in a matter of seconds.

As his heart climbed back into his throat, Micah tripped on his way to Andrew's side, his fiancé's complexion drained and shining with a layer of sweat. Deep, oozing punctures bored down to white wrist bone in half a dozen places. Andrew reached out with his uninjured hand and clung to Micah's arm, lips pressed into a thin line and tears standing in his eyes.

Chamomile entered the periphery of Micah's vision, and without looking up, he held out his hand for her herbs. He pinned his staff under his knee. Swallowing his nausea, Micah withdrew a handful of basil leaves which he and Chamomile wrapped around Andrew's wrist like bandages. Murmured pleas for healing and relief left Micah's lips as he suppressed the shuddering of his fingers. Chamomile held Andrew's hand and elbow delicately in her fingers while Micah wrapped Andrew's forearm in actual bandaging and taped it down.

She glanced at Micah. "He'll need human medical attention. This is good for now, but you need to take him in."

"You guys keep stuff under control for a couple hours." Micah looked between Ingrid and Chamomile. "I'll take him now, and then—"

"Not now." Andrew shook his head sharply, his words coming out in a breathless whisper. "We need to end this." He released a ragged sigh, the leaves wrapping his arm slowly tamping down the throbbing intensity of pain.

"Andrew, no, I can't—"

"Don't argue with me." Andrew gripped Micah's chin and pressed their lips together. He moved back and said with a ghoulish smile, "I've got a crazy amount of adrenaline right now. As long as I stay conscious, I'm good to go." Folding his wrapped arm against his chest, Andrew shifted to sit more comfortably even though the moss underneath him was bloodstained. He looked up at the *faoladh*, who was hyperventilating as Liath wiped Andrew's blood off her face with a rag from Ingrid. Fionna howled, the sound ripped from a deep well of misery and shame. Ingrid whispered to her, holding the girl's hands in her graceful fingers. Soon the blood on her cheeks was gone, but it was quickly replaced by tears and snot.

Andrew crawled over to her, butting his forehead into Fionna's temple so the girl was forced to respond to him. She nuzzled into his neck, the tang of his blood stronger when she came near to his arm. Fionna resisted the urge to lick at the wound, instead allowing him to hold her tightly as their racing heartbeats synchronized, as they curled into each other, comforting despite the horror that was inflicted upon them.

Micah took one step back from them, then another, and it seemed like he was stepping away from his body as much as from them. A buzzing filled his ears and made his muscles vibrate as he slowly lost feeling in his hands.

Then Ingrid's cool touch fell around his shoulders. She gently smoothed his hair beneath his bone circlet. She didn't say anything. She didn't need to. Her maternal caress did enough, brought him back to his unfinished task, and he allowed her to turn him back to face the fire pit.

While Micah had fixed up Andrew's wrist, the hawthorn had finished growing. Roots twined across Cirrus's prone body like a macabre quilt, dimpling into her flesh, tucking her in as if for an eternal slumber. Micah shot Syabira a dirty look where she squatted beside the fire pit.

Syabira glared back at him with her liquid doe eyes. "This is my last plea to allow her to be buried beneath it forever."

Micah sighed, pressing his hand flat against his sternum, glancing up at Ingrid. The faerie's expression was impassive as she twirled a burgundy curl around her index finger. He returned his gaze to the frustrated gnome. Some of his warning was directed at the hawthorn tree, whose energy was feral, carrying visions of death and destruction.

"Cirrus is just a girl. She's stupid, and guilty, but she's just a girl. She isn't my mother." Though this would be easier if she were. If he could simply leave her to become detritus, to allow her flesh and bones to feed the soil beneath Lilydale and grow a glorious bed of chrysanthemums atop the memory of her.

"Look at your knight and his pup," Syabira said through her teeth. "Is the girl who did that to them not wicked?"

"He told you his decision." Ingrid's narrowed eyes snapped down to the gnome.

Chastised, Syabira set her jaw and gazed in silence at her for a moment before deferring. The hawthorn was reluctant as it loosened the net over the girl, undoing the thickest knots and slithering into the soil. As the roots burrowed down, the hawthorn formed into a grown, creaking, swaying tree with a claustrophobic cage of sharp branches and knotted trunk formed overtop of the unconscious girl. Snarls of hairlike roots imposed on her space, brushing her skin with each rise and fall of her chest. Heavy red berries drooped among dark green leaves.

Micah formed a mound of roots for himself where he took a seat beside her cage and laid his staff across his knees. The scraggly bars separated as he reached through them, so when he wound back his arm, the force he brought down to slap Cirrus across the face was loud enough to stop all conversation among the Folk behind him. Cirrus spasmed, moaned, and shook her head, blinking hard. A blue bruise smeared across her forehead from Micah's staff, and her cheek and jaw turned pink from his slap.

"All right, now that you've had your fun." Micah steepled his fingers, elbows on his knees as he leaned forward. "Let's talk."

"Fuck you!" Cirrus wept, clutching her face. She tried to sit up, but she didn't have enough room in her cage. She was forced to remain on her hands and knees, roots snagging in her hair. "What is this? Why am I in a tree?"

"Oh, the hawthorn?" Micah gazed up at it. "Hawthorns have a wicked reputation, said to contain bad luck. But it depends on your perspective. As it stands, it's a container, for you. The wicked one."

Cirrus's eyes widened. "Am I gonna rot in here forever?"

"Oh." Micah's lips curved. "You've heard? I do have a track record of doing that, don't I? Well, the idea has been thrown around. But I'm more curious about your origin story. Every villain has one. Go on. Tell me."

"No!" She spat and hissed like a cat, her breathing getting frantic, like it did before she forced Fionna to bend to her will.

Impatient, Micah grabbed Cirrus's chin so their eyes met. "You made an innocent girl rip open my fiancé's wrist. I'm done asking nicely. *Tell me* what I need to know." A whiff of mulberries carried on his breath. Evergreen ringed his luminous nightshade eyes for a flash, and then it vanished.

Cirrus's pupils dilated, reflecting a dozen torches within their black depths as her jaw went slack and her lips rounded between his fingers. She blinked the last of her tears away with a dreamy sigh. Ingrid and Andrew exchanged a look, sharing wonder over how easily Micah had charmed Cirrus. Over his head, though he didn't notice, the whistling wind masked the creaking of the redwood as it stretched taller in the darkness.

Cirrus chewed on her cheek as if trying to fight his compulsion, biting through the thin skin with a pop of copper spreading over her tongue. She swallowed. "I heard about the bluffs in high school and used to think it all sounded so magical and mysterious," Cirrus whispered. "I was wrong. All you guys bring is chaos and fear."

"According to whom?" Micah demanded.

"My dead brother." Cirrus's voice cracked. "We were told three years ago he died by suicide. But I found out last year that he was fucked out of his mind on a slice of Fae-spelled fruit and he jumped off the High Bridge thinking it was a fucking water park. You don't care! You'll never *have* to care."

"You're wrong." Micah spoke as if to a child. "And it sucks that your whole revenge mission against me was built on a misconception. I'm sorry about your brother—nobody should lose somebody like that, but—"

"Oh, you think you're different because you've got a sad human dad?" Cirrus sneered.

Micah stiffened. A crease appeared between his eyebrows. "How the hell do you know about my dad?"

Cirrus rolled her eyes, propping her cheek on her fist as if the pose could give her some power despite being stuck on her belly in the bowels of a tree. "Sam talks to him *all* the time."

Micah wouldn't have needed to hear Andrew's hissed profanity to feel his fiancé grow tense behind him.

Andrew came to stand near Micah's hip, fire in his eyes. "How did you make him cooperate? Did he want to?"

"No, of course not." She snorted. "Little bitch was stupidly loyal to you, you crabby asshole."

"Then what?" snapped Micah.

"Easy." Despite the charm making her spill her secrets, Cirrus clearly reveled in their uncertainty, in their rapidly mounting fury. "Threatened him. Said if he didn't give me the vial of your blood, I'd feed pathetic old Julian Fae-spelled foods till he died."

Micah recoiled as if she hit him, eyes bulging. He was no longer himself, skin lit from within with glowing fury, muscles corded like a lynx that found its prey. The roots of the hawthorn stirred and constricted on her like snakes. Micah lunged and seized her throat, her delicate skin so tempting to crush under his palm, under his curled fingers. Turning red and then violet, Cirrus choked, but his grip on her tightened, holding her fast.

"You are a worm!" His voice was the cracking of a falling tree. His features were contorted, teeth bared, spittle flying from his lips. A deep and rumbling creaking almost distracted him—almost. "You are *nothing*. You flounder for meaning and lash out like a mangy dog, and it has changed nothing about how small you are!" A blood vessel burst in her eye with a rush of red flooding her sclera.

Holding his breath, Andrew slipped his hand along the corded, twitching muscles of Micah's flexed forearm. Micah flinched, swinging back his free hand as if to strike Andrew away before he sniffed Andrew's almond and tea scent and caught himself.

"You will regret killing her." Andrew's tone was matter-of-fact, a barely audible whisper that tickled Micah's stubble. "You don't want her death on your heart."

Micah gave the girl a vicious shove with a growl and released her to fall heavily onto her belly. She wheezed and sobbed, the charm on her effectively broken but the fight gone from her too as her complexion turned from deep red to pink and back to clammy white. Red scribbles marked her face where more blood vessels burst.

"I curse you," Micah snarled, the root cage parting with a groan to allow Cirrus to depart, though he stayed where he was and blocked her way. He swiped his thumb through the illuminated tip of his birchwood staff and came away with a fingerful of glittering moisture that he painted across Cirrus's forehead. The girl was too startled and addled to move away; the mark faded into her skin but for a dark green line like a permanent marker would have left. "I curse the memories you have of Lilydale so they fade to a dream and you can't meddle in our affairs ever again. I curse you to sit in the misery you have wrought like perpetually wet socks. I curse your feet to turn you away from this place and keep you pointed toward the boring mediocre life you deserve." He grabbed her by the collar of her dirty shirt and dragged her forth from beneath the hawthorn tree, putting her on her feet. The evergreen rings returned to Micah's eyes as he leaned close enough that his nose brushed the girl's. "Now you will walk home and may your feet be frostbitten and sore by the time you get back into your miserable little bed. Goodbye forever, Cirrus."

He gave her a shove toward the Brickyard Trail, easily two miles north from Lilydale on a treacherous path made worse by the winter and the dark. But if she slipped and fell, that would be her own damn fault. Micah's gaze landed on the moth-winged male, Reave. "I want her watched around the clock. If there's seeing devices we can set up, fine, but for now, follow her home and report back when someone's swapped you out to relieve you." The pixie nodded his understanding as his brown and white moth wings flapped between his shoulder blades and carried him into the stars in pursuit of Cirrus, who shrank swiftly into the distance until she was swallowed up in the dark.

The fluorescent hospital lights ached against the backs of Andrew's eye sockets. The sterile smell made his sinuses hurt, and the constant phones ringing, pagers dinging, and doors slamming made him yearn for the quiet wildlife in Lilydale. He sat in a scantily padded waiting room chair while Micah bounced his leg in the neighboring seat, his thumbnail grinding between his teeth till he snapped it off. He rolled the nail between his fingertips before moving in on his index finger.

"Micah," Andrew hissed.

Micah jumped. His distant gaze sharpened. "Hm?" He looked down as Andrew tugged his hand away from his mouth before he groaned. "Sorry." Andrew nodded, forcing Micah to hold his hand while the questionnaire clipboard balanced precariously under their knuckles on his knee. Underneath Andrew's makeshift sling, Micah had topped the dressing of leaves and cloth with the birchwood staff, which had honestly dampened the throbbing down to a faint sting. And it kept changing, too. The pain. Waves of soothing warmth coursed inside his veins and his torn ligaments. But Micah wouldn't hear of it, wouldn't allow Andrew to follow the violent urge to curl up in bed and sleep until Ostara.

"Andrew?" A small nurse in pink scrubs stood back as an automatic door hissed open, her pink and purple braids pulled neatly over one shoulder. Micah jumped up and helped Andrew to his feet, murmuring false pleasantries as he dragged Andrew along after the sleepy, polite nurse. She dropped them off in a cold exam room with a curtain instead of a fourth wall, took his blood pressure and temperature—too low, and too high, respectively—and then left them to wait for the next provider. Micah had another fingernail between his teeth as he paced in tight circles next to the exam table where Andrew kicked his feet and scrolled through news articles on his phone.

"Why are you acting so nonchalant?" Micah finally demanded. He planted his hands on his hips, head cocked. He looked so different now than when he was interrogating Cirrus, as a powerful Fae lord harnessing the land to his bidding. Now he was a mother hen, worrying incessantly, guilt plain on his pinched features.

Andrew looked up slowly. He pushed his hair off his brow, tucking it behind his ear. "I told you that it doesn't hurt that bad."

"That's *shock*, babe. Your vitals say so." Micah waved a hand that sent his flannel flapping near his elbow.

Andrew stifled a laugh. "Whatever you say, love."

"Don't—" Micah growled and turned away, arms crossed. "Maybe Syabira was right, and I should've..."

Andrew leaned forward to catch Micah's wrist and tugged him over to the table. "Let me lay on your chest." Tense as he was, Micah was forced to oblige. He held Andrew delicately as if he might break, chin on the crown of his red hair. Cheek to chest, Andrew listened contentedly as Micah's frantic heartbeat gradually slowed.

Then someone spoke from the curtain and peeked inside, and a young Somali doctor in a hijab stepped into their space and pulled the curtain shut behind herself.

"I hear you have a potential broken wrist," said the doctor as Micah stepped out of her way. "Can you tell me what happened?"

Andrew's face went blank. "Um—"

"We rescued a wolf dog," Micah said without hesitation. "She came from a bad situation. We're still working on rehabilitation. She bit him."

"We don't blame her," Andrew added hurriedly. "We'll get her there."

The doctor nodded as she pulled around a metal tray to rest Andrew's elbow on it. "What's all this? Is this bark? And leaves?"

"Naturopathic treatments." When the doctor moved to pull gloves from a cardboard box fixed to the wall, Micah nudged the birchwood bracelet so it climbed up to sit on Andrew's bicep instead of his wrist. "We dressed it about four hours ago."

Once she had on a pair of thin blue gloves, she carefully unwrapped the leaves and used a salt-smelling pad to dab at the caked on blood, working in silence for a while and going through several pads to clear it all away. When it was cleaned, she sat back, blinking long curly eyelashes. "I...don't see any open wounds." She carefully pressed on Andrew's delicate wrist bones, checking for the fracture that Andrew and Micah both knew had been there earlier. "I don't feel a break. We can do imaging, but..."

Andrew stared at his wrist with his mouth hanging open. Experimentally, he flexed his fingers into a fist. The oozing puncture wounds from earlier had closed up into dark brown scabs that could have been two or three days old.

"Oh." A giddy spark lit in Micah's chest. He quickly met Andrew's eyes, the trace of evergreen so fleeting in Micah's aubergine gaze that Andrew almost missed it. "Hey, what a relief it's not more serious. You know, I think we're going to go. Hey, you did great work. Come on, Andrew. Let's get home."

Andrew smelled the mulberries overpower the sterile scent of the hospital and saw the quizzical arch of the doctor's brow, but she didn't fight them as they hustled from the room and wove through orderlies and patients and wheelchairs until they made it out the front doors.

"I told you!" Andrew giggled as Micah dragged him past the drop off zone, hanging a left until they got to the street parking spot where Micah's hybrid was parked. "You—we—this wild and magical night healed me itself."

"I don't understand." Micah combed through his hair with his fingers. "What does the birchwood do for you? It should really be a conduit to help access magic more easily. If we gave it to, say, my dad, it would just be a walking stick. So you must have something of your own that it communicates with."

Andrew shrugged as Micah put him in the passenger seat and buckled him in. Truthfully, he was limp with relief as he stared at the minor wound on his wrist. No cast for his wedding day, no lasting damage to Andrew's sword hand. He nestled into Micah's plush leather seat. "I'm so excited to be in bed."

Untwisting from checking his blind spots, Micah slipped onto the road to follow West Seventh back to his brownstone, streetlights flashing against his windshield, staining them gold between slanting slashes of navy blue. He glanced at Andrew and sucked his teeth. "I'm not going to stop bringing this up until we have some explanation."

"Why?" Andrew's gaze was shot with mahogany when he lazily met Micah's eyes. "I don't need answers. I just know it's there." Micah scrutinized the hue of Andrew's eyes, feeling a sense of unfamiliarity. It was like the soil-brown of Andrew's eyes had spun on the color wheel of his irises, what had once for so long been honey was now more like wine.

Micah hummed, returning his attention to the road until he came to his parking spot behind the row of brownstones on Saint Claire. He kept a protective hand on Andrew's back as they entered the dark house, Cinnamon coming to greet them with a tremble in his feathery tail. He was excited to tell Micah about their additional visitor, how she smelled like shortbread cookies and wore warm flannels and wool socks that Cinnamon wanted to sleep on. Micah smiled and bent to scratch his head as they moved with extra caution through Julian's level of the brownstone. For years it had only been Micah's father sleeping on that level, but now Liath slept in the room on the end next to Fionna's room. Fionna had her door open, so Andrew peeled off from Micah's grip to go check on the slumbering girl. Her little bed was buried beneath a mountain of stuffed toys, fluffy blankets, and cartoon pillows. Snoring softly, she hardly stirred when Andrew brushed his fingers over her forehead, her stray hairs tickling the pads of his fingertips. Micah threaded their hands together and kissed Andrew's jaw before they slowly backed out of the girl's room.

Liath's low murmuring voice drifted beneath the crack of her door as she talked to someone on the phone. Andrew listened for a moment, just to hear her talk, his eyes suddenly stinging.

"What's wrong?" Micah whispered.

"My mum and your father are sleeping under the same roof." Andrew glanced between the parallel doors as Cinnamon wound between his legs. "Isn't that wild?"

Micah chewed his lip, leaning into Andrew's side as Andrew draped his arm around his shoulders. "I kinda like it."

# CHAPTER EIGHTEEN
# THE TRUTH

"WHY'D YOU DO IT, Sam?"

Sam jumped. He hadn't heard Andrew open the back door to Magic's Repair, so when Andrew dropped into the chair next to him and spoke, it was to very unnerving effect.

Pushing his glasses up his nose, Sam sniffed and asked, "Can you be more specific?"

It was several days since Micah had erected the tree ward and cursed Cirrus into obscurity. Things were calm, for the most part, aside from the thrilling chaos of planning a short-notice wedding. Andrew had promised himself he would get some work done for his business, but that wasn't his main reason for coming into the shop.

Sam remained uncharacteristically still, suggesting he knew quite well what Andrew meant. It made him smile faintly.

"You didn't hand over the vial out of spite," Andrew said. He slid his brown bomber jacket off the short sleeve button-up he had underneath, making it so he matched Sam's outfit quite well. Collared shirts with novelty prints and jeans had been their unofficial uniform for seven years, after all, give or take a tastefully clashing necktie, like the one Sam was wearing that was covered in rainbow twenty sided dice. Sam's eyes returned to his computer, scanning the code as he chewed on his lip and tapped the backspace twice.

Andrew pressed, "You could have saved yourself from several lectures from several people if you'd mentioned the fact that you were protecting Julian."

Sam swallowed. "It didn't matter why I did it. I still effectively got Micah killed. Twice." He clicked the run button on his software, and then gave the program a dirty look before returning to the code.

"Did you know that's what she was going to do with it?" Andrew asked.

Sam shook his head, just slightly, barely noticeable.

Arwen jumped up on Sam's end of the desk. She raised her small black nose and sniffed lightly in Andrew's direction before narrowing her eyes. Andrew didn't need Micah to translate the expression: Andrew smelled like dog.

"I'm sorry you were ever put in a position like that because of me," said Andrew.

Sam glanced at him and said quickly, "Don't quit. Please."

Andrew paused. "I—"

Sam stared at his keyboard. "Do you want to, or are you trying to do it to protect me?"

Andrew wheeled closer to him, considering the best way to explain himself.

Glancing over at him, Sam did a double take, peering seriously into his eyes. "You look different."

"How's that?"

"Your eyes used to be gold-brown. Now they're, like...mahogany," Sam said. "And you...I don't know, there's something else. You seem a little blurrier around the edges." When Andrew began to protest, Sam waved a hand. "Anyway, continue."

Resting his cheek on his fist, Andrew said slowly, "I don't *want* to quit. I put everything on the line when I opened this dumb little shop. You know for the first few years, I only got three customers a day—maybe? And two of them—"

"—Were asking for directions to the convention center," laughed Sam. "I know. You tell that story all the time."

"Sorry. I'm going senile."

Sam rolled his eyes.

"Just because my life has changed a lot in the last nine years doesn't mean I don't still want this place."

"Well, that's good," said Sam. "Now save yourself the 'but.' I'm not accepting your resignation. You're going down with the ship."

Andrew frowned. "I'm afraid my shifted priorities will put you at risk. You said it yourself that I'm different. Now more than ever. What if I keep bringing around trouble like Cirrus?"

Eyes on his screen, Sam's lips twitched. "Cirrus." He shook his head slowly. "Cirrus was a special kind of bitch. I learned a lot from getting screwed over by her, you know?" He glanced sidelong at Andrew with his hazel eyes flashing. "I'm hoping it's improved my judgment. And you know who else improves my judgment?"

"Arwen," said Andrew automatically.

On her bed between the monitors, Arwen lifted her head and blinked slowly, making them both laugh.

"You, ya bloody goof," said Sam, exaggerating Andrew's accent. Andrew socked him in the shoulder, making him grin. "You've always looked out for me." Sam paused, his smile fading. "Kinda like how I wanna look out for Julian."

"He's crazy about you," agreed Andrew.

Sam's lips twitched slightly as he leaned back in his chair, picking a cat hair off his keyboard. "He and I are oddly kind of similar these days, you know?"

Andrew wanted to agree, but confusion furrowed his brow instead, and he waited in silence for Sam to elaborate.

Pushing his glasses up his nose, Sam glanced at Andrew. "We're both in the same orbit, circling around you and Micah, the brightest goddamn sunspots of all time."

Early spring in Micah's back garden normally meant trying not to cross the line by bringing all his perennials back to life *too* soon after the first thaw. But this year, magenta coneflowers blossomed right before his eyes as soon as he approached. By the time he sat next to Liath in the dry brown grass, fat pink peonies reached for him, tickling his spine through the thin fabric of his striped tee.

Holding a smooth beige stone, Liath stole a glance at him with afternoon sunlight sparkling in her crinkling eyes.

Micah grimaced sheepishly. He stroked the silky petal of a peony with two fingers, and the blossom swelled under his touch. "I usually offer to help the neighbors garden, but this might raise some red flags."

Over their heads on the patio bench, Julian swigged an Arnold Palmer and said brusquely, "Anyone nosy enough to say something would clearly just be jealous." It was so rare that Julian was out in the sun enough to transition the lenses of his glasses that the effect made him ooze confidence. That, or he was trying to impress Liath, which was a delightful development Andrew and Micah had noticed over the last few days. With Fionna staying in Lilydale under the supervision of Nox, Cosmos, and Spirulina until the cairn waypoints were activated, Julian and Liath had been spending most of their quiet time together under the guise of tying up the last of the wedding plans for the grooms.

Dirt smeared Liath's forearms up to her rolled up sweat-shirt sleeves. A bandana held her short auburn hair out of her eyes. She knelt on a gardening pad in a well-worn pair of jeans and her feet bare, despite the nip still in the air. Slowly, she laid the twelfth stone on the top of the child-sized tower in the corner of Micah's garden under the shadow of the patio overhead. It was a surreptitious monument, unlikely to attract attention any more than Micah's superb gardening did.

"So—" Micah looked up as Julian leaned between his knees to peer at them through the slats of the wooden deck. "Are there going to be Folk busting through there around the clock now?"

Urgently, Micah waved both hands. "Absolutely not. It's mostly for me, Andrew, and Fi. The Folk have been told to still generally use the shadows or travel in and out of Lilydale on foot."

"Oh." Julian frowned.

Cocking his head, Micah smiled faintly. "Did you...want visitors from Lilydale, Dad?"

Julian turned his head deliberately to glare inside, away from Micah. "N-no."

Micah's smile widened. "I'm sure if you ever want to leave out any food for the Folk, they'd be happy to stop for a snack. We didn't get any of our engagement cake leftovers. It was spirited away. They loved it."

Julian looked down through the slats. "Really?"

"Really." Micah savored the pleased smile Julian tried to suppress before returning his attention to Liath. "What's next, ma'am?"

Liath shook her head. "Nothing except to test it."

"It just works, just like that?"

"Aye. You created a leyline," Liath told him.

Micah stared blankly at her. She didn't know him well enough to identify the confusion on his face; to her, he just looked a little ditzy, so she stared back at him without supplying more explanation.

"He doesn't know what that is." Julian's amusement was stuffed aggressively out of his voice to avoid riling his son up. Based on the sharp nightshade glare Micah sent up between Julian's feet, that was unsuccessful.

Liath patiently set her hands in her lap. "Whatever you did to anoint your home has the same magic as your tree circle in Lilydale, so there's now a sort of...energetic string stretching out between here and there. So I merely used the stones as a doorknob."

"Ma'am, all due respect, but how can you do this stuff?" Micah demanded, equal parts impressed by her wisdom and humiliated by his own ignorance. He settled himself by pruning a dried iris bud off the stalk at his hip. As soon as he snipped off the tip with his fingernails, an infant bud unfurled like a sleepy purple bird between the pads of his fingers.

"What do you mean by 'this stuff'?" She was as exacting as her son.

"Magic." Micah carefully plucked free the new blossom and held it out to Liath. "I've seen what witches have to do in order to access magic. Borrowing from powers already there and bending it to their will with spells and demands. You don't quite do magic like a faerie, but you don't do it like them. And Andrew—" When Liath gently took the iris from his fingers, she lifted it to her slender nose and breathed in its sweet, fresh scent. "Andrew seems to get some benefit from using my staff." To ensure there was no double entêndre, Micah pulled the birchwood off his wrist and extended it to its full length before laying it at his knees between him and Liath. "But my understanding is that, to someone with no magical inclination like Sam, this would be no more useful than a walking stick. It's an enhancement to magic. A paintbrush to an artist—useless without ability. But it's helped Andrew heal on two occasions so far, which means it's enhanced an ability that's already there. How? What am I missing about Druids?"

Liath shifted uneasily. "There are books that might answer your question, Lord Heartwood."

"So you're hiding something."

"No! No—" Liath held up both hands, eyes wide. "No. Not to be deceptive." When she paused, Micah stared her down until she swallowed. "I—I grew up burdened by the knowledge. My Ma told me when I was a girl about our

Druid lineage. It was at times a boon, but when it wasn't, it made my mistakes go septic. I resented it and myself. It often took away my sense of agency, making me feel as if I failed to live up to some higher purpose. I never wanted to do that to my son. So I never disclosed it. But I would never have lied if he'd asked."

Realization dawned on Micah like a sunrise. His lips parted. Everything aligned like a solar eclipse. Chamomile called Andrew 'Tall One' the moment they met. His easy grace with a blade...his use of runes of protection...his lanky elegance, unnatural stillness, how much he looked and acted like Ingrid. Eda had almost told Andrew a few weeks ago. "Druids are descendants of the Folk. Aren't you?"

Liath's pink tongue darted out to moisten her slender lips. She dropped her eyes, her shoulders sagging as she wrung her hands together. Relief, shame—Micah couldn't be sure what he saw. "Aye."

Micah sat back heavily, the peonies eagerly clambering about his shoulders like a rustling shawl so fragrant he could taste them. "Whoa."

She swallowed. "Was I wrong? To withhold that."

Andrew Vidasche, descendant of Fair Folk. Micah wanted him home this instant, but to blurt out this news? Not necessarily. "N...No, actually. I think he...at least—at least some part of him would be glad he didn't know."

True relief brought glittering tears to Liath's lashes. "Aye?"

Micah nodded. "He said on the way home from the hospital that he wasn't looking for answers. He just knew what he could see, and that was all he said he needed to know." He brushed a speck of soil off his staff. "But, Miss Ryan, I'm not sure I can...just...*not* tell him. Honesty is humanity to me."

"I'm sorry," said Liath.

"It's all right."

They both jumped. Micah followed the elegant line of Liath's throat and her tipped back chin to the balcony over their head, where Andrew stood in a bomber jacket and a button-down, gripping the railing with white knuckles, auburn hair billowing around his shoulders. Julian, always minding his business, focused on a pointedly long pull of his Arnold Palmer.

"Child—"

"Really." Andrew tucked his hair behind his ear before he thumped slowly down the steps to the garden where his mother and fiancé sat in the grass. Micah gaped silently at him as the peonies shifted toward Andrew as if he brought the sunlight with him. Andrew stopped next to Micah, leg brushing his shoulder. Micah twined his arm around Andrew's calf. They shouldn't have, but those lean runner's muscles felt different now. Andrew had a composed, intellectual look on his alabaster features suggesting to Micah that this would be something processed slowly, probably later tonight in the dark in their room, and that Andrew was firmly shielding himself with neutrality.

Liath grimaced. "Forgive us for discussing you without you."

Shrugging, Andrew carded his fingers through Micah's hair. "I know this one wanted some answers. Best they came before I married a faerie prince, I suppose. Might I ask some more questions?"

"Of course. Anything you'd like."

Andrew remained silent, jaw working. His hand fell away from Micah's head as he slowly curled his fingers into fists, eyes round, looking lost. "I...I don't actually know, at the moment." Micah rubbed the back of his thigh with a reassuring smile when Andrew glanced down at him.

Liath leaned into the grass and started to rise. Quickly, Andrew helped her up with his hand on her bicep. She gave him a shy, appreciative smile before stooping to brush off her knees and ankles. Lifting her eyes to study Andrew's face, she held her dirt-caked hands as if she was trying her hardest to abstain from offering him a comforting touch.

"This has always been the truth for you and it always will be. You needn't push yourself to form an opinion or know your feelings in any sort of rush."

Andrew nodded, blinking several times. Distantly, he gestured toward the cairn. "Can I help?"

"It's done." Liath was about to prop her hands on her hips before she noticed her dirty hands. "Right. I'm going to go wash up. Excuse me, lads." She slipped around them and thudded quietly on the stairs, pausing to speak to Julian, who prompted an immediate laugh from her.

Julian tapped his foot against the wood over their heads. "Make sure you're back in time for dinner, and bring Fionna!"

"Yes, Dad." Standing and tucking his staff under his armpit, Micah clasped Andrew's hand before looking up and quickly calling to the woman before she could disappear inside. "Liath, how do we do this?"

"Draw a circle round yourselves in the dirt, and then step toward the cairn." Liath had her own glass of Arnold Palmer—either that, or Julian had given her his. Saluting her and winking at his father, Micah obeyed using the end of his staff in the dirt. When he completed the circle, he urged Andrew forward with an arm around his narrow waist. And just like that—no racing over the land or tripping out again, no jerking or vertigo—they were in Lilydale. Like stepping through a doorway. The upper cairn was right outside Micah and Andrew's hut, so it was almost like they could have been inside it the whole time. Micah sneezed enormously, while Andrew sniffed as if trying to fight his back.

Andrew took a step, faltered, and then fat, gleaming tears leaked from his eyes. They raced down his cheeks as his mouth screwed up and his eyes squeezed closed. Nearby, Ingrid, Chamomile and Fiona looked over from the basket of flowers they were stringing together. Fiona yelped and scampered over, throwing herself around Andrew's waist with a whimper of concern.

"Look at me," choked Andrew. He rubbed at his eyes with his jacket sleeve while tangling his fingers in Fionna's coarse hair. His stomach cramped as if the new information clattering in his brain wanted to expel itself out of his body. "I'd rather cry in Lilydale than in front of my own mother."

"But why, Dad-Andrew? Why are you sad?" Fionna nuzzled his stomach.

Andrew dropped himself onto the rug outside their hut. Fionna crowded into his lap while Micah stepped inside to fetch one of the water bottles from their nightstand. "I–I'm not sad, pup...I just..." He took the bottle from Micah, but his hands trembled so badly that he couldn't unscrew the cap.

Micah laid his hand over Andrew's and held them there. "Some part of you knew." He kept his voice a low purr in Andrew's ear, lips ghosting over his soft earlobe before he laid his chin on Andrew's shoulder. "Just breathe, babe. You've got plenty of time."

Andrew took a few hiccupping breaths before he gave up and focused on Micah's warm hand cupping his, and the heavy weight of the girl curled up in his lap, clinging to his chest, golden eyes on his face. The air up here smelled like

Micah's newly grown trees, like summer, like venison stew cooking in a cauldron. Andrew slowly unscrewed his water and took a few small sips, holding the cold on his tongue. After he swallowed, he sighed and shut his eyes. "My ancestors were Fae." Saying it aloud cemented it, assured him he didn't imagine the whole conversation between Lord Heartwood and his mother.

"You *know?*" Chamomile's songbird voice drilled directly into his teeth, loud and sharp.

Andrew opened one eye and glared at the goblin, who was throwing flower stems into the air with glee.

Ingrid pressed her hand to her breast. "Ugh, *finally.*"

Micah groaned, and then he and Andrew both started to laugh.

# Chapter Nineteen
# The Rings

The sun came out for them, and the last week had been mild enough to prompt the trees to bud and the snow to melt. In Minnesota, it was just as likely there would be a blizzard the week after, but they weren't concerned with that possibility.

Insulated in his tightly-laced Docs, Andrew stepped unafraid through shallow, mirror-bright puddles.

Sam, Liath, Andrew, and Fionna left the Saturn parked on the street that ran through Cherokee Park and overlooked the bluffs and the city. Cherokee was nearly deserted, so Andrew was able to park in the same spot as his first time coming to Lilydale with Micah.

Sam and Andrew wore brown tweed suit coats and dark brown slacks, Andrew's blazer with maroon elbow patches. He was going once again for his 'professor' energy, but with how much he was glowing, he might as well have been dipped straight into liquid gold. Andrew's Leinster scarf crossed around his neck and through the coat. The top part of his hair was pulled back in Celtic braids Liath had fixed in place with Ingrid's black enchanted thread and a forest-green ribbon that fluttered in the wind.

"So, what's the plan here? Wander around the park till you figure out where your wedding is?" Sam's tone clearly carried his opinion on Micah's secrecy around the site of the wedding ceremony.

"I'll be able to tell." Andrew slipped his hands into his slacks. He was following the tickle in his nose, the taste of mulberries that coated the back of his tongue, getting faintly stronger as he headed southward towards the Brickyard Trail. "I already have a good—"

Leaping far higher than most girls her size could, Fionna stomped into a puddle with a howl. Unbothered in her galoshes and shiny jacket protecting her puffy dress, she looked up with delight in her eyes and tucked a stray gray hair up into her braid crown.

"Child." Liath *tsk*ed, swiping the beads of water easily off her wool skirt. It bore the same Louth tartan as Andrew's scarf.

Andrew stopped next to a black chain-link fence and gazed up at a familiar archway of trees that led to the switchback Brickyard Trail. The soles of his feet tingled with anticipation. He took a deep breath and put an arm around Sam and an arm around his mum and squeezed them both to his sides.

"What?" Sam blinked. "Is this it?"

"You don't feel anything?" asked Fionna, tilting her head back as she leaned into Sam's legs. "Micah's magic tastes like berries!" Fionna took his hand and pulled him away.

Andrew slid Liath's hand through the crook of his elbow. She blinked and caught his left hand in her fingers, pulling it closer to her face. Her moonstone ring glinted on his finger.

She looked up, eyes damp. "You kept the ring I gave you."

"Er..." Andrew tried to tug back his hand. "Is that okay?"

"Andrew..." Liath turned toward him and cupped his face in her hand. "You honor me more than I deserve, and I am so happy for that. It means the world to me that I get to be here for this today."

"Me, too, Mum."

Arm in arm, they stepped off the paved walkway and under the trees, which were still mostly barren. Blushing pink honeysuckles stood out in stark relief among the gray and brown landscape. As they drew close, the honeysuckles vibrated, radiating a powerful fragrance and making the air around them draw aside like a veil.

Andrew was right: this was the spot.

Blossoms of every color fenced in a path plush with emerald green moss, smelling like balmy high summer rather than the early kiss of spring. Faerie lights floated like snowflakes. The two dozen Folk of Lilydale started to cheer when Andrew appeared. They were arranged in a processional aisle and dressed in fine gossamer and silk. Uncannily beautiful music drifted from the lyre which Cosmos held between their rosy pink knees and plucked skillfully with their eyes closed and their angular head cocked toward the sweet, slow notes. Liath let out a wistful sigh at Andrew's elbow, leaning her head on his shoulder. As lovely a party as the Folk made, Andrew's gaze found Micah and all else faded into smudges of color and distant murmurs.

Lord Heartwood wore a green velvet suit, a bow tie at his throat bearing the County Louth tartan. His skull and nightshade crown sat prettily on his brow; delicate gold lined his lower lashes and brushed his tawny cheekbones, drawing out the rosy hue of his flushed cheeks. He beamed through a sheen of tears, which reflected like a thousand mirrors over his lilac irises. Andrew tried not to break into a run to reach the quivering archway of white flowers curving over Micah's head. Micah's slim brocade boots rocked restlessly within a ring of red-capped mushrooms, which had just enough space to let Andrew in as he handed Liath off to stand beside Sam.

Micah caught his lip between his teeth. "Did you know where to look?"

"Of course." Andrew scoffed. "This is where I first kissed you." He drank in how Micah's lip glistened when released from his sharp ivory canine, drawn into the citrus ambrosia of Micah's euphoria. He felt himself lean forward, wanting Micah's lips on his own, fully in control of his faculties yet helpless against his desires.

Micah's sage lashes fluttered as he tipped back his chin, pillowy lips curling. "You're intoxicating."

Chamomile cleared her throat pointedly. She perched on a fallen oak tree which crossed through the edge of their clearing, crisply dressed in a wool suit that was certainly from the seventies. Her silver hair was bound in a low ponytail and decorated with tiger lilies bright and vivid as the sunlight trickling through the branches overhead. When the couple hushed and turned their attention to her, she began, "You two put me in charge of this ceremony, so you'd best keep your hands off each other till I say so."

"Aw," Andrew whined. Over Micah's shoulder, Ingrid laughed. It was a sound like a bubbling stream flowing over colorful pebbles. Her lips, painted a pink that matched the honeysuckles growing magically in the woods, spread to reveal her straight white teeth, and when they drew the attention of Julian's amber eyes, he didn't flinch.

Her laughter was a sound he'd never heard in the Redwoods, never from the lips of the Queen nor from her daughter. Something clicked, some door opened to reveal that this woman was no longer the same as the Redwoods which grew her, as much as her lithe body and burgundy curls may have looked it. Her dress complemented Micah's green suit, a velvet so dark green it was black in the shadows of the canopy of branches. Her dark makeup was already smeared with tears, another sight never beheld in the Redwoods. Julian, positioned at Micah's elbow and cozy in a knit cardigan over a dress shirt and a green tie, looked up at her and smiled.

Chamomile sighed prettily, grasping for her words with a vague gesture as she studied Andrew and Micah in lengthy turns. "I felt it the moment you two collided." She wetted her plump lips. "I felt something momentous starting, but I wasn't sure what it was going to be. Some love that cleaves on so quickly is just as quick to burn out."

Micah raised an eyebrow at her.

"It's clear yours is not one such love," she assured him with a grin. "To have Lilydale led by two people so empowered by one another will yield great things. To lead the rest of your days in love will give back tenfold the bounty to you and yours." Her light voice broke like a flower stem snapping. "You have asked to perform a handfasting ritual when you exchange vows. This is something Folk have carried with us for millennia, and we have passed it onto our Druid kin." She gestured briefly to Liath, who inclined her head in silence. Then Chamomile looked past Micah's shoulder toward Ingrid, who stepped forward holding a shimmering green ribbon.

She laid Micah's left hand atop Andrew's right hand and then wound the ribbon from Micah's elbow, down around their joined hands, and then up to Andrew's elbow. The ribbon had a heartbeat, which lured in the lifeblood of the men joining hands until the beat was one singular rhythm coursing between them.

"Andrew," said Chamomile, "go ahead with your vows."

"Okay, well, I wrote some stuff down, but I'm not going to read from a paper." Andrew slid his free left hand around Micah's waist, and Chamomile didn't stop him. He gazed down at Micah's full rosy smile, his squared chin, the column of his throat now healed and unblemished. Then he found his way home to Micah's lavender eyes. "It feels more right to hold your hands and look you in the eyes and tell you how wonderstruck you make me feel." He took a breath. "My vow to you, Micah Stillwater, is that you will always have all of me. I vow to choose you every single day, as you chose me since you first laid eyes on me. I don't know why I'm lucky enough to be yours, but I thank the stars and the earth every day for that. I vow to fight for you, as I have since we met, and to fight with you, if you need me to." He grinned, his soul capturing Micah's returned smile like a suncatcher that blazed into a rainbow of sunshine. "I vow to grow with you, not out of you. And I vow never to give up on you, or on us."

Micah kissed his knuckles with his eyes bright with tears.

"Micah, you go ahead now."

"Okay, I vow to try not to cry too much," laughed Micah.

"Let it out," Andrew said warmly. "Men ought to cry more."

Micah giggled at Andrew's nod to their first date. Then he took a steadying breath. "I knew, too." He tipped his head toward Chamomile as he gazed into Andrew's mahogany eyes. "When I saw you, I knew you were my person. I know it was probably magical intuition. Or maybe something in my soul vibrated in time with yours. But I know that isn't gonna cut it. The love may have been easily won, but I'm ready to fight for it.

"I vow to work for us every day no matter how difficult you're being." He winked, and Andrew laughed. "I vow to protect you and build you up, and to let you protect me if you choose. I also vow to choose you every single day until I stop breathing. And I'm so, so excited about that."

When he concluded, the ribbon around their arms vibrated and began to dissolve into their sleeves, into the delicate skin of the backs of their hands. It settled on their flesh like dewdrops, and then the rope disappeared. Their hands, though, were marked with twin green stripes like an intricate knot made from grass stains on a summer day.

Chamomile nodded in satisfaction. "It's time to exchange rings. A ring has no beginning or end. Within the ring, the wearer is protected from forces that oppose what it represents. For you two, let it serve as a visible reminder of the vows you have made for each other today."

Julian held out a small velvet sachet to Micah, who took it with fingers that trembled slightly. Sam held out a matching sachet to Andrew, which Andrew tipped into the palm of his hand.

He gently lifted Micah's left hand. Micah's band was delicate gold and designed to tuck under the edges of his moss agate stone. Andrew slid the band onto his finger as he tried to see through his tears.

Rather than Andrew's left, Micah picked up Andrew's right hand. As the cool band slid onto his slender ring finger, Andrew's mouth dropped open. He could *feel* the real wood beneath the golden sheen. A little stone was set into the metal, bark-brown with flashing amber banding.

Micah explained, "It's a twig from my heartwood. I grew it for you from my staff, then Ingrid electroformed it with gold." Andrew caught his breath. "Then the stone is a Tiger's Eye. It's supposed to represent wisdom, courage, and protection. Obviously all things that made me think of you." Micah sheepishly dropped his gaze. "Tiger's Eye is also said to help alleviate depression. I don't want to change you, but I want to help how I can."

Andrew burst into tears. They leaked down swiftly as he wiped them with the edge of his scarf, still staring at his ring. Smiling warmly, Micah used the pad of his thumb to catch the last salty drop.

"This concludes the wedding ritual, which binds you to one another like a promise," said Chamomile. "I have nothing to do with the legality of Andrew taking Micah's family name, but this also marks the beginning of your life together as one another's husband. And I've been led to understand that you only consider this ritual complete if you get to kiss. So, I hereby conclude this declaration of marriage and invite you to..."

The word didn't leave her mouth before Micah bounced up to throw his arms around Andrew's neck. Lips tasting of hope, of new beginnings, of life and love, pressed together over the cacophony of Folk and human cheers. For as wonderful as the support was, Andrew and Micah hardly heard them. Within their embrace, all they felt was the heat radiating between their bodies, and all they heard was the thunderous pounding of their synchronized heartbeats.

The celebration in Lilydale lasted long past sundown. White flower petals drifted lazily from the ivy canopy overhead. Syabira had grown mushrooms on the trunks of the trees which glowed green in the dark among paper lanterns hanging from the branches of the trees and the ivy. The Folk drank deeply from goblets of golden wine and ate from a lavish setting of fruits and pastries and cheeses on the log table near the blazing fire pit. Every instrument in the compound was given a part played by wandering Fae between drinks or bites.

Adorned with crowns of delicate white flowers, Andrew and Micah slipped away to their shelter. The Folk had placed at their door—which was now a slab of dark oak on a pair of antique hinges—fresh flowers and baubles and plastic-wrapped foods they'd gotten from the store out of respect for Andrew.

"The walls are finished," said Micah, gesturing. The limestone walls were eight feet tall and maybe twelve square feet. They merged with the thatched roofing, which was now speckled with toadstools and bright little wildflowers. "They won't hear a thing." Micah grinned suggestively, and then his hands roamed up beneath Andrew's blazer and untucked the dress shirt beneath it.

Color rose on Andrew's cheeks as he tingled under Micah's touch. Micah toed open the oak door, pushing Andrew inside as the lanterns blazed to life. Andrew was just barely able to pull the door closed behind Micah before he was whisked off his feet and carried over their deerskin rug, arms and legs twisting around Micah, who held Andrew aloft with his hands under his thighs.

"Sorry—" Micah's voice was a husky half apology. "But I am very eager to make love to my new husband."

Andrew couldn't respond before Micah pressed a new kiss to him as they crossed the room and laid across their blankets. White flowers sprinkled across the bed and provoked a heavy fragrance when their bodies rubbed against the oil of the petals.

They unbuttoned trousers and dress shirts together with alacrity. Leaning over Andrew and spreading his legs, Micah beamed at him with the warmth of a thousand suns, tracing his fingers along the faint freckles across the bridge of Andrew's nose, brushing his red eyelashes with the pad of his finger. Andrew felt his eyes sting and his throat tighten at the intensity of Micah's admiration. He clenched Micah's hips between his thighs and then laced his fingers together behind his neck, tugging Micah down, touching their foreheads together while trying to collect himself. They were completely still for several ragged breaths, chest to bare chest, skin scorching hot with desire. But it was more than that now, after everything they'd made it through, after the handfasting tattooed green ribbons on their skin that merged on their hands.

Andrew took a deep breath of Micah's musk of sage and spring as he pressed his lips into the curve of Micah's neck.

"You smell like...cinnamon," said Micah, pulling back and inhaling deeply. "That's new. Is it a cologne?"

Andrew shook his head. "Not wearing anything."

Micah raised one moss-green eyebrow before his lips quirked in a smirk. "Must be magic."

"You've *always* given off different magical smells." Andrew's hands roamed across Micah's bare muscled chest, tracing one of the antlers on his tattoo. "Maybe it's my turn to join you."

Micah's eyes brightened into shining coins when Andrew said *join.* He gathered his attention back to the task at hand, sinking his fingers into Andrew suddenly enough to elicit a trembling gasp from him. Micah brushed their lips together, flicking his tongue into Andrew's mouth while he flicked his thumb over Andrew's nipple. When he made Andrew twitch, Micah deepened the kiss and slid his arm under the small of Andrew's back.

With his flower crown askew on his braided hair, Andrew hooked his ankles together behind Micah's hips and threw back his head when he felt Micah fill him. Micah kissed and nipped his way up from Andrew's collarbone while he drove a steady rhythm; they both moaned. Andrew looked up to meet Micah's eyes, silver as the moon, craning his neck and reaching for a kiss, which was obliged. Softly at first, and then deeper, tongue swirling, Andrew practically purring.

Pulling back, but only slightly, Micah growled against Andrew's lips, "You're *my* husband." He let go of Andrew's left hand so he could stroke him, eliciting more frantic gasps as Micah made short work of him. They finished together with a shuddering sigh.

"Well?" Andrew asked breathlessly.

"What?" grunted Micah, flopping onto the blankets beside him, slicking back his sweat-damp hair.

"Am I different now?" Andrew rolled to face Micah, playing with the wooden plug in Micah's ear. "As Andrew Stillwater?"

"Different?" Micah repeated hoarsely. "Mm, perhaps. I don't know how you could amaze me more than you do, but every day...every *second*, I love you more than before." The way Andrew's eyes glowed like sun-soaked tea made the pit of Micah's stomach clench.

Andrew shook his arms free of his blazer and dress shirt. He began pressing kisses and light licks to Micah's smooth, tattooed chest. He ran his hands down Micah's muscled torso and then over his thighs. He scraped Micah's nipple with his teeth.

Breathlessly, Micah clutched Andrew's shoulders and managed, "Wait, wait, wait. I know. I'm there with you. But we can't."

Andrew protested and dropped his head on Micah's stomach with a *whump*. "But I want all the wedding night sex."

"The night's not over." Micah flicked Andrew's nose. "C'mon. Let's wash up. The stream running inside the east tree line has warmed up since my trees grew. It's a regular watering hole."

Andrew peered up at Micah. "You want to take a bath in front of everyone?"

"We're their lords," Micah answered with pride. "They'd be honored."

"I don't know if I'm...uh...precocious enough for that, love."

Clutching Andrew's chin, Micah assured him, "If someone looks at you wrong, I'll string 'em up a tree for an hour."

"Oh my."

"Come on. We don't have time to lose."

With a groan of displeasure, Andrew shook his head. He nudged Micah onto his back and laid his hands flat against Micah's chest, planting a line of kisses up Micah's sternum, to the hollow and to the apple of his throat, and along his square jaw. Micah's breathing hitched repeatedly, and he got hard again. With a wicked grin, Andrew sat up and lowered himself onto Micah before he could protest.

This time they went slowly, tender, never out of breath so much as inhaling each other's delight and affection. Their twined fingers made an uninterrupted tattoo from the marks left by their handfasting.

After they finished, Andrew climbed off and sat on his knees and said, slurred with pleasure, "Okay, fine. I'll take your bath, but only because you're my husband." He combed Micah's hair back from his forehead, picking a flower petal loose from the pale green locks. He ran the pad of his thumb over Micah's damp, flushed cheek, and Micah caught his fingers and kissed Andrew's wedding band.

They clambered unsteadily to their feet, leaning against each other, and pushed open their oak door. Andrew picked up an unopened bottle of champagne as he passed the gifts stacked around their shelter as if they lived inside an altar.

Spirulina and Leif both glanced their way with surprise and warm amusement from outside their own tent, which had been remade after Andrew and Micah colonized theirs.

Andrew shrugged in feigned nonchalance as Micah scuttled with his hand in Andrew's toward what was once the stream marking the eastern edge of Lilydale's territory. Now the water was turquoise and still, with flowers and lily pads drifting across the surface. It had gotten deeper, condensing itself into four shallow feet of water over smooth stones. It was currently empty, so Micah splashed his way in with Andrew in tow.

They heard a familiar whistle and Andrew glanced northward to Chamomile's hut. She sat on her roof with her legs crossed next to Reave, where they picked at a large frosted pastry. With a wink, Chamomile called, "Andrew, you've got a cute little ass, don't you?"

"You know I threatened to string up gawkers from a tree," called Micah.

"You could certainly try," drawled Chamomile.

Andrew popped the bottle of champagne and took a drink straight from the lip of the glass and then handed it to Micah.

"Why are we in a rush tonight?" asked Andrew. "We don't have a honeymoon planned or anything."

"Oh." Micah leaned his head back and dunked his hair into the water. His flower crown melted apart and drifted away on a gentle current. "Yeah, we do."

As he lowered himself into the pond, Andrew asked with eyes widening, "Come again?"

Micah lifted his head so water ribboned off his hair and down his shoulders, trickling over the faint green sunbeam scar on his back. "We're going to Ireland."

"We're what?" demanded Andrew. "No. What? No."

Micah grinned and nodded.

"Micah! What?"

"I started planning it as soon as your mum got here. Our flight leaves at four in the morning, so sorry, we won't be getting any sleep tonight until we're on the plane. Your bags are all packed at the brownstone. Julian and your mum also helped me renew your passport. Fionna's staying here and is now calling Cosmos her auntie, so that's good."

Andrew stared at Micah with his jaw slack. "I...Ireland."

Micah took Andrew's face between his hands and kissed him lightly. "It seems wrong that you've never been."

"This is amazing." Andrew ran his hands over his cheeks, eyes bulging. "I haven't been in Europe for twenty years."

Micah nodded. "Yup. I've never been. We'll be there for three weeks."

Andrew's mouth opened further.

Looking a little embarrassed, Micah confessed, "Only catch is that Ingrid got really jealous and wanted to be in Leister with you, so...I told her she could come for a few days, before she goes back to the Redwoods. And since she was going, Chamomile decided she wants to come too."

"For their own romantic trip together in Ireland," said Andrew with a knowing nod.

"Watch it," called Chamomile.

"Undoubtedly. Now, they're not flying like us. We're going to be normal about this. Business class, though, since you're tall. And no layovers. They'll meet us there in, like, five days or something. I don't remember. Is that okay?"

"That's great!" laughed Andrew.

Micah added more solemnly, "I didn't want saying goodbye to Ingrid to come anywhere near the joy of our wedding, so I convinced her to hold off a few weeks. That's why I compromised when she found out about Ireland."

Andrew paddled closer and wrapped his arms around Micah's neck and kissed him tenderly. "I don't even know what to say. I have the best husband."

"Now, I expect we'll get into some amount of trouble when we're there, because that's what we do." Micah thumbed Andrew's chin. "But I'm excited to travel with you again, and sink ourselves into the magic there and see what happens. It's going to be amazing. Our whole life together is going to be amazing, Andrew. I love you so much."

Andrew bumped their foreheads together. "I love you."

They climbed out of the pond and shook themselves dry in the mild, luminous air.

"Andrew!" Ingrid appeared out of nowhere, her eyes wide and slightly crazed as she held a golden plate piled with food. Her cheeks were rosy red apples.

Andrew jumped. He tried to cover himself. "What's wrong?"

"I had this revelation," she explained, stripped down from her velvet dress into a slip of black silk. "Wouldn't salt neutralize the spelling effect of Fae-made food?"

"Oh." Andrew furrowed his brow at the boughs of trees overhead. "Well, yeah. Presumably."

"I'm so smart!" squawked Ingrid. "Here, try." She sprinkled from a salt shaker Micah didn't know she owned and coated a piece of Fae-grown apple.

Andrew glanced uncertainly at Micah. "I think I'd rather not mess with that on my wedding night," he said carefully, looking back at Ingrid. "I like our method now, bringing me in food. Can we wait? Like...a year or two?"

"Ah." Ingrid sobered, withdrawing the plate, popping a cherry into her mouth. "I suppose you have plenty of time here."

Nodding, Andrew said, "Thank you very much for thinking of me, though, Ingrid."

"I always will," she told him seriously, but her voice slurred a bit. "I think you're my best friend."

"Rude," called Chamomile.

"You're not my best friend," called Ingrid, pointing. "You're my partner. My *lover*." She clapped her hands over her mouth. "Oops."

"*What?!*" screamed Micah. He shook Andrew's arm. "Oh my god. We were *right!*"

"What?" exclaimed Chamomile. She jumped from her roof and padded over to them. "You two have been talking about us?"

"We've literally been speculating about you two since we were in Montana together," Andrew told her gently.

"If only you knew what *we* say about *you two*."

"Red here doesn't actually hide her feelings all that well," said Micah, ignoring Chamomile's attempt to regain her standing. "We have that in common. The only difference is that Ingrid doesn't have as many feelings as me, except where you're concerned, Chami."

"Aw." Chamomile's cheeks turned pink.

Andrew asked awkwardly, "Also, can I please put some clothes on?"

"Nothing to be modest about, babe," said Micah as he patted Andrew's flat stomach.

Reave fluttered from the roof of Chamomile's hut on his moth wings and said, "I'll get naked too, if that helps, Lord Andrew."

Andrew grimaced. "Thanks, Reave."

"What kind of thing are you two?" Micah asked over his shoulder as he hurried to their hut, ducked inside, and returned with a blanket which he wrapped Andrew within. He pulled on his own pair of rather short track shorts. He held two French macaroons from one of their offerings, one he popped in Andrew's mouth, the other he ate himself.

"Well, I'm not particularly interested in sexual relations," admitted Ingrid, munching on a flaky pastry. "That's problematic for partners, I'm finding." She turned in a circle, spotted an unsupervised jar of golden mead, and picked it up to take a deep swallow.

"I don't want to ask her to give what she's uncomfortable giving. And anyway, I would not be an acceptable lover in the Redwoods," said Chamomile. "Tall Ones only engage in true relations among themselves. As a goblin, if they suspected I was expecting affection freely from the Ruby Daughter, they'd kill me."

"It's gonna be so difficult to resume acting with dignity," said Ingrid, swaying. "You all have made me so easygoing."

Andrew said with a scoff, "Ah, yes. How dare we."

Chamomile smirked. "Ingrid and I knew as soon as she arrived here it was likely she wouldn't stay forever, so we knew whatever we did together was not forever, either."

"Does this mean I kind of kissed my sister?" Micah's complexion paled.

"That means I've kind of kissed both of you," sighed Andrew. He took a long drink of champagne.

"We've all kissed," said Ingrid, screwing up her features. "I dislike that a lot."

"It's just body parts touching body parts, everyone," said Chamomile with a shake of her head. "Reave and I touched body parts twenty minutes ago, and everything is fine."

"I'm in love with her," cried Reave as he stalked away from them before flapping his wings and climbing into a hanging basket in the grove of trees, disappearing inside with a mournful sigh.

Chamomile shook her head wearily.

"Maybe you need to find someone special," said Micah, patting her head.

"Oh, I'm completely in love with Ingrid," Chamomile told him dismissively. "Everything else is just to pass the time."

Ingrid looked away, blushing.

Andrew's jaw dropped.

"It's fine, you romantic twit," muttered Chamomile, punching Andrew in the back of the knee so his leg buckled. In exchange, Andrew whipped her with the edge of his blanket cape.

"This is weirdly bumming me out." Micah took a drink of champagne.

"Then come and dance until you must leave!" exclaimed Ingrid. She grabbed Micah's bicep and hauled him away as he tripped through the grasses and over limestone planes.

Andrew and Chamomile stood beside each other quietly for a moment, as Chamomile's expression sobered.

"I envy you," she admitted to him.

Andrew glanced down at her.

"What you have with Micah." Chamomile scratched her cheek awkwardly. "I probably confessed my love to Ingrid twenty years ago. But it's not her path to love deeply like you or Lord Heartwood. She's given all the love she has to give to him."

Andrew bent his knees, swooped a blanket-draped arm around her, and picked her up in a bone-popping embrace. Chamomile went feral, pushing back his head at a painful angle and kicking her short legs. He fought her for a moment to hang onto her before he dropped her back to the ground. "I'm sorry," he said to her.

"For what?" demanded Chamomile, trying to tame her mussed hair.

"Unrequited love is the greatest tragedy of all time," Andrew said.

Chamomile let out a soft sigh and shrugged one shoulder. "I have the privilege to spend a few nights of my life with the Ruby Daughter. I'm content with that." She glanced up at him and added, "It's something of a balm for me to know I get to watch you two give each other everything for so many years to come. It warms me and my cynical old heart."

Andrew smiled.

# CHAPTER TWENTY
# THE STILLWATERS

IN THE PARKING LOT of Two Rivers High School, Fionna Stillwater shouldered her gym bag as she walked between Andrew and Micah. She'd come home with Andrew a decade ago, but the couple was nearly unaffected by time. Andrew had a beard now, and Micah stretched his ears a bit bigger, wearing earrings made from polished limestone from the bluffs.

Andrew beeped the doors unlocked on their pickup truck. She was the same height as Micah now, with muscular limbs and a slender waist. Last year, Chamomile helped her cut most of her tawny hair into a pixie cut that emphasized her many ear piercings. Nobody in Lilydale had let her dye her hair, though, insisting that she keep her hair matching her wolf pelt, that people could deal with her unique appearance rather than making her hide.

Slipping behind Andrew, she snatched the keys out of his hand. Fionna jangled the keys out of his reach, smirking proudly as she pranced away toward the driver's side of the truck.

"Hey! Fi, give 'em back," exclaimed Andrew.

"Aw, c'mon." Micah strung an arm around Andrew's waist, holding him back from snatching the keys from Fionna. "Let her drive. It was a good tournament for her! Second place, just good enough not to arouse suspicion."

"It's all about balance, right?" Fionna's golden eyes glinted. She pranced back to them and licked Micah's temple in a habit she refused to give up.

"The family motto," remarked Micah, waiting until Fionna looked away before he wiped off his temple. Andrew grinned at him, arm around his neck. He stooped and licked Micah's other temple, laughing and dodging out of the way when Micah took a swipe at him.

As Fionna opened the driver's door, she waved sweetly at a brunette girl and a boy with an afro.

"See you at the indies," the boy said. He was part of the youth wrestling league that met at the community center. "Maybe I can beat you next time."

Fionna cast him a wry smile and didn't say anything.

He kept walking with the brunette, who whispered, "See! I told you Fionna's dads are super hot."

He replied in more of a hushed exclamation, "Are you sure those are her dads? They look *maybe* thirty."

"They adopted her, Treyvon. Obviously."

Micah, Andrew, and Fionna all snickered when she closed the driver's side door.

"Idiot humans," Fionna said with a snort.

"Watch it, miss." Andrew shot her a nasty look.

"You hardly qualify as human anymore, Dad."

Andrew glowered, but Fionna wasn't wrong. Ever since he'd married Micah, he wasn't aging like a human anymore. And sometimes, his walnut-brown eyes had a purple cast to them. Not that he complained. It was a relief knowing he wasn't going to wither before Micah's eyes while his husband remained the same as the day they met twelve years ago. As Micah had always explained, it was unknown whether he as half-Fae was completely immortal, or if aging would just occur slowly. But at least now, they were going to find out together.

"I need to get dropped off at Saint Kate's," Andrew told her. "I'm teaching the rest of the day." Professor Stillwater had an interesting mix of classes he taught, primarily using his Master's degree in Folklore and European Mythology, but occasionally picking up an information technology class for the undergraduate program when he wanted to keep his computer skills sharp. Since he was currently finishing up his doctoral program, he wasn't running Magic's anymore—Sam was a much better business owner than him, especially with Micah as an on-call business consultant. Sam's girlfriend Xena worked with him now, too, and they added oddities and quirky gifts for sale to build more revenue beyond the computer services.

Glancing at Andrew with pride in his eyes, Micah said, "I think I must be able to see the future. Kinda like Chami."

Fionna snorted. "Okay, Dad."

"I called your dad Professor Vidasche on our first date," said Micah, pulling on Andrew's collar and kissing his high freckled cheekbone.

Andrew blushed.

"Ew." Fionna gagged.

"You have to decide where you're setting up for tonight," Andrew told her more seriously. "Lilydale or Saint Claire?"

"I want to hang out with my partner," sighed Fionna, "and they are in Lilydale."

"Don't remind us," Andrew said mournfully from the middle seat, laying his head on Micah's shoulder. "It makes me feel dreadfully old. I remember when you couldn't even speak a full sentence."

Fionna got the truck on the road with a steady hand, the morning sunlight shafting through jeweled leaves and casting golden shadows across the fields to their right. "I know, Dad. And don't worry. Cosmos makes sure I get my homework done. I wouldn't *dare* get any B's. Grandpa Julian would wring my neck."

As Fionna drove them onto the 35-E bridge that went over the Mississippi, the bluffs of Lilydale spread out toward the north with the Smith Avenue bridge arching in the distance. Their eyes drifted off the traffic and toward the singular towering redwood tree rising out of the forest. From here, you wouldn't be able to guess there was a thriving magical community within a magical ring of trees. But as always, Lilydale didn't need to be seen to be felt.

# Ogham Alphabet

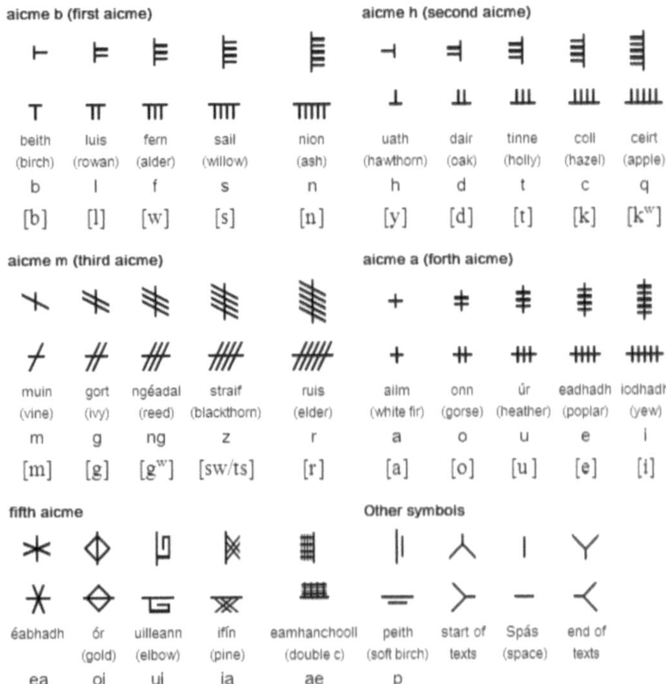



source: *https://www.omniglot.com/writing/ogham.htm*

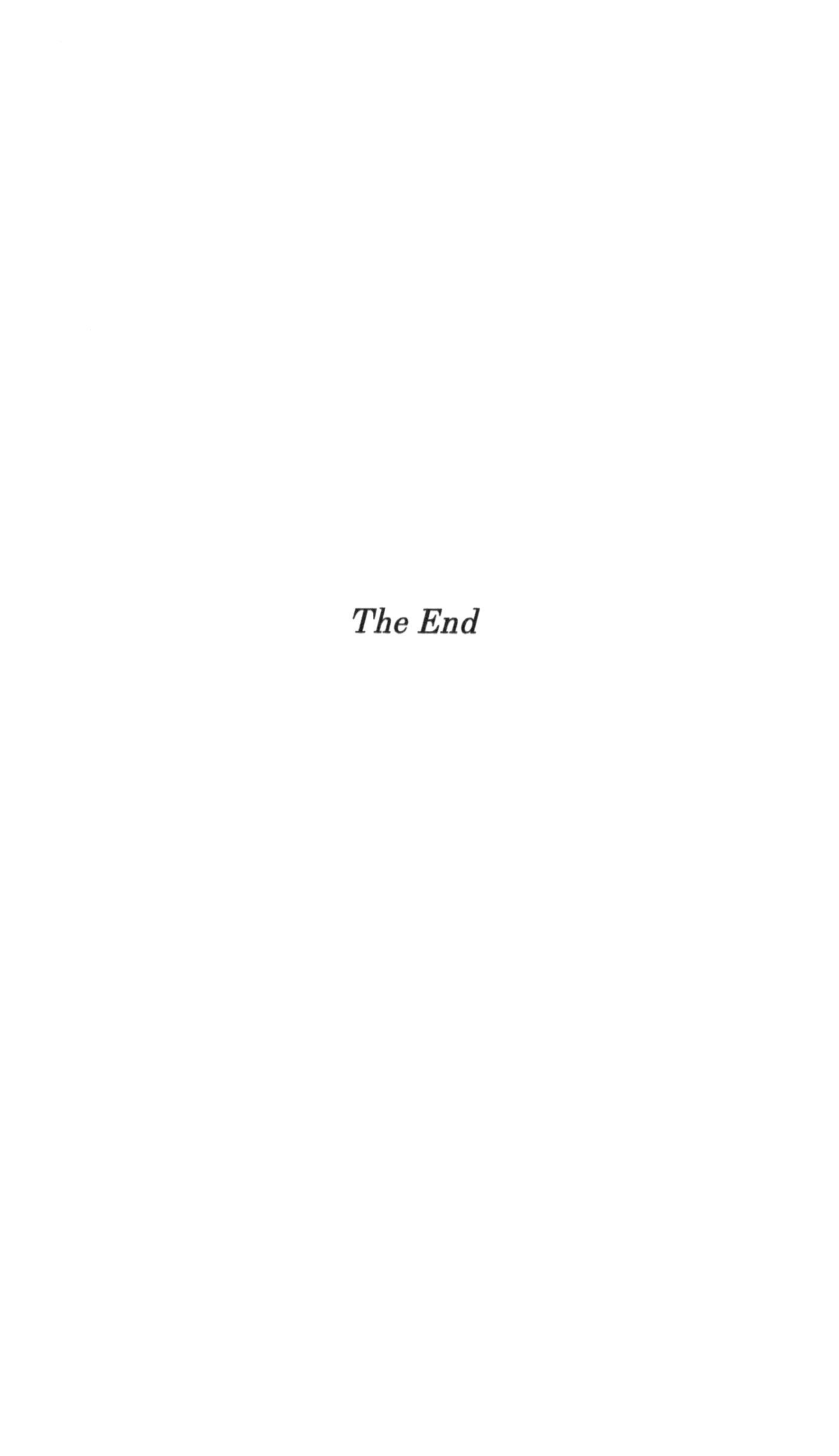

The End

*THANK YOU FOR COMING on this journey in Lilydale with me. I am honored to see it through to the end, but remember: the Folk are always watching.*